Rules of a Rebel
and a
Shy Girl

By Jessica Sorensen

Rules of a Rebel and a Shy Girl

For information: *jessicasorensen.com*

Cover Design by Najla Qamber Designs

The very first kiss...

Chapter One

Willow

13 years old…

My mom's new boyfriend is screaming again, either yelling at her or simply yelling because he's drunk. I want to leave my room and check on the situation, but I'm afraid of going on the other side of my door. As long as the door's shut, I have a barrier from the madness. As long as my door is shut, I can pretend he's playing a game and that the nonsense is out of excitement. Once I step foot out of my room, reality will smack me across the face. Hard. So, instead of going out there, I sit on my bed, hugging my legs against my chest and keeping my eyes on the door.

I've been down this road before with my mom's many, many boyfriends. She's accumulated so many over the years that I sometimes wonder if she likes to collect them like other moms collect figurines, books, or shoes.

She wasn't always this way. Up until I was six years old, my life was normally decent. Sure, my mom had her ups and downs, but when my dad was still around, she didn't seem as miserable. She was stable. She did stuff with me, like took me to the park and the movies when we could afford it. We didn't have a ton of money, but I never felt like I was missing out on much. I was happy to have a mom and dad living with me under the same roof, unlike some of the other kids I went to school with.

But then my father decided he didn't want to be a dad and husband anymore, and my life was dropkicked like a soccer ball, spinning out of control. Seven years later, that ball is still spinning, my dad is gone, and my mom spends more time at the bar or with her new boyfriends than she does me.

"Just leave her alone, Bill," my mom's voice flows from the other side of my bedroom door. "She's not bothering anyone."

The doorknob jiggles and the door rattles. "I don't want her here, Paula," Bill snaps with a slight slur. "Kids repeat everything they see and hear. Do you know what could happen if she goes to school and tells one of her friends I was over here? What if my daughter found out and told my wife?"

"She won't tell," my mom tries to reassure him. "Willow knows the rules."

"I don't give a shit if she knows the rules. Kids never obey the rules."

A hard object slams against the door and I jump, pressing my back against the headboard, wishing I could vanish through the walls to the outside. Then I would run and run and run until I found my dad and begged him to come back and fix everything.

"Bill, just calm down," my mom begs. "I'll talk to her again and make sure she understands. I'll do that right now."

"I don't want you to talk to her," he slurs. "I want you to get her out of here for the next few days. That way, we can have some fun without worrying she'll open her mouth. I don't come over here to worry about kids. I come here to have fun. If I wanted to worry about shit, I'd be at home with my family."

"I know, hon. And I'm so glad you're here. I really am. I love you. You know that."

"Well, if you love me, then get her out of here."

I hold my breath, waiting for my mom's answer. While she's been a pretty crappy mother lately—drinking a lot and bringing home random guys from the bar—I don't think she'd kick me out of the house.

Would she?

It wouldn't be the first time.

The house grows silent, and I start to wonder—hope— that perhaps they decided to take off and do whatever they do when they disappear for hours in the middle of the night. Then there's a soft knock on my door.

"Willow, can you please open the door?" My mom uses her sweet, gentle tone to try to persuade me. "I need to talk to you."

I hug my knees more tightly against my chest and don't answer, worried she's going to tell me to leave. Maybe if I pretend I'm invisible, she'll forget I'm here and so will Bill. It's actually happened before.

Once, when I was ten, my mom took off to a bar with some of her friends. She didn't come back for three days. When she finally returned, she apologized for being gone so long, telling me that it wasn't her fault. She said she found out her boyfriend was cheating on her and her friends talked her into going to Vegas to ease her broken heart. I felt bad for her, remembering how my dad had broken her heart, so I told her I was fine, that I knew how to take care of myself, which was true. I had been doing it for years.

She seemed relieved by my words and, after that, started staying out more. I was left wishing I never felt sorry for her to begin with.

"Willow, please just open the door, or I'm going to pick the lock. Then I'll be upset, and I hate getting upset with you." Her voice is calm but firm, carrying a warning.

Sucking in a breath, I scoot away from the headboard and slide to the edge of the bed. The linoleum floor is ice cold against my bare feet as I stand up and walk to the door, probably because my mom turned down the heat to save money.

"Is Bill out there?" I ask quietly as I reach the door.

"No, he went to my room," she says. "But he might come out soon, so hurry up."

My fingers tremble as I place my hand on the door-knob and crack open the door.

My mom immediately shoves her way in, shuts the door, and turns to face me, her glassy eyes scanning my organized desk, my made bed, and the alphabetized books on the corner shelf.

"You're always so organized," she remarks, complete-ly getting sidetracked, something she's good at. "You definitely get that from your father."

I don't like when she compares me to my father, partly because I don't like him and partly because she doesn't like him, so the comparison isn't a compliment.

"Mom, I don't have to leave the house, do I?" I ask, chewing on my thumbnail.

She doesn't make eye contact as she ambles over to the window and draws back the curtains to stare outside at the night sky. "Remember when your dad left, how sad I was?"

I start to answer, but she talks over me.

"I was really upset. He didn't just break my heart; he smashed it to pieces." She releases the curtain and twists around. "He bailed on you, too, you know."

"Yeah, I know that." I frown, unsure why she's bring-ing the painful subject up. I hate thinking of my dad, how

11

he bailed on me and destroyed my fun, loving mom.

"It's okay, sweetie." She crosses the room and pulls me in for a hug. She reeks of cigarette smoke, whiskey, and some sort of spice that makes my nostrils burn and my eyes water. "I wasn't bringing that up to make you sad. I just wanted to let you know that I'd never leave you, no matter what. I promise I'll be here for you no matter what happens. I won't become your father."

I circle my arms around her and hug her tightly as relief washes over me. *She isn't going to make me leave.*

"But," she starts, and my muscles wind into tight knots. "In order for me to keep my promise, you're going to have to meet me halfway."

"Okay … How do I do that?"

"By giving me some space when I need it."

Tears burn my eyes as I slant my chin up to meet her eye to eye. "You mean leaving the house right now?"

She sighs as tears stream from my eyes. "It's not a big deal. You can come home on Monday when Bill goes home."

I wipe the tears from my cheeks. "But where should I go?"

She glances from the window to the door then back at me. "You can go hang out in the car. That could be fun. You could take your sleeping bag out there and pretend you're camping."

"I don't like camping," I say pointlessly. "And the last time I slept in the car, some guys started banging on the window and trying to get me to let them in."

"Oh, yeah, I forgot about that." She taps her finger against her bottom lip. "Maybe you could go spend the weekend at one of your friends'." Excitement lights up in her eyes. "That would be fun, right?"

I glance at the alarm clock on my dresser. "I doubt any of my friends are even awake."

She steps back, reaches into the pocket of her jeans, and retrieves her phone. "Well, you won't know until you try, right?"

I warily eyeball the phone. "Their parents might get mad if I call this late."

"I'm sure they won't." She urges me to take the phone. When I don't budge, she grimaces. "Willow, this promise thing isn't going to work if you're not cooperative. I can't keep my side of the deal if you don't keep yours."

I open my mouth to tell her I don't want to do the promise, but then all the times my mom has disappeared for days on end flash through my mind. I've often worried that one day, she won't come back, and I'll be all alone.

While I try to act tough and pretend I can handle living on my own, I sometimes get scared, like at night when our neighbors are having parties or when someone knocks on the door, trying to get me to let them into the house.

13

"Fine, I'll call one of my friends." I take the phone from her. "But if they don't answer, you still have to keep the promise."

She holds the phone out to me. "If they don't answer, I'll find somewhere else for you to go."

Grimacing, I take her phone, flip it open, and debate who to call. My friend Luna's parents are super strict, so she's a no-go. Wynter and Ari might let me stay over, but then I'd have to explain why my mom is kicking me out of the house, and I'm not ready to tell them about my home life yet.

Only one person knows about what goes on at my house, and that's Beckett. He's been one of my closest friends since grade school. I told him about my mom a couple of years ago when he came over to my house to work on a school project and my mom wasn't home by the time he was leaving.

"Are you sure you're going to be okay being here all by yourself?" he asked, reluctant to leave even though his mom had honked the horn five times already.

I nodded, cringing at the shouting floating through the walls from the neighbors. "I'll be fine. I'm home alone a lot, actually."

He slung his backpack onto his shoulder with worry in his eyes. "Really? That doesn't seem okay. I mean, my parents aren't that great, but they don't leave me home this late unless the maid or Theo is there with me."

"It's fine." I felt stupid and silly and embarrassed, not just for having to defend my mom, but because of how loud the neighbors were screaming. It was bad enough bringing Beck to my tiny, broken house located on the crappy side of town when his house is so fancy and big. But we needed some rocks from my rock collection to do our project, so I didn't have much of a choice. "I can take care of myself."

"But you shouldn't have to." He lightly tapped me on the nose, something he did to try to cheer me up. "Why don't you come over to my house and hang out until your mom gets home?"

My shoulders slumped even lower. "She might not be home until morning." Or maybe even for a couple of days, but I didn't want to tell him that.

He blinked in shock, and I waited for him to call my mom a weirdo and a freak like other kids did, but all he said was, "That's okay. You can spend the night."

I almost smiled. I should've known Beck would never call me a freak. "You think your mom will let me?"

He shrugged. "I'll just tell her that we have to finish our project and your mom will pick you up in a few hours. She'll be asleep by then, so she won't notice."

"But what about in the morning when I'm still there?"

"She has tennis practice at, like, eight and won't be back until noon."

15

I nodded and then packed my things, glad I didn't have to sleep in the house alone again and thankful Beck was my best friend.

I glance at my mom, wondering how she would feel about me spending the night at a guy's house or if she found out that I had already done that a handful of times over the years. Honestly, I don't think she'd care.

I dial Beck's number, crossing my fingers his dad doesn't get angry that I called. He can be kind of grumpy sometimes.

The phone rings four times before Beck picks up.

"Since when do you stay up this late?" he asks in a teasing tone. "I thought you were on a schedule so you could get maximum study hours in or whatever."

"I am on a schedule." I turn my back to my mom as she examines me inquisitively. "But the schedule got interrupted."

He sighs. "Let me guess. Boyfriend number twenty-seven is over and is being loud and annoying."

He knows me too well.

"Yes to the last." I glance at mom out of the corner of my eye. "No to the first … I'm pretty sure she's above twenty-seven."

A pucker forms at my mom's brow. "What are you saying to him?"

I shake my head. "Nothing."

"Okay …" Her gaze roams to the doorway. "I'm going to go check on Bill. I'll be right back."

After she walks out, I wander toward the window and close my eyes, shame washing over me. While I doubt Beck will judge me, it doesn't make asking for help any easier.

"I need a favor."

"Sure," he replies easily. "What's up?"

I rest my head against the frosted window. "I need a place to crash for a few days."

"Why? What happened?" Nervousness creeps into his tone. "This boyfriend dude didn't try to get into your room like the last one did, did he?"

"No … Well, he did, but only to try to get me out of the house," I say quietly, "which is why I need a place to crash."

"Your mom's letting him kick you out of the house?" He doesn't sound that shocked.

"They're not really kicking me out …" My cheeks warm with my embarrassment. "My mom just asked me if I could sleep in the car or go spend the night at one of my friends' houses for a few days. I don't really like sleeping in the car … so I called you." I shrug, even though he can't see me. I feel so pathetic.

"Well, I'm glad you called me. I don't want you sleeping in a car, especially because your neighbors are so crazy.

17

I just wish your mom didn't treat you like this. You deserve so much better, Wills." He pauses. "Maybe you should tell someone that she kicks you out all the time. It isn't right."

"It's fine … I'm fine," I say, not really knowing what else to say. Sure, I know my home life isn't normal, but it could be worse. She could've left me by now. "So, you don't care if I stay with you?"

"You can always stay with me. In fact, I want you to promise that you'll never sleep in the car again. Always call me if you need help."

"I can do that." I blow out a stressed breath, the weight on my shoulders feeling a tiny bit lighter. "Thanks. You're the best friend ever."

"Well, duh," he jokes. "When are you heading over? I'll order pizza or something. How does that sound?"

As if answering, my stomach grumbles, reminding me how the cupboards and fridge are empty, so I had to skip dinner again. "You don't have to do that."

"I know, but I want to. Besides, I bet you skipped dinner."

"You know me too well."

"That's because I'm your best friend. If I didn't know you, then I'd be the worst friend ever."

A tiny smile forms on my lips, but contentment nosedives as my mom pokes her head into my room.

"Is your friend letting you stay over?" she asks, her

eyes more bloodshot than they already were.

I nod, covering the phone with my hand. "Yeah."

"Good." She steps into my room, swaying a little. "They'll have to come pick you up. I can't drive right now."

I want to argue, but I'm pretty sure she's either drunk or high. "My friends aren't old enough to drive."

"They have parents, though, right?" she asks as she grasps the doorframe to regain her balance. "See if they'll come pick you up."

I waver, not wanting to ask Beck for such a huge favor. But staying in the car doesn't sound that fantastic, either.

"Please stop being difficult." Her bleary eyes plead with me to understand. "Bill already thinks you're gone, so you need to get out of here before he finds out I lied to him."

Tears of mortification sting my eyes as I put the phone to my ear. "Beck?"

"I heard," he says tightly. "I'm already heading out to the car with Theo."

A shaky breath falters from my lips as I fight back the waterworks. "Your brother got his license?"

"Technically."

"What does that mean?"

"It means he has his learner's permit. But don't worry. He's a really good driver."

"What if your parents find out?" Guilt gnaws at my stomach. "Won't you guys get into trouble?"

"They won't find out," he promises. "Now chin up, princess. We'll be there in about twenty minutes."

By the time I hang up, tears are slipping down my cheeks. I quickly wipe them away with the back of my hand.

"All good?" my mom asks as I give her back the phone.

I nod, though nothing feels good. At all. In fact, the whole situation makes me feel terribly icky inside.

A droopy smile forms on her lips as she stuffs the phone into the pocket of her pants. "Then you should probably get packed and wait for him on the steps. I don't want Bill to start yelling at you again. I'm sure that probably scares you." She wraps her arms around me. "Thank you so much for doing this, sweetie. You're such a good daughter. How did I get so lucky?"

I wish I could believe her, but if her words were true, then why is she always kicking me out of the house and leaving me all the time? I don't ask, though, too afraid of the answer.

She hugs me before walking out of my room. I hurry and pack, slip on a jacket and sneakers, and wait outside on the porch, but I quickly bail when a couple of kids a few years older than me try to persuade me to get high with them.

When Beck finally pulls up, I'm standing at the edge of the parking lot in the dark, hiding near the entrance sign to the single-story apartment complex I live in.

"What're you doing out here?" Beck asks as he hops out of the fancy sports car that belongs to his older brother Theo.

I rush toward him, scuffing my sneakers in the dirt. "Some guys were trying to get me to do drugs, so I thought I'd be safer out here."

He shakes his head, taking hold of my hand. The second his skin touches mine, a calming warmth spreads through me.

"Next time, wait inside," he says, eyeing the guys loitering near the door to my apartment. Their attention is trained on us, smoke is lacing the air, and when one guy whispers something to the other, my legs turn into Jell-O.

Beck must sense my nervousness because he hauls me closer and steers us toward the car.

"I would've waited in the house, but my mom told me I had to wait on the porch." I clutch his hand, wishing I never had to let go.

I can't see his face, but he tightens his fingers around my hand as he opens the back door and slides into the backseat, pulling me in with him. Once the door is shut, Theo drives out onto the street.

"Are you okay?" Theo asks, casting a quick glance in the rearview mirror.

Theo usually teases Beck and me, making kissing faces and cracking jokes about liking each other, so his niceness throws me off.

"I'm fine." But I'm shaking, which can't mean I'm fine, right?

Beck notices, shucks off his hoodie, and places it over my shoulders. "It's going to be okay." He drapes an arm around my shoulder and kisses the side of my head. "I won't ever let anything happen to you. I promise."

I know it's silly, but a guy has never kissed me before, not even on the cheek. My skin burns from where his lips touched, and all I can think is, *I feel so cared for.*

Safe.

I lean into him, resting my head on his shoulder, believing his promise way more than I do my mom's. "Thank you, Beck," I whisper, "for everything."

"You're welcome." He gives me a sideways hug. "I'll always be here for you, Wills."

I hope he's right. I don't know what I'd do without him.

While Rule #1—the very first list—is

in play...

Chapter Two

Willow

Five years later…

Sometimes, I wonder if luck has a vendetta against me. Perhaps I unknowingly offended it, and now it's pissed off and determined to break me down. That would explain a lot about my life.

I know how cuckoo I sound. And in reality, I don't actually believe luck exists, at least in a physical sense. But pretending it does makes situations like this easier. Then I don't have to deal with the truth: that my life is just really, really shitty and that lately, I've made it shittier by making shitty choices.

"Goddammit, not again," I curse as I steer my car over to the side of the road.

Smoke funnels from the hood, and the engine growls like a dying Gremlin as I shove the shifter into park and shut down the engine. Leaving the headlights on, I unbuckle my seatbelt and slip on a hoodie over my work uniform, trying to cover up one of the many bad decisions I made tonight: not changing out of my outfit before I left work. In my defense, I was in a rush to get home and check on my mom who hasn't texted me in over six hours. And that would be yet another bad decision: leaving my mom home alone after she spent the entire night sobbing and drinking away her broken heart, searching for the pieces in the bottom of a bottle.

I really should've called in sick.

But then how would you pay rent?

I send my mom another text, but she doesn't reply. Shoving down my anxiety over something possibly being really wrong this time, I climb out of the car to check out the damage. The cool November air nips at my bare legs and stings my cheeks as I go to the trunk and grab the flashlight I put in there after the last time my car broke down. Then I walk around to the front of my car and pop the hood open.

Smoke plumes into my face as the engine hisses, which probably means it overheated, something that's been happening on and off for a month now. I need to take it to a shop to get fixed, but my mom hasn't been able to hold a steady job since boyfriend number forty-five dumped her for someone half her age. And with me starting college, our financial situation has gone from crappy to desperately nonexistent, which leads me to my third bad decision: my new job.

I pull the jacket securely around me as I glance up and

down the dark, desolate highway that stretches between Ridgefield and Fairs Hollow. Fairs Hollow is where I attend college and work, but I've been staying at home in Ridgefield because I can't afford to pay my mom's rent and mine. Plus, I really need to keep an eye on my mom after her boyfriend just dumped her. That may not sound that bad, but my mom doesn't handle breakups very well. No, scratch that. My mom doesn't *handle* breakups at all. She buries her pain in alcohol until the next guy comes along. Then she either gets high with him or gets high off the relationship, and for as long as that lasts, she's happy. But when they break up, she sinks into a pit of despair. This has been going on for years, and I've spent many nights making sure she doesn't die in her sleep after days of binge drinking and drugs, something she was doing before I left for work earlier.

Uneasiness crushes my chest, and I retrieve my phone from the pocket of my shorts to send her yet another message. Then I get back into the car and send Luna, Wynter, and Ari, three of my best friends, a pleading text that I'm stuck out on the highway and need help.

While I wait for them to respond, I lock the doors and flip on my emergency lights, crossing my fingers no one stops. That might sound crazy, but the last time my car broke down, a guy stopped and offered me twenty bucks if I sucked him off in the backseat. He was forty-something with a godawful comb-over, and he was sporting a shiny wedding ring. So, not only was he a complete creeper, but a cheating bastard, just like a lot of the guys my mom dates.

When I told him just that, he looked as if he wanted to slap me. Thank God Wynter showed up, or who knows what would've happened?

I shiver at the thought, nausea winding in the pit of my stomach. The ill feeling expands as my mind wanders to my job and how many creepers I've met there over the last couple of months. It's my own damn fault. I chose to work at the shithole when I knew the shitty rep the place has. I chose to put myself in that situation in order to pay mine and my mom's bills and still afford to attend school, which will hopefully help me get ahead in life instead of continuously being behind like I've been for my entire childhood.

I chose, I chose, I chose my luck.

I lower my head to the steering wheel. "God, what I wouldn't give to have just one single moment when it doesn't feel like an elephant is sitting on my chest. Is that too much to ask? To just have one lucky day when my cards align?"

I don't even know who I'm talking to, but they definitely answer with a big fat no as my phone buzzes with messages from both Luna and Wynter.

Wynter: I'm actually at the airport, getting ready to head to New York to see my grandma, so I can't :(

You should try Luna, though. I think she's in Ridgefield for the week.

I soon discover that Wynter is wrong about Luna as I open the other message I received.

Luna: Oh, my gosh! That sucks! I wish I could come get you, but Grey and I are already on the road to Virginia. We're about three hours out, but we can totally turn around and drive back if you need us to.

Despite the panic strangling the air from my lungs, I can't help smiling. Luna's one of the nicest people I know, and if I told her to turn around, she would. But I'm not about to make her bail out on her road trip with her boyfriend so she can come pick up my pathetic ass.

I text back and tell her it's okay. Then I message Wynter to have fun in New York with a tiny flame of jealousy burning in my chest.

It's Thanksgiving break. I should be going on trips to spend the holiday with family or at least doing something other than being stuck on the side of the road after getting off from a job that makes me feel disgusting inside.

I shut my eyes and take a few measured breaths, but the memory of a few hours ago flashes through my mind and my chest constricts.

Music booming, lights flashing, and the air reeks of alcohol and dirty money.

As I walk by the bar, a man slips a twenty in my back

29

pocket. "Let me buy you a drink, gorgeous," he says with a toothy grin, his hand resting on my hip.

I fight back the urge to smash my fist in his face for putting his hand on me and, instead, smile sweetly. "Sorry, but I can't drink on the job."

His other hand finds my waist, and he drags me toward the stool he's sitting on. He smells like stale peanuts, and his bald head reflects the neon ceiling lights.

"How about this, then." He leans in, dipping his lips toward my ear. "When you get off your shift, you meet me out back." His hands wander toward my ass. "I promise I'll make it worth your while."

I lift my hand instinctively to slap him across his face, but Gus, the manager, shoots me a warning look from behind the bar. Correcting myself, I plaster on the fake smile that's starting to feel more real with each passing day.

My phone buzzes in my hand, startling the bejesus out of me. My fingers tremble as I swipe open the message, hoping upon hope it's from Ari, replying that yes, he'll come pick me up. But Luna's name pops up across the screen again.

Luna: I texted Beck and he said he stayed home instead of going with his family to Vail, so he'll come get you. Just let him know where you are. And make sure to text me when you get home, so I know you made it back safely :)

Her text is sweet, but the mention of Beck makes my stomach ravel into knots. Beck is still one of my best friends in the entire universe, maybe more than even Wynter, Luna, and Ari combined. But even though I tell him almost everything, I've never mentioned and never plan on mentioning my new job. And if he sees me in my uniform, reeking of sweat, beer, and disgustingness, he'll know something's up.

I flop my head back against the headrest and stare up at a hole in the fabric ceiling. What the heck am I going to tell him? I usually bring an extra change of clothes, but I stayed up for half the night, trying to track my mom down at the local bar, and ended up sleeping in later than I normally do. I was in a rush when I left the house and forgot to grab my normal clothes.

Before I can come up with a solution, my phone rings, and the screen illuminates the dark car.

"Speak of the devil." Summoning a breath, I answer, "Hey."

"Hey," he replies in a light tone. "I heard you got yourself into a bit of trouble."

"Yeah, my car broke down again, but can I point out that you sound way too happy about the fact?"

"I'm just happy I get to come play knight in shining armor for you again."

"Haven't you done that enough? I thought you'd be

31

tired of it by now."

"Is that why you didn't text me yourself? Because you thought I was a lazy knight in shining armor?" he jokes, but a drop of hurt resides in his tone.

"No, I thought you were in Vail," I reply, eyeballing a car driving by.

The truth is that I wasn't sure if he went to Vail or not. I just didn't call him because 1). Beck already does too much for me. And while that seemed okay when we were younger, I feel pathetic for still needing his help all the time when I'm now an adult. 2). The whole seeing me in my work outfit thing. And 3). Beck comes from a very wealthy family and sometimes has a hard time understanding financial struggles, like why I don't just get my piece of shit car fixed. Answering with a "because I can't afford it" leads to an offer to give me the money, which I'll never accept, despite his persistence.

There's also a number four, but I hate thinking about that one, mostly because I hate that the number exists. But it has to. Otherwise, Beck and my friendship would become too complicated. The middle of senior year was a perfect example of this.

We were at a party, and after way too many drinks and way too much time dirty dancing, we ended up in Beck's bedroom, which wasn't odd—we did that a lot—but that night felt different. That night, his touches and smiles caused my stomach to flutter.

"You seem nervous," he said as we sat on his bed, facing each other with our legs crossed. Music vibrated through the floorboards, and soft light filtered across the room.

"I'm always nervous," I admitted. This was Beck, the only person who truly understood the depth of my anxiety. "You know that."

"I do know that." He tucked a strand of hair behind my ear. "But that doesn't mean I want to know why any less, so spill."

"You're just making me a little nervous tonight." I didn't know what else to tell him other than the truth, even if it had to do with him.

He pressed his hand to his chest in shock. "I am?"

I nodded, staring down at the comforter. "I don't know why, though." Or maybe I did, and I just didn't want to admit it.

He cupped his hand underneath my chin and angled my head up. "I don't ever want you to be nervous around me. What can I do to make it better?"

I shook my head, and for some wildly weird reason, my gaze roamed to his lips. I'd been doing it all night, wondering what kissing him would be like. I knew he'd kissed a handful of girls and heard rumors that he was a great kisser. I was curious, not just about kissing Beck, but

33

kissing in general. I hadn't done it. I had rules against it. Rules saved me from turning into my mother. Of course, with alcohol in my system, breaking rules seemed easier.

"I really don't know," I whispered, unable to remove my focus from his lips.

Silence took over except for the booming music playing downstairs. I wondered what other people were doing right now, what my friends were up to. Were they having more fun than me? Doubtful since my most fun moments were with Beck. Plus, he made me feel so safe, especially when he hugged me. Sometimes, I wished I could stay in his arms forever. Life would be so much easier that way.

"Wills." His voice was low and husky.

I tore my eyes away from his mouth and met his gaze. His eyes were blazing with an indecipherable hunger. I couldn't figure out what was causing the look until he leaned in and grazed his lips against mine.

I squeezed my eyes shut, parted my lips, and for a heart-stopping, soul-burning, mind-blowing moment, life was perfect. Then I snapped out of my stupidity and remembered life wasn't perfect. I had lived in imperfection since I was six.

Panic rose inside of me, and I ran like a coward.

For weeks afterward, I could barely look Beck in the eye. Those were some of the loneliest days of my entire life. The only reason I was able to be friends with him again was because of the rule. A simple rule. At least, it seemed so on paper.

Absolutely no lip-to-lip contact.

Yep, that was my rule. I gave Beck a copy and keep the original in my glovebox. Having that boundary written down seems to be working for us.

Sort of …

"You sound stressed. What's going on?" Beck's troubled voice lures me out of the memory.

Fear scorches through me as a car zooms by, and I sink even lower in the seat.

"I'm always stressed. It comes with the territory of being a worrier," I tell him. "But the place I'm broke down isn't helping my anxiety, either."

"Where are you exactly?"

"On the highway between Ridgefield and Fairs Hollow."

"Fuck, that's in the middle of nowhere."

"Yeah, I know. I was …" *I was what? Coming home from work? Because he thinks you work at a library, which is far, far away from here.* "I had to run a few errands for my mom, and my stupid car decided it was going to overheat again." *God, I hate lying to him. It makes my heart ache.*

"You really need to get your car looked at," he says over the chatter and piano music rising in the background.

35

"I will," I lie. Like I pointed out earlier, trying to explain not having money to Beck doesn't work. "Where are you? I hear a lot of noise."

"I'm at my sister's. She's throwing a week before Thanksgiving party."

"Is that a thing?"

"Apparently. At least to her. But you know how Emmaline is. She throws parties for every holiday and the week before. Remember she did that for Easter a couple of years back?"

I smile. "Yeah, I remember. You made me go to it with you and told all the kids at the kid table that we were eating rabbit. They freaked out and started to cry, and your dad got so pissed."

"My dad is always pissed," he reminds me with slight bitterness. The only time Beck ever sounds bitter is when he's talking about his dad, a cold, unemotional man who loves to work more than be a father or husband. "But that time, it was kind of worth it just to see the look on those kids' faces."

"You can be so evil sometimes."

"So can you. That's why we're so great together. In fact, I think we might create the epitome of perfection."

Deep down, I know he doesn't mean we'd be a great couple, but my lips tug downward, anyway. Not because Beck would be a horrible boyfriend; I just prefer not to think about boyfriends: of having one, of ruining my life to have one, of getting consumed by one, of ending up like my mom because I get so consumed by one. And Beck, he could definitely consume me. I can feel the magnetic attraction, the overwhelming sense of drowning every time I'm near him.

I glance at the glovebox, thinking about the rule. Knowing it exists makes me breathe easier.

"Maybe I should try texting Ari again," I change the subject. "I don't want to make you leave your sister's party."

"Too late for that. I'm already in the car."

If I had a penny for every time he said that to me, I wouldn't be in this mess to begin with.

"Besides," he continues. "I'm not about to pass up my chance to be your knight in shining armor just so I can stick around and listen to my sister's friends babble about the stock market."

"Is that what you rich folks are talking about these days?" I tease, hunkering down in my seat as headlights shine through the rear window of my car.

"Oh, my God, you have no idea," he gripes. "I swear if I heard any more about exchanges and volumes and yields, I was going to start singing Linkin Park's 'One Step Closer' at the top of my lungs."

I giggle. "Man, I'd love to see that go down."

"One day, I'll make that happen for you."

"I'm going to hold you to that," I tease then suck in a sharp breath as the headlights move closer.

I turn around to glance out the window, but I can't tell if the car is driving absurdly slow or has stopped. I double-check to make sure the doors are locked then sink lower into the seat.

"It'll have to be at one of your parties, though. That kind of stuff would fit right in with the stupid parties my mom throws all the time. Someone is always screaming about something." I bite my tongue as soon as I say it. While Beck knows how my mom is, he doesn't need me whining to him about my pathetic life. "I'm sorry. I didn't mean to bitch about my mom. She's just been giving me a headache lately."

"I'm guessing Claude the nose picker broke up with her?"

"Was he the nose picker? I thought that was Wally."

"No, I'm pretty sure Claude was the nose picker. Wally was caterpillar brows."

"You know what? I think you're right." I'm on the verge of smiling, something only Beck can get me to do when we're talking about my mom's many ex-boyfriends.

He actually came up with the idea of giving them nicknames after I divulged I had a difficult time remembering their names. We started giving them quirky names based on their habits and weird characteristics, like Claude the nose picker, Wally the caterpillar brows, and Ed the wedgie picker.

The headlights spotlight my car as a vehicle pulls up right behind me.

Fuck, someone stopped.

When I turn in my seat, someone raps on my window. Whirling back around, I damn near bump my head on the ceiling.

"You need some help?" A guy in his late twenties smiles at me through the window. "I'm not very good with cars, but I can give you a ride somewhere."

I swallow down a shaky breath. "I'm fine. My friend is actually on his way to pick me up. He'll be here in a few minutes," I lie. It'll take Beck at least twenty minutes to get here.

"You sure?" he asks, squinting through the window to get a better look at me.

I gulp. "I'm fine. I promise."

His gaze travels across my exposed legs, and I shift in the seat, tugging the hem of my jacket lower.

"Well, all right, then." He stares at me for another slamming heartbeat before hiking back to his car.

"Willow, what the hell is going on?" Beck asks through the phone I'm clutching.

Letting out an uneven breath, I put the phone back to

39

my ear. "Some guy just stopped to see if I need a ride." I cast an anxious glance in the rearview mirror at the unmoving car. "How far away are you?"

"I'll be there in about ten minutes," he says. "Did the guy leave?"

"No. He's just sitting in his car right now … I'm sure he'll leave soon, though." *I hope.*

"Are your doors locked?"

"Yes."

"Do you still have that pepper spray I gave you?"

"Yeah, it's in the glovebox." I lean over the console to get it out. "I hope it still works. You gave it to me forever ago." It was about a year ago after I had to pick up my mom from some sketchy bar and got harassed by a group of drunken guys. When I told Beck about what happened and how scared I was, he went out and bought me a can of pepper spray and made me take a self-defense class.

That's Beck for you, always looking out for me. He has been since we were kids, and he promised me in the car that he would always be there for me.

At the time, I believed he'd never break the promise. Now that I'm older, I understand that one day after he falls in love, he'll become a knight in shining armor for someone else. Whoever she is, she'll be very lucky because Beck is great. Perfect. But not for me.

No guy is perfect for me. And I'm not perfect for any

guy.

Nothing is ever perfect.

I really need to learn to stop relying on him so much. Stop spending so much time with him.

The last thought makes me feel sick.

I clutch the can of pepper spray in my hand. "I wonder if pepper spray expires."

"I'm not sure." He sounds unnervingly worried, a rare occurrence for Beck, and my uneasiness skyrockets. "Is he still there?"

"Yeah." I don't even have to look to know. The blinding headlights announce his presence.

"If he gets out of the car again, hang up and call the police."

My heart rate accelerates so rapidly I worry I'm about to have a heart attack. "Beck, I think—"

The guy knocks on the passenger side window, and I'm startled, dropping the phone.

"Shit."

"Hey, I was thinking that maybe I could sit with you until your friend shows up." His lips curl into a grin. "I'm Dane, by the way."

Like telling me his name will somehow make me more willing to let him in my car.

Keeping my eyes on him, I lean forward and feel around for the phone.

"Come on," Dane continues, grinning at me. "I don't bite. I swear."

"L-look, Dane, thanks for the offer." *Take deep breaths, Willow. Deep breaths. Find your phone and call the police.* "B-but, like I said, my friend will be here any minute."

He glances up and down the empty road then back at me. "Are you sure about that? Because I don't see any cars coming."

"Y-yes, I'm sure." *Calm down. Steady your voice. Stop panicking.*

His eyes drink in my uniform. "Your outfit looks like the ones those girls wear at Crazy, Crazy Morelliesin's. Do you work there?"

I swallow hard. Crazy Morelliesin's is what the regulars call the club I work at. Regulars are the worst. Sometimes, they wait out back to make illegal offers to the dancers and waitresses we get off work. Some of the girls accept. I'd never get that desperate for money, though. At least, that's what I tell myself. But sometimes, I question how much I am like my mother. Perhaps I'm living in denial when I say I'll never be like her. After all, this sort of job is something my mom has done to make cash.

"No," I lie to the guy. My fingers brush across the phone, and I exhale shakily as I sit back up and put the receiver to my ear. "Hey, Beck, are you about here yet?" I say loudly enough for the guy to hear. I try not to let my expression falter when I realize the line is dead. "A couple of minutes? Yeah, okay. Sounds good."

The guy eyes me over, as if debating whether I'm full of shit. Well, either that or he's calculating a way to break into my car and not get doused by the pepper spray in my hand.

"Are you sure your friend's coming?" he questions. "It seems like it's taking him an awfully long time to get here."

I'm starting to move the phone away to call the police when a BMW pulls off to the side of the road, parking right in front of me. The driver's side opens, and Beck hops out.

Thank God. Thank God. Thank God!

I glance at the dude. "See? My friend …"

He's already jogging back to his car.

Beck strides down the side of the road, passes my car, and heads toward the guy with a look on his face that screams I'm-about-to-beat-some-ass. Beck's not much of a fighter, so despite the fact that I'd love to see creeper dude's ass get kicked, I scurry out of the car to stop him.

"Just let him go," I tell Beck, chasing after him.

"No fucking way." He continues marching forward as the guy jumps into his car.

I snag hold of Beck's sleeve. "I don't want you getting into a fight on the side of the road, out in the middle of no-where, with some strange, creepy dude. It's not worth it."

43

He tries to wiggle his arm out of my grip, but I clutch on for dear life, refusing to release him until the guy peels out onto the road.

Beck curses as the car zooms by, leaving a cloud of dust behind.

Releasing his sleeve, I rush to the side of the road and squint through the darkness to try to make out the model of the vehicle. I manage to spot a metal horse on the back of the trunk and make a mental note to keep an eye out for Mustangs in the club parking lot. At least then I can have a warning that he's there.

My stomach twists with nausea at the thought of seeing creepy Dane again.

"You should've let me beat his ass," Beck growls, storming up to me.

"No, I shouldn't have." I cross my arms over my chest. "You don't get into fights. And I'm not about to let you turn into that kind of a person because of me."

"It wouldn't have been your fault. He deserves to get his ass kicked." His tone is surprisingly sharp and very un-like the calm, collected Beck I know. He inches closer to me, and even though I'm tall, I have to tip my chin up to meet his blazing gaze. "I could hear every damn thing he was saying to you. Trying to get you to let him in the car …" He shakes his head, opening and flexing his hands. "We should report him to the police."

44

"I only got the make of the car, not a plate number. So they probably wouldn't be able to track him down." My body quivers, either from shock or from how upset Beck sounds. "Besides, what would I tell them? That some guy stood outside my car and talked to me? Technically, he didn't do anything wrong."

"Yeah, because I pulled up and scared him off." He roughly rakes his fingers through his blond hair. "God fucking knows what he would've done if I hadn't …" He shakes his head for the thousandth time, glaring daggers at my car. "I wish you'd let me just buy you a new damn car."

And here we go. "You're not buying me a new car, so don't be weird."

He steps toward me and tucks a strand of hair behind my ear, the fury in his eyes shifting into something unreadable, but it makes my heart skip a beat. "Then let me pay to get yours fixed."

I shake my head, telling the flutter in my chest to shut the hell up. Flutters that haven't left since our kiss. That doesn't mean I have to listen to them, though. They're just that: silly and insignificant. It's when I act on them, allow them to control me, that I have a real problem.

"It's not your responsibility to take care of me."

"Why not? I promised you I would."

"Yeah, but … That was a long time ago. We were kids. You didn't even know what you were getting yourself into."

"I don't feel obligated if that's what you're getting at."
He taps the tip of my nose with his fingertip, his lips tugging into a half-smile. I swear my heart glows. "Taking care of you is one of my favorite things to do, so quit arguing and let me do what I love."

"Beck …" I rack my brain for the right thing to say. "You're my best friend, and best friends aren't supposed to pay for each other's cars to get fixed. It's not right, no matter how much you love doing it."

He cocks a brow. "Who says it's not right?"

"Me." I rub my hands up and down my arms as the cool night air works through the fabric of my jacket. "I need to start taking care of myself more and stop relying on you so much. I'm too old for you to still be rescuing me." There, I said what I needed to say. I should feel better, right?

Then why do I feel so sick?

He splays his hand across my cheek, looking me in the eye. "I'm not trying to rescue you. I just don't like you driving around in an unreliable car, especially when you work late and take a road that's out in the middle of fucking nowhere." His brows abruptly dip as his gaze drops to the shorts I'm wearing that barely cover my ass. He blinks a few times before his eyes meet mine again. "Wait … Where were you tonight? I thought you were working."

Panicking, I search for a lie to tell him. At a party? Dancing at a club? Ha! Like that would ever work. I rarely go out partying, and I wear shorts this short even less frequently.

Unable to think of a good lie, I decide a party is my best option.

"I was at this party a girl from my Chemistry class was having. It was a pool party, but you know how much I hate swimsuits, so I just went in shorts."

God, I hate lying to him.

But telling him the truth would be way worse.

His gaze falls to my legs again. Biting his lip, he reaches out and brushes his knuckles against the outside of my thigh. "How come you never wear stuff like this to my pool parties?"

I shiver from the unexpected touch, and good Lord, those silly flutters just about lose their damn minds. "I, um …" I clear my throat, trying to clear the flustered tone out of my system. *It's not like he's never touched your leg before. Jesus, get a grip on yourself.* "I don't know … because I know you and know you won't get mad at me for not following the party dress code."

Rubbing his lips together, he drags his gaze up my body to my face. I search his eyes, attempting to get a vibe on him, see if he's buying my lie. If anyone can read through my bullshit, it's Beck. I can't pick up his vibe at

47

all, though. I used to be able to all the time, but lately, something's changed. Either I've lost the ability to read my best friend, or he's been more closed off.

His lips curve into a devious grin. "Well, not anymore."

"Huh?"

"From now on, I'm going to be pissed off if you don't follow my party dress code." He crosses his arms, seeming pretty damn pleased with himself. "So, on Friday, you better show up to my place wearing a sexy black dress."

I crinkle my nose. "You're having a party the day after Thanksgiving that requires people to wear sexy black dresses? What kind of theme is that?"

"The do-whatever-the-hell-I-want theme." His eyes sparkle in the glow of my hazard lights. "And since you're such a party girl, now I don't have to beg you to come."

Crap. I didn't think this through very well at all.

Why do I get the feeling he knows I'm lying about where I was tonight and is just trying to get me to confess?

He gives me a second to admit I'm full of shit, but being the huge chicken I am, all I do is nod.

Sighing disappointedly, he strolls past me. "Come on; let's get you home. I'd ask if you want me to have a tow truck come get your car, but I already know the answer." He stops near the front of my car where I left the flashlight balanced on the bumper and leans over to inspect the engine. "So, either I can come pick you up tomorrow and we can drive out here and try to fix this, or we can borrow Ari's truck and tow it to your mom's house."

"Towing will probably be better since I'm not a hundred percent sure what's wrong with it." I move over beside him, feeling shaken up about what happened and craving his comforting nearness.

He stares at the engine with his head tucked down, his mouth set in a thin line. I don't know what's running through his mind, but I'm not fond of how upset he looks, and I hate that I might have played a part in it.

"Thank you for saving my ass," I feel the need to say as guilt stirs in my chest. "And for being my knight in shining armor again."

He takes a deep breath before elevating his gaze to me, a smile playing on his lips. "Anytime, princess."

I restrain a sigh. "Beck … I thought we had an agreement that you weren't going to use that nickname anymore. I'm getting too old for it."

"I never agreed to anything. You just told me I had to stop, and I did for a while." He slips an arm around my shoulders, and all I can think is safe, safe, *safe*. "But I figure, since I'm your knight in shining armor tonight, you have to be my princess. It's part of the rules, and you can't argue with the rules."

I shake my head, deciding to let him win this one, even

49

though the nickname makes me feel like a little kid or a damsel in distress.

"Fine, but this princess needs to get home," I tell him through a yawn. "She's really sleepy."

"All right, my lady. Your chariot awaits." He bows, and a laugh bubbles from my lips, a sound I didn't expect to hear on such a cruddy night.

He smiles proudly, and I start to question if getting me to laugh was his intention all along. He really is the best friend ever. I'll never be able to thank him enough. Still, I want to try so maybe I won't crumble when he finds the love of his life.

I wrap my arms around him and embrace him with gratitude. "Thank you. I really do appreciate everything you do for me, even if it doesn't always seem like I do." I breathe in his scent. *Calm. I feel so calm.*

He hugs me back, slipping an arm around me then pressing our bodies closer. "You know I'll always be here for you, Wills. Even when we're seventy years old and can barely walk, I'll use my cane to keep the bad guys away."

I smile, but sadness weighs on my heart. He may mean that now, but one day, he'll have other people he'll want to care for more than me. Or worse, one day, he'll find out how big of a liar I am and decide I'm not worth saving anymore.

Chapter Three

Beck

Willow. Willow. Willow. She's the most amazing, brave, strong, beautiful girl I know, even if she doesn't think so. She also gets herself into some of the most unnerving situations. Then again, most of the time, it isn't her fault.

She's had a difficult life, starting from when her dad walked out when she was six. I met her not too long after that happened. She was so quiet, sad, and broken back then. Sometimes, she still looks that way, her big eyes so crammed with pain, sadness, and the stress of a difficult life. All I want to do is hug her, which I try to do as much as she'll let me.

But the touching thing is becoming a real problem lately. For me, anyway.

Somewhere along the road of friendship, I started seeing her as more than a friend. Way, way more.

After we get into my car, I drive toward her house, taking subtle breaths to try to calm the fuck down. I'm normally a fairly calm guy and prefer talking things out in-

stead of throwing punches. But when I heard that guy trying to coax Willow into opening the door, uncontrollable
anger blazed through me. Then I pulled up and saw him
running to his car, and I lost any ounce of calm I had left. If
Willow hadn't stopped me, I don't know what I would've
done. Probably rammed my fist into his face until my
knuckles broke. I should feel rattled by that, but thinking
about what that guy probably wanted to do to her …

I open and flex my fingers, sucking in an unsteady exhale.

"Are you okay?" Willow fixes her big eyes on my
hands. "Why're your hands shaking?"

"They're just having a spasm," I lie, tightening my grip
on the steering wheel. "Too much typing up assignments, I
think."

She gives me a dubious look. "Since when do you even
do assignments?"

I press my hand to my heart, mocking offense. "Are
you saying I'm a slacker?"

"No … but you did get away with only taking tests
during our senior year."

"Hey, it's not my fault the tests were so damn easy.
And if I can ace them without doing the homework, then
why do the homework?"

She shrugs. "I don't know … I guess I can kind of see
your point. Although, I could never get away with doing

that."

I reach over and lightly tug on a strand of her hair. "Of course you could. You're the smartest person I know." I offer her a lopsided smile. "You're just an overachiever."

Her face scrunches. "Sometimes, I wish I wasn't, though."

"Since when?" I search her sad eyes, wondering what's bothering her tonight.

"I don't know … since forever, I guess." She shrugs, picking at her fingernails. "I just think life would be way easier if I wasn't always trying so hard and just didn't care."

"It's not," I tell her. "Trust me, I know."

She gives me *the look*, the one that means she's about to defend my slacker actions and stroke my ego. "You're not a slacker. You just don't like wasting time by doing stuff you don't like. But you work so hard and always do what you love." She sighs, resting her head against the window, dazing off into her own little world. "I wish I could spend my life having more fun and being less stressed out."

"You could." I reach out and place my hand over hers. "You just have to stop worrying about everything so much."

"Yeah, but I don't have just me to worry about," she mutters, her hand twitching underneath mine, but she doesn't pull back.

We sink into silence as Willow stares out the window, lost in thought, probably stressing over her car, her mom, school, bills. At eighteen years old, she has more responsibilities than most people have in a lifetime. I wish I could take some of the burden away for her, but she rarely accepts my offers to help. I love helping her. I wish she'd stop being so stubborn and let me fix her car so I wouldn't have to worry about her getting into another situation like tonight. Until she does get her car fixed, I'll spend my nights worrying about her safety.

Then again, at this point in my life, I should be used to it.

Ever since grade school when we first became friends, I felt a need to protect Willow, like when other kids teased her because she wore old clothes and glasses that were too big. Plus, she was so shy and rarely stood up for herself. That quickly became my job, and I spent many recesses warding off anyone who dared come near her on the playground. During middle school, though, my warding off days diminished, mostly because Willow changed.

So did the way I looked at her.

I remember the moment clearly. My mom had dragged me to France with her for the entire summer, and I didn't see Willow for three months straight. By the time I returned, I was excited to go back to school, to return to normalcy, to eat a cheeseburger, and to see my friends, particularly Willow. Partly because I wanted to check up on her, and partly because I simply missed her.

I didn't get a chance to see her until the first day of school, but a couple of our other friends, she, and I all agreed over the phone to meet out front so we could walk in together.

Wynter showed up first. She looked pretty much the same as she had at the beginning of summer. Her blonde hair was a little longer, and she was wearing a dress like she usually did.

"Hello, Beckett. Long time no see." She plopped down beside me on the short wall that ran down the side of the stairway that led to the school.

"I wish you'd stop calling me that." My lip twitched. I hated when she called me Beckett. My dad used my full name when he yelled at me, telling me how much of a screw-up I am. Wynter knew I loathed the name, but she loved getting under my skin.

"Why?" Her eyes sparkled mischievously in the sunlight. "It's your name, isn't it?"

"Yeah, but you know I hate it."

"Which makes it even more appealing."

I blew out an exasperated breath, keeping my lips sealed. It was too early in the morning to argue with her, something we did a lot. Some of my friends said we acted this way because we were so much alike. Perhaps that was true. Wynter came from a wealthy family like me, and our parents could sometimes be neglectful. But they made up for their absence by showering us with gifts. Still, I thought Wynter acted more spoiled than I did.

She crossed her legs, fiddling with her diamond bracelet. "So was Paris any fun? I bet it was. I wish my parents would take me there. They hate taking me on trips with them, though. You're so lucky your mom takes you places sometimes."

"Yeah, I guess so." I didn't mean to sound grumpy, but going on trips with my mom meant sitting in a hotel room while she went shopping. The only reason she brought me was because my dad didn't want to be responsible for me.

I sat back on my hands and stared at the people walking up and down the stairway in front of us. "The food kind of sucked, though."

"Whatever. I bet it didn't. I bet you were just being … well, you."

I shot her a dirty look. "What's that supposed to mean?"

She gave a half-shrug. "That sometimes, you don't appreciate the finer things in life."

I shot an insinuating look at the bracelet on her wrist. "Isn't that like the pot calling the kettle black?"

She covered the bracelet with her hand. "That's different. I appreciate my parents for getting this for me."

"And I appreciate my mom for taking me to Paris. That doesn't mean I have to lie and say I liked the food or say I had a blast when I didn't."

"God, you're so spoiled."

I resisted an eye roll, biting my tongue. Again, it was too early in the morning for this shit.

"Do you know what time Willow and Luna are supposed to be here?" I glanced at the parent drop-off section at the bottom of the stairway. "I really want to go see where my locker is before the bell rings. Oh, yeah, and I met this guy—Ari—the other day when I was hanging out at the skate park. He just moved here. He seems pretty cool. I told him he could hang out with us."

"What's he like? Is he cute?"

"What do I look like, a girl?"

"Sometimes, you act like one."

God, I really need more guy friends.

"And you can be such a brat sometimes, but you don't see me pointing it out every two seconds." I waved at Levi and Jack, two of my other friends, ignoring Wynter's withering gaze.

Levi cupped his hands around his mouth. "Yo, Beck, you coming in?"

"In a bit," I called out. "I'm waiting for Luna and Willow to show up."

"So, which one of them are you dating now?" Levi teased, and Jack laughed.

I flipped them the middle finger, and they howled with laughter before pushing through the entrance doors.

"I can't believe people are still giving you crap for hanging out with girls," Wynter said, frowning. "They really just need to get over it."

"You mean like you just did?" I questioned.

She shrugged. "That's different."

"How do you figure?"

"Because I'm your friend."

I didn't even bother trying to understand her logic. Instead, I asked her what classes she was taking, which seemed like a safe topic.

Wynter and I talked until we spotted Luna's mom's van pulling into the drop-off area. The side door rolled open, and Luna hopped out. She was wearing a godawful yellow turtleneck and baggy jeans. Poor girl. I didn't know why she dressed in such hideous outfits. I figured her mom made her. I didn't know for sure, though. Other kids made fun of her a lot, and I stuck up for her when I could, but it never felt like enough.

Slinging her backpack over her shoulder, Luna moved to the rolled down passenger window to talk to her mom while Willow jumped out. Well, I thought the tall girl without glasses was Willow, anyway. I wasn't so sure.

She looked way different. Her long brown hair was down and wavy, and she was wearing tight black jeans, a thick pair of boots laced up to her knees, and a plaid shirt over a fitted tank top.

I assessed her as she waited for Luna to finish talking to her mom. The clothes weren't flashy, but Willow usually wore loose-fitted jeans, baggy T-shirts, glasses, and her hair was always in a ponytail. She looked so different that it was kind of wigging me out.

When the two of them headed up the stairs, I hopped off the wall to meet them halfway. The closer I got, the more I noticed that Willow had gotten taller, and she filled out her clothes more. She looked good. Really, really good.

I quickly shoved the thought away. No fucking way was I going there. Getting a crush on my best friend would be stupid. And there were plenty of other girls around, ones who wouldn't destroy my life when we broke up. And that's what would happen if I dated Willow and we broke up. I'd lose the only person who knew most of my secrets, who knew how crappy I felt when my dad told me I was a screw-up, who knew I secretly cried during sad movies sometimes, who knew I got lonely a lot. Who would break just as much if she lost me, too. Because Willow needed me as much as I needed her.

Clearing my head of Willow's sudden hotness, I continued down the stairway straight for her. When Willow spotted me, her eyes lit up as she bounced and threw her arms around me.

"I'm so glad you're back." She hugged the crap out of me. "I missed you."

I hugged her back, spinning her around until she laughed. "I missed you, too." *And I was so worried about you while I was gone.*

Wynter glowered at me as I set Willow down on her feet. "Why didn't I get that kind of hello?" she asked.

I shrugged, and her eyes narrowed even more. I didn't have an answer to give her, not one I was going to share.

The truth was, ever since the day Willow confided in me about her home life, I felt an overpowering connection to her, enough that I told her some of my secrets, too.

"So, how was Paris?" Willow asked me excitedly. "Was it as cool as it sounds? Because it sounds pretty cool."

"It was okay." I stuffed my hands into my back pockets. "It would've been more fun if you were there."

"See? Again, he's nicer to Willow," Wynter whined to Luna. "Why can't we get that kind of treatment?"

"Beck is nice to us," Luna said, fidgeting with the collar of her turtleneck.

Ignoring them, I pulled out a small box from my backpack. "I got you something." I handed the box to Willow. "I saw it in the airport, and it kind of reminded me of you."

"You didn't have to get me anything." But she smiled and opened the box. "Oh! Cool." She picked up the miniature snow globe and gave it a shake. Then her eyes met mine, her smile practically glowing, which made me feel like I was glowing. "Thanks, Beck. You're the best. Seriously, you spoil me too much."

I shrugged, playing it cool, but really, I felt super proud that I got her to smile. "I figured you could add it to that collection your dad gave you."

The happiness in her eyes faded to sadness as her eyes traveled to the snow globe. "Yeah, I could."

Crap. I didn't think it through very well. "Sorry. I didn't mean to remind you of your dad." I reached for the snow globe. "I can get rid of it if you want."

She tucked it behind her back, shaking her head. "No way. I love it too much. Plus, it's from *Paris*."

I relaxed, wondering why I was so nervous. "Good. I'm glad you like it. My mom tried to talk me into buying you a bracelet, but I told her you weren't a bracelet kind of girl."

"No, I'm definitely not." Willow fell into step with me as we headed up the stairway, staring at the snow globe in her hand. Luna and Wynter followed, lost in their own conversation.

"So, how was your summer?" I asked, hoping to distract her from thoughts of her jerk of a father who bailed on

61

her and her mom. "You didn't have any problems, right? I mean, with your mom?"

"I guess not … Her new boyfriend moved in with us about a month ago … He has a cat …" She sighed, rotating the snow globe in her hand. "I think I'm allergic to cats. I wake up every day sneezing, and my eyes are always red."

"Aw, Wills, I'm so sorry." I draped an arm around her and steered her to the side as I maneuvered the door open. "What can I do to make you feel better?"

"I don't think there's anything you can do." Her frown deepened as we wandered down the busy hallway with Luna and Wynter still trailing behind us. "You know how my mom gets … And it's just a cat." Another stressed sigh. "It just sucks because her stupid boyfriend doesn't even like kids. He told me that when he moved in, that he hates kids and that I need to make sure I stay out of his way or he might have to send me off to boarding school." She shook her head, folding her fingers around the snow globe. "Like he could really do that. He doesn't even have a job."

I hated that her mom put her boyfriends above Willow and that she brought such sketchy guys into the house. I once offered to let Willow live in one of our five guest rooms so she could get away from her mom's creepy boyfriends. I doubted my parents would notice her living with us, considering they were hardly ever home. But Willow declined like she usually did when I tried to give her things.

Even when she needed my help, she had a hard time asking.

I massaged her shoulder. "I should get you a dog, one that's well-trained and will keep that guy away and the cat, too."

"My mom would probably get rid of it." She tucked the snow globe into the side pocket of her backpack then looked at me, forcing a smile on her face. "Tell me more about Paris. Did you see the Eiffel Tower? Oh, please tell me you went to the catacombs."

Noting the desperate subject change, I started telling her about my trip, even though I really didn't want to talk about it.

By the time we reached my locker, I noticed quite a few people, particularly guys, glancing in our direction. I figured they were looking at Wynter because that happened a lot. And sometimes guys would come up and ask me about her, see if she had a boyfriend. Later, when I was doodling in math class, I found out that the staring wasn't about Wynter after all.

"Hey, Beck, can I ask you something?" Levi plopped down into the desk in front of mine. "It's about that girl Willow you're always hanging out with."

I peered up from my doodling, confused. "Okay."

He twisted in his seat and rested his arms on my desk. "Does she have a boyfriend?"

His question threw me off guard.

Willow?

My Willow?

I wasn't sure how to respond. Normally, with Wynter, I answered honestly. Now, I found myself desperate to lie, to say that she did have a boyfriend so Levi wouldn't ask her out. Not that I didn't like Levi; I just didn't want Willow to have a boyfriend.

"She does, actually." I sat back in my seat. "I think he's a grade ahead of us."

"Really?" Levi frowned, thrumming his fingers on top of the desk. "Well, that sucks. She seems pretty cool. Plus, she's hot."

I shrugged, feeling a little guilty for lying. What would Willow do if she knew what I did? She always trusted me. Did I just break her trust?

What if she wanted to date Levi? Then I'd see less of her, and I barely survived the summer without her.

She trusted me so much, and she hardly trusted anyone.

I sighed and decided to tell her at lunchtime, even though I didn't want to.

"Levi likes me? Really?" she asked after I sat down at the lunch table and reluctantly told her what happened in math class.

"Yeah. That's what he said." I stuffed a handful of

chips into my mouth, eyeing her over. "You don't seem that happy about it."

"That's because Levi's not her type." Wynter squeezed between Willow and me while Luna took a seat across the table.

"You have a type?" I asked Willow.

She shook her head, but a blush crept up her cheeks. "No."

"Yes, you do." Wynter popped the tab of her soda. "You told me this summer that you liked—"

Willow threw a carrot at Wynter, pegging her right in the face. "Shush. You promised you wouldn't tell."

I frowned. Willow told Wynter a secret that she didn't tell me?

"Hey," Wynter whined, chucking the carrot back at Willow. "That wasn't very nice."

Willow ducked out of the way, and the carrot fell onto the floor. "Well, you promised you wouldn't tell anyone."

"What's the big deal?" Wynter asked, tearing open a bag of chips. "So, you like a guy? It was bound to happen sometime."

Willow glared at Wynter. "Stop talking about this in front of everyone."

My frown deepened. Okay, now I'm part of the *every-one*.

Then the craziest thought occurred to me. What if Willow had a crush on me, and that's why she was so mad at Wynter? The idea should've made me uncomfortable, but honestly, I kind of liked it.

A few moments later, though, Wynter blabbed that Willow had a crush on Dominic, a guy who was a grade above us and wore studded bracelets and, I was pretty sure, eyeliner. That was the day I realized Willow had a type, and I was far from it.

I also realized I had a crush on my best friend.

My crush lasted all through middle school up to our junior year of high school. That year, everything changed. I went from thinking of Willow as my hot best friend to thinking she was a beautiful, kind, smart, caring girl I wanted to kiss all the time.

And I mean, all the fucking time.

I remember the first time I actually considered doing it. We were hanging out at my house, watching some stupid soap opera that was boring as shit, but there was nothing else on. Willow muted the volume and began ad-libbing for the characters. I joined in, and by the time the show was over, we were laughing our asses off.

That's when my dad walked in and ruined the moment by being his douchey self.

"What the hell are you doing?" He grabbed the remote from my hand and shut off the television. He was wearing a grey suit and red tie, ready to go off to work, on a Sunday, something he did every single week, never taking days off, always worrying about work, work, work. "Get off your ass and do something. Quit wasting your life."

He wasn't a horrible guy, just a huge believer that people should spend life working their asses off. The problem was, I loved to mess around, have fun, party, and play sports. I didn't have big goals or any real plans other than to pass Algebra and kick ass on the soccer field. I knew a lot of people my age who didn't have any major life goals yet.

"We were just watching TV." I frowned at the disappointment on his face. "It's Sunday morning. There's nothing else to do."

He crossed his arms and stared me down. "Well, if you had a job, then that wouldn't be a problem."

"I have a job," I argued, lowering my feet to the floor.

He laughed, and the noise made my muscles constrict. "Selling shit and lending out money isn't a job."

"Why?" I questioned with a crook of my brow. "I make money. Isn't that what a job is?"

"Watch your tone," he warned. "And no, that's not a job … unless you want to work in sales. Is that what you want to do for the rest of your life? Spend hours in a store, trying to bullshit people into buying stuff? And doing so for a crap salary?" His tone dripped with sarcasm. "Sounds pretty rewarding, doesn't it?"

"Some people have to work in sales. There's nothing wrong with that. And I'm sure it's just as hard of work as what you do." I wanted to add that his job wasn't all that rewarding, either, that his career as a lawyer had turned him into a liar, a jerk, and a snob. Whatever. There was only so far I could push my father before I had to pay some extreme consequence.

"Get your ass up and come help me at the office," he snapped. "I'm going to teach you a thing or two about hard work."

His gaze shifted to Willow, and I had the strongest compulsion to move in front of her, protect her, though I knew my dad wouldn't harm her. I didn't even like that she had to sit here and witness his shit-fit.

"You should take my advice, too, young lady. There are better things to do than sit around, wasting your time and my son's." He eyed over her cut-offs, her unlaced boots, and the worn T-shirt she was wearing, and disgust flashed in his eyes. "Although, I'd suggest cleaning up a little before you tried to apply for jobs. Most companies won't hire people who look like they spend their nights sleeping in a cardboard box."

My hands balled into fists, and I started to rise. I rarely yelled at my dad, but as my lips parted, I knew I was about to scream at him to shut the fuck up.

Before the scream could leave my lips, however, Willow beat me to the punch.

"First of all, I don't think spending time with your son is a waste of time." Willow held her chin high, her voice wobbling slightly. "I learn a lot from spending time with Beck. And second, I have a job. Two, actually. So I don't need your advice."

My dad blinked, thrown off. Then his eyes narrowed. "What could you possibly learn from my son?" His eyes swept the room littered with candy wrappers and soda cans. "Other than how to sit around on your ass all day and be completely useless?"

God, I hated my father. Nothing I ever did was good enough. And I hated that Willow was here to witness this. Sure, she knew my dad was a dick from the stories I told her and from witnessing him ream me occasionally, but he'd never directed his douchiness on her before.

"He taught me how to play soccer the other day, which let me tell you, took a lot of patience." Willow counted down on her fingers, her eyes burning fiercely. "He taught me how to drive a stick, helped me open a savings account, showed me how to make interest in it. He's actually really smart with numbers, but you probably know that already since you're his dad." Her lips spread into a smile. "Oh, yeah, and he taught me how to eat cookies and drink milk at the same time, which doesn't sound like a big deal, but when you're having a cookie eating contest, it really comes in handy. And winning cookie contests is really important to me. In fact, I'm thinking about going pro. That is, if they'll let people who look like they live in cardboard boxes enter the competition. I'm not really sure about that. Maybe you know, though, since you're so smart."

I wasn't sure whether to jump in front of her, laugh, or kiss the freakin' shit out of her.

Steam practically fumed out of my dad's ears as his gaze shot to me. "Beckett, you have five minutes to say good-bye to your little friend and get ready to go to the office with me. And make sure to dress properly." Then he turned and stormed out of the room.

Once he was gone, I let out a breath I didn't even realize I was holding and turned toward Willow. "I'm so fucking sorry about that, Wills. Seriously, I can't believe he did that."

"You don't have to apologize," she insisted. "I already knew your dad was a dick."

"Still … I should've told him to go fuck himself when he said all that stuff to you. I was planning on it, I swear. You just beat me to it." I grinned. "You're kind of a badass when you want to be."

She smiled back at me. "I figured I could return the favor for all those years you stood up for me when kids called me a four-eyed freak. It just sucks that he's making you go to work with him. I know how much you don't want to work in an office."

"I'll be fine." I tried to sound convincing and failed epically. "A few days isn't going to hurt me."

"Still, if you need me to rescue you, call me." She scooted closer to me on the couch, and when our knees brushed, my gaze flew to her legs.

She was wearing shorts, something she rarely did and something I had more than fully noticed when she'd showed up at my house. Her legs were so long, and her skin looked so soft. She was gorgeous. I swear to God, some days, it drove me crazy. I thought about touching her all the time, running my fingers up the sides of her legs, maybe even the inside of her thighs. I often wondered, if I did, would she shudder? I imagined she would. Of course, that might have been because I wanted her so badly.

"You're okay, though, right?" Her voice was crammed with concern as she placed her hand on my leg, drawing my attention away from her legs. "You know what he said wasn't true, right?"

I blinked the desire away, knowing she'd probably run the hell out of here if she knew my thoughts. Well, either that or kick my ass.

"Yeah ... I'm used to his shit by now." My miserable tone suggested otherwise. I wasn't even sure my miserableness was because of my dad or from how much I wanted her without having the nerve to make a move.

71

She poked me in the side, and I flinched but laughed.

"Don't let him turn you into a wallower. That's not you. Don't let him take away who you are."

"It might be better if he did. I mean, everything he said was kind of true. I don't really have any direction or goals or anything." I was being overdramatic. At the same time, I kind of liked hearing her defend me. It made me feel all good inside. I wanted to hug her … kiss her … run my finger up the inside of her thigh …

See? There I went again.

"You have direction and goals," she said. "They're just different from his."

I forced myself to focus on the conversation, carrying her gaze. "And yours."

"Yeah, so? My goals are boring. You're so much more fun than I am. Sometimes, I wish I could be more like you." She twisted a strand of her hair around her finger and chewed on her bottom lip, drawing all of my attention to her mouth.

Unable to control myself any longer, I started to lean in to do just that.

Her eyes snapped wide. "What are you doing?" she sputtered, slanting back.

Holy fucking shit, this is getting out of hand.

I tried to settle the hell down. Moving away damn near killed me. It went against everything I wanted.

That's when I realized how much I liked her. And not just because she was hot. I liked her for everything she was, for everything she did for me, for everything that we were. Some of my favorite life moments were experienced with her.

She made me laugh. She told me things I tried to convince myself I didn't need to hear. She got me. And I got her. I got her so much that I knew I could never act on my feelings because it would break her rule to never date anyone, at least until she finished college. She created the rule over the belief that it would help her not end up like her mom. I knew she never would. But when Willow made up her mind about something, she threw all of her effort into it, which meant there was a slim to none chance that me acting on my feelings would end well.

And so began the last three years of my self-torment, of wanting something I couldn't have. Something that was always right in front of me, reminding me how perfect life could be.

And, for a while, my self-torment was working.

Until the day I broke.

We were up in my room on my bed during a party, a little drunk and alone. I kept picturing myself laying her back, kissing her while exploring her body. I knew I couldn't act on my desires. At least, I did until she told me I was making her nervous, staring at my mouth like she

73

wanted to taste me as badly as I wanted to taste her.

Hope rose inside me, and I went in for the kiss.

For a microsecond, everything was perfect as our lips connected for the first time.

And then she broke the kiss and took off, taking the perfection with her.

She's kept a hold of it ever since, and I question if I'll ever get it back, even after she gave me a piece of paper that pretty much informed me that we'd never kiss again.

A stupid piece of paper with a stupid rule: absolutely no lip-to-lip contact.

I'm not much of a rule follower. Never have been. But for the last year, I've tried to be … for her.

Always for her.

Chapter Four

Beck

I'm not sure how long I zone off, thinking of all the times I almost kissed Willow and destroyed our friendship. Probably way too long, though, because by the time I'm yanked back to reality, we're close to her apartment. I hate that I get so consumed with wanting her and wish I could just figure out a way to talk to her and tell her how I feel without her freaking out.

"Beck, are you okay?" Willow asks.

My gaze moves from the narrow street to her. "Yeah. I was just thinking about stuff."

She twists in the seat, bringing her knee up. I try not to stare at her long legs that I can't stop picturing around me, but she rarely wears shorts—though she really should—and I can't help sneaking a glance or two. Or three. Or four. Or twenty. Still, I can't help wondering why she's dressed like this. She said it was for a party, but I know when she's lying.

"What kind of stuff?" She rests her chin on her knee. "You have that look on your face."

"What look?" *The look where I'm thinking about how much I want you and how you'll never want me back? At least, not the way I want you to. Do I have a look for that?*

"The look when your dad is being a pain in the ass." Her mouth curves downward. "Is he bugging you about working at the firm again?"

That wasn't where my thoughts were, but I'll take talking about my dad over telling her the truth.

"Princess, he's never stopped bugging me. He likes yelling at me way too much," I say. "And I'm pretty sure he won't ever stop until I agree to do what he wants."

"Please don't let him force you to do anything," she begs. "You deserve to do what you want. And you'd be miserable as a lawyer. I know you would."

"Oh, trust me; I know that, too." I flip on the blinker to turn onto the side road that runs through her rundown neighborhood. "And I've tried to explain that to him. I told him that I'd be the suckiest lawyer that's ever existed. But you know my dad … His way is the only way."

"Why does he even think you need to go into law?" she asks, tangling a strand of hair around her finger. "Just because he did?"

"I have no idea." I shrug stiffly. "I stopped trying to figure out what the fuck goes on in his head when I turned twelve and realized he loved his job more than his own family."

"I'm sure he doesn't love work more," she tries to convince me. "He's just a workaholic."

"Wills, I love that you're trying to make me feel better, but I already accepted a long time ago that my dad will never like me as much as he likes his clients … and money, which kind of coincide."

Her lips part, but then shut. A moment of pitying silence ticks by, and I start to feel like shit. Then she grins.

"Well, he's an idiot. You're way better than money. In fact, if I had to choose between you and having all the money in the world, I'd choose you."

"Really?" My lips quirk. "All the money in the world, huh? Man, I must be extremely valuable."

She bobs her head up and down exaggeratedly. "You're at the top of the list, Beck. Way, way up at the top where no one else is." The lampposts reflect in her eyes, highlighting a hint of sadness. "You always will be."

My chest tightens in the most wonderfully agonizing way. God, what I wouldn't give to just kiss her again. *All the money in the world and then some.*

"What about Theo?" she asks, already moving on from the moment. Me, I wonder if I'll be stuck there forever, consumed by wanting her but knowing I'll never have her. "Is he only going to law school just to please your dad?"

I shrug. "Probably. I haven't really talked to him about why he decided to go. Theo always seemed like he was go-

77

ing to become someone who needed a lawyer, not the one who would become one."

She giggles, and the sound makes me want to spend all night cracking joke after joke. She looks so beautiful, especially when she laughs. I wish she would do it more often. I wish she wasn't so stressed all the time so she could.

"Theo did get into a lot of trouble," she agrees, her smile fading. "But, anyway. All I'm saying is that maybe if you and Theo were on the same page, you could talk to your dad together and try to make him see it your way."

Leave it to Willow to try to find a solution to my problem.

"I love the suggestion, but I doubt it'll work." When she frowns, I add, "You know my dad. He never hears anything unless he wants to. I don't even know how many times I've tried to have a conversation with him, and he completely ignored me and just walked out of the room." I make a right down a narrow side road lined with small, older houses. "The guy's got a serious case of selective hearing. I swear, it's a fucking gift or something."

"Or maybe they taught him that in law school," she jokes, a small but beautiful smile pulling at her lips.

"Maybe. Or maybe he's just an asshole."

"Aren't those two supposed to be one and the same?"

"They are, actually. In fact, I heard they make you take a class in law school that teaches you asshole skills. I think it's called *learning how to channel your inner asshole so that you bully people into doing things your way and become a real prick*."

"See? All the more reason for you not to go. You'd never be able to pass that class." She reaches over and cups my face with her hand. "Face it. You're too sweet, Beckett."

It takes every ounce of my willpower not to lean into her touch and shut my eyes.

"*Beckett*? Since when did you start calling me Beckett?"

"I was just trying it out." An evil glint twinkles in her eyes. "I figure, if you end up becoming a lawyer, Beck isn't going to work for you anymore. I don't even know if Beckett will work. You might have to change your name to Greg or Chad or something equally douchey."

"Greg and Chad are douchey names?" I arch a brow. "Since when?"

She removes her hand from my face, leaving my skin—my entire body—cold. "I have a Greg and a Chad in my Women's Literature class, and every single time they come to class, they make a point to walk by my desk and"—she makes air quotes—" 'accidentally' knock my books onto the floor. I don't even know why they take the class to begin with. I don't think they ever do any of the assignments."

I thrum my fingers on top of the steering wheel, a little annoyed with Greg and Chad, though I've never met them. "Yeah, I might know why they're doing that."

"Really …? Wait … Do you mean taking the class or knocking my books off my desk?"

"Both."

"Okay …" She looks at me expectantly. "Are you going to tell me?"

Honestly, I'm not sure I want to. As wrong as it is, I like that Willow is clueless about how attractive she is and that she doesn't notice when guys check her out. I worry, though, that she'll one day become aware, and then she'll meet a guy she decides is worth giving up her no dating rule for.

When she stares at me with her lip jutting out in a pout, I cave.

"They're doing it so they can check out your ass when you pick up your books," I explain. "And they probably took the class because they thought there'd be a ton of girls in it."

Her nose crinkles. "Really? That doesn't seem like it could be true."

"Trust me; I'm right."

"But it doesn't make any sense. I mean, they knock my books off every single class. And for what? Just to look at my ass? It's not that great." She faces forward in her seat, shaking her head. "No, I'm pretty sure they're being ass-holes. They always laugh when they do it, too."

"Trust me on this one. I'm a guy. I know how guys think, and I promise you that guys check out your ass all the time … It's a really great ass." My gaze wanders to her legs as she crosses them. "And if you were wearing those shorts, Chad and Greg would probably knock your books off before and after class, maybe even take a few bathroom breaks …" I force my eyes off her legs to find her gaping at me. "What?" I ask innocently. "You tell Wynter when guys are checking her out. Why can't I do the same thing for you?"

She self-consciously tugs on the hem of her shorts. "Because I don't tell Wynter she has a great ass."

"Well, maybe you're not as good of a friend as I am," I say, slowing down to turn into the parking lot of the apart-ment complex. "And FYI, you never tell me my ass is nice, either."

She looks completely unimpressed. "I don't tell Wynter her ass is nice because that's not what friends do."

"Says who?"

"Says everyone."

"Well, I think everyone is wrong and I'm right. Telling your friend that they have a nice ass should be done daily to boost their self-confidence. That's what life's about, right? Making other people feel better?" I flash her my best charming smile. "And when people feel better, the world is a better place."

She gives a dramatic eye roll. "Okay, maybe you should become a lawyer, Mr. Overdramatic."

"Hey." I playfully poke her side, and she squeals through a laugh. "No going over to the dark side." I'm about to laugh with her when her smile suddenly vanishes. "What's wrong?"

She rubs her lips together. "It's nothing. I was just thinking about some stuff."

"What kind of stuff?" I ask as I park in front of her apartment. The sound of thudding music and the sight of empty liquor bottles on the steps cause me to immediately frown. "You want me to come inside for a while?" *So I can find out what's bothering you and so you don't have to be alone at one of your mom's parties.*

She scrutinizes the smoke snaking out the open window of her apartment. "No … I'm fine. I just didn't know she was having a party." She fiddles with the hem of her shorts again. "I was trying to get a hold of her all day … I thought she was passed out drunk, but I guess we made it to the rebound stage already." Heaving a sigh, she unfastens her seatbelt. "Thanks for the ride. I'll see you tomorrow." She reaches for the door handle then pauses. "Unless you have other stuff to do. I can always just have Ari come over here and pick me up and we can tow my car. It should only take two people."

"No way. Ari doesn't get to take away doing my favorite thing." I catch her wrist. "What's with the mood dive?"

She tips her head downward, her long, brown hair veiling her face. "It's nothing. I'm just really tired. With work and school and stuff, I haven't been sleeping very well."

"Willow," I summon my best warning tone, "fess up the truth or pay the consequences."

She peers over at me, restraining a smile. "You know, that used to work on me until I found out what your"—she makes an air quote with her free hand—" *'consequences'* were."

"Hey, tickling can be a good form of punishment, especially when *someone* almost pees their pants."

"I did that one time," she argues, holding up a finger. "And that was after you tickled me for five minutes. Anyone would've lost bladder control in that situation."

A cocky grin spreads across my lips. "Not me. And you want to know why?"

"No," she answers, having heard it all before.

I brag, anyway, trying to get her to smile. "Because I'm not ticklish."

"So you say." Her eyes travel across my arms, my chest, my legs, and she sucks her bottom lip between her teeth. "But it's never been proven, at least that I've seen."

Fuck, what I wouldn't give for her to look at me like

83

that all the time.

"I'll tell you what. If you come home with me and spend the night at my place, I'll let you find out the real answer."

"Aren't we a little too old for sleepovers?"

"You just spent the night at my house last month."

Wariness floods her eyes. "Yeah, but only because my car broke down, and I didn't want to make you drive me home."

"You used to stay at my house all the time to get away from this shit," I remind her, nodding at the house. "What's the difference now?"

She sucks in a shallow inhale. "The difference is, I'm starting to realize that this shit is just part of life, and I can't escape it by running away for the night."

With that, she climbs out of the car, slams the door shut, and rushes inside the apartment.

My lips part in shock. Never has Willow run away from me like that. Well, except for the time we kissed. Never mind running away *into* her house. It's usually the opposite.

I rewind through everything I said, trying to figure out where I went wrong. All I can come up with is perhaps I pushed the whole flirting thing too far. I did mention her ass a lot, but seriously, it's an incredibly hot ass.

I need to make sure she's okay, that she's not freaking

out. Then I need to lie, lie, lie, lie and pretend I don't like her so much it hurts.

I get out of the car, make my way up the path, and knock on the door. No one answers.

Figuring the music is too loud, I decide to walk in, but the door is locked. People laugh from inside, and the music is turned up more loudly as the front window slides shut.

Through the thin walls, I hear Willow's mom shout at the top of her lungs, "Holy shit! Look at my daughter, everyone!" The request is followed by, "She's turning into a little slut!"

"Just like her mama!" a male voice says.

Goddammit, I hate this place. I hate that Willow's in there.

Fighting the urge to break down the door, I return to my car and send Willow a text.

Me: Just want to make sure you're okay before I take off. Things sound pretty intense in there ...

A couple of minutes tick by while I wait for her to respond. A few guys carrying beers and passing around a joint exit her place, a couple a few doors down are yelling at each other, and a woman is trying to sell herself to everyone who passes by. Everything about this area is sketchy, so when a brand spankin' new Mercedes pulls into the parking lot, I have to question if perhaps it belongs to a drug lord. Then again, I'm sitting in my BMW. Perhaps the

85

driver's here to try to save someone they care about.

I keep throwing glances at the car, curious to see who gets out until my phone pings, distracting me.

Wills: Yep, I'm fine. It's not as noisy in my room. And I have the door locked, so no one will bother me. Thanks for the ride, Beck. I really do appreciate everything you do.

What she doesn't say, but I swear is written between the lines, is she feels guilty I have to help her. She wishes she didn't have to be here while feeling obligated to because her mom is smashed.

One day, though, I'm going to get her away from this life, no matter what it takes. Until then, I'll keep doing what I can, helping her as much as she'll allow me to, and hope to God nothing bad ever happens to her.

I fear I'll one day drop her off here or she'll break down on the side of the road, and I'll never see her again.

Chapter Five

Willow

The disastrous night was becoming okay, even after Beck made the remark about my ass. Then he joked about me going to the dark side, and the ominous words struck a deeply embedded nerve.

God, if he only knew how right he was, he wouldn't be here.

Guilt about my new job rose over my head, drowning me in shame, and I bolted from the car. As soon as I stepped foot into the apartment, though, I wished I never left Beck's car.

I wished I never had to.

"Holy shit! Look at my daughter, everyone!" my mom shouts the second she spots me standing in the trashed kitchen. Her eyes are bloodshot, and she's wearing nothing but a leather mini skirt and a red lacy bra as she stands in the middle of the room, twisting. "She's turning into a little slut!"

I glance down at my clothes and wince. Shit! I forgot I was wearing my uniform.

I tug on the bottom of the hoodie as eyes fixate on me. Most of the people in the room are men twice as old as me, but the age difference doesn't stop them from ogling me with their bloodshot eyes.

"Just like her mama!" a taller man with hairy as fuck arms shouts, fist-pumping the air.

They all laugh. Even my mom.

She continues laughing as she twirls and twirls around in the center of the messy kitchen. Empty whiskey and beer bottles cover the brown countertops, the linoleum floor is littered with cigarette butts, and pieces of broken glass are scattered across the table, from what I'm guessing used to be a crack pipe. Before I left for work, I cleaned the place spotless. Ten hours later, it looks like a crack house, and maybe it is. I really don't know anymore.

I want to run away, go back to Beck, and let him take me to his house, put me in his bed, and fall asleep in the peaceful bliss of comfort and quiet. But two things stop me: One, the promise I made to myself to stop relying on him so much. And two, I don't feel comfortable leaving my mom alone in this condition. When I was younger, I used to all the time, but now I'm older and better understand the severity of the situation.

Taking a measured breath, I squeeze past people, slapping hands away that brush against my ass, and push my way up to my mom.

"How much have you had to drink tonight?" I ask her loudly over the music.

She stops spinning, swaying tipsily from side to side. "Oh, I haven't had anything to drink tonight."

I watch her worriedly as she zigzags toward the fridge.

"Then what did you take?"

She shrugs, yanking the door open. "A few things ... Don't worry, though. I feel completely fine. Great, actually." She smiles at me to prove her point. The problem is, her point is lost in the droopiness of her eyes and how big her pupils are dilated.

"Maybe we should tell people to go home," I suggest. "It's really late, and the neighbors might make a complaint again."

She waves me off, ducking her head to look inside the fridge. "Those neighbors moved out, like, a month ago. And all I have to say is good riddance. They were ruining the unwritten rules of this apartment."

The hairs on the back of my neck stand on end as someone moves up behind me. "What rules?"

"The keep your mouth shut rules." She grabs a beer from a six-pack in the fridge, which is pretty much the only thing in there. "Where the hell did all the food go? I thought you went grocery shopping."

"I did a few days ago." I shuffle forward as my personal space gets stolen away. "And there was way more food in there when I left for work."

"Well, you should probably go again because there really isn't much left." She closes the fridge and faces me, unscrewing the lid off the bottle. "Where do you work, anyway? And why are you dressed like that?"

"You mean like a slut?" I ask with bitterness, wrapping my arms around myself.

A drop of remorse emerges in her dazed eyes. "I'm sorry about that, sweetie. I was caught in the moment. I get that way sometimes."

When I was younger, I latched on to her apologies and the rare moments when she resembled the mother I had before my dad left. Now I understand that most of the time, she's either trying to butter me up because she wants something, or she's blazed out of her mind.

"It's fine," I lie, ramming my elbow into the guy behind me. He curses and calls me some not-so-nice names, but thankfully, backs off. Still, the confrontation makes me feel out of control and breathless, and not in the good kind of way, like when I sometimes look into Beck's eyes and feel like I'm spinning out of control. "But I still think maybe you should ask everyone to leave."

"Nah, the fun's just getting started." She downs a swig of the beer then steps toward me. "Don't worry. We probably won't stick around for very much longer. There's supposed to be live music down at the corner bar. We'll probably go check that out."

"Please don't drive," I plead. "Take the bus or walk, okay?"

"Of course." Her dismissive tone leads me to believe she's lying. And she already has a revoked license because of too many DUIs.

Once she leaves the kitchen to do shots with her friend Darla in the living room, I sneak into her bedroom and steal her keys out of her purse before heading for my bedroom. On my way down the crowded hallway, a guy smirks and reaches for me.

"Look, it's a mini-Paula," he tells one of his friends.

I smack his hand away, my heart an erratic mess. "I'm nothing like my mother."

Then I glance down at my clothes, painfully reminded of what I was doing only hours ago.

Maybe I am.

Tears flood my eyes as I shove the guy away, run into my room, and lock the door. Then I peel my clothes off and change into my pajamas, wishing I could take a shower and wash tonight off me. But the last thing I want to do is go into that madness again.

Before I climb into bed, I receive a text from Beck.

Beck: Just want to make sure you're okay before I take off. Things sound pretty intense in there …

I tiptoe over to the window and peer out, wondering if

he's still out there. I spot his BMW almost instantly. It stands out here like a cheerleader at a Goth club. Strangely, though, a Mercedes is parked beside Beck's car.

Two fancy cars in one night. So weird.

I wouldn't think too much of it, but here, I worry some rich drug dealer is inside, staking out my apartment because my mom owes them money.

It wouldn't be the first time that's happened.

Fear lashes through me, causing my heart to pound violently in my chest. I want to confess everything to Beck, admit I want him to come inside, throw me over his shoulder, and carry me out of this hellhole. I want him to save me. On my way, I'd tell my mom I'm never coming back. And I'd mean it. I wouldn't care.

The problem is I do care about my mom, even if I don't want to. And besides, asking Beck to save me isn't what I want. I want to be able to save myself. I want to be a strong person who doesn't break when they're alone.

You can handle this. You've done it a thousand times.

Me: Yep, I'm fine. It's not as noisy in my room. And I have the door locked, so no one will bother me. Thanks for the ride, Beck. I really do appreciate everything you do.

He doesn't reply, and I lie down in bed, staring at the snow globe collection my father gave me before he left. They are the only items I have left that are connected to him since my mom pawned off everything else he left behind.

Front and center is the snow globe Beck gave me after he came back from Paris. It's my favorite one because it came from him. Beck is my favorite person in the entire world, and knowing that is scary.

Tumbling, falling, out of control—that's how I feel when I'm around him.

I like him too much.

I try to convince myself that Beck's silence is for the best. Maybe he's finally giving up on being my knight in shining armor. The stinging ache in my heart has nothing to do with the fact that maybe, just maybe, he's finally moving on. Still, my heart twinges.

I rub my hand across my chest, willing the pain away as I lie in my bedroom, battling sleep.

About ten minutes into the battle, a light tap hits my window. I don't budge, terrified I was correct about the drug lord.

The tapping happens repeatedly, and then my phone hums with an incoming message.

Beck: Would you please just come to your window? I can see through the curtains, so I know you're awake.

My gaze darts to the window as I climb out of bed.

Padding across my room, I pull back the curtains, seeing Beck smiling at me, his posture stiff.

"What are you doing out there?" I ask as I slide open the window.

"Making you a real, live princess," he jokes, tossing a glance over his shoulder at the parking lot.

"How does this make me a real, live princess?"

"Because I'm your Prince Charming, here to rescue you." He motions for me to move. "Now move back so I can climb in."

I want to argue, but loud music and yelling makes me easily step back.

Lowering his head, he ducks inside then straightens, brushing some dirt off his sleeve.

"This is very chivalrous of you," I tease, nervous.

While Beck does make me feel safe, he hasn't been in my bedroom in ages, a room that's probably about as big as his closet and smells like stale cigarettes. The whole apartment does.

"I'm just glad you weren't on the second floor." He scans the bare walls and my unmade bed. When his eyes land on my snow globe collection, he smiles. "Mine's in the front."

For some dumb reason, my cheeks heat like he just discovered a dirty little secret or something.

"It's my favorite one," I say to cover up my mortification.

His smile grows as he lightly taps my nose. "Good.

I'm glad."

I return his smile, feeling a little lost. "I don't mean for this to sound rude, but why are you here?"

His smile disappears. "Because I couldn't bring myself to drive away and leave you alone in this shit."

"It's fine," I lie. "It's not anything I haven't dealt with before."

"That doesn't make it right." He wanders around my room, looking at my locked bedroom door and then at my bed again. "I have some work stuff to do really early, but I want to stick around for a few hours if that's okay with you. At least until the party dies down."

"I'm not sure if it will die down. It might. But sometimes, my mom can keep it up for days."

"Well, I'll stay as long as I can."

I fiddle with the hem of my short pajama bottoms, glad the lamp offers limited lighting. "You really don't have to do that."

"I know I don't have to, but I want to." He plops down on my bed and leans over to untie his boots.

"What are you doing?" I squeak like an idiot.

He peers up at me with amusement dancing in his eyes. "Taking off my shoes."

I remain near the open window, terrified of getting any closer to him as memories of the last time we were alone in a bedroom storm through my mind. "But why?"

"I figured I'd lie down with you until you fall asleep." Once he gets his shoes off, he sits up and reaches for the hem of his long-sleeved shirt.

My breath lodges in my throat as I watch him pull it over his head. Then I try not to frown disappointedly at the T-shirt he has on underneath.

When he notices me staring, he presses his lips together as he drops the shirt onto the floor. I worry he can read my dirty thoughts all over my face, so I hastily look away from his chest.

"This is okay, right?" he asks. "I don't want to make you nervous. That's kind of the opposite of my intentions."

"You're fine." Deciding to stop being a coward, I force my feet forward and make my way to the bed. "It's just weird having you in my room."

"Why?" He slides over, so I can sit down beside him. "You've been in mine a thousand times. You've even slept there."

"I know." I tuck my hands underneath my legs. "But I like going to your place. This isn't the kind of place anyone likes to go. Well, except for my mom's trashy friends."

He unbuckles his belt. "I don't mind being here. Sure, I'd way rather us be at my place or somewhere else that's safe, but I like being around you. You should know that by now." He slips his belt off and drops it to the floor.

So much clothing coming off. When will he stop?

Hopefully never.

I dropkick that thought from my brain and scoot back onto the bed toward the headboard.

"You really think you can sleep through all the yelling and music?"

"I'm not going to sleep." He stands up and pulls off his T-shirt, tossing it to the floor. "I'm just going to lie down next to you until you fall asleep."

Holy flutterville all freakin' mighty.

I try not to gawk. I really do. Yet my gaze strays a few times to his lean chest and solid abs.

Finally, I manage to fix my attention elsewhere as I pull back the covers and climb under them.

"That doesn't sound like much fun for you."

His eyes sparkle with amusement as he lies down beside me and pulls the blanket over us. "You have no idea how wrong you are."

I want to ask him what he means, but the fierceness in his expression keeps my lips zipped.

I roll onto my side, and he does the same, so we're facing each other. We aren't quite touching, but close enough that his body heat and scent engulf me.

Music and shouting fill up the quietness between us, along with my shallow breathing.

"Are you nervous?" he asks unexpectedly. "I can lie on the floor."

I want to nod, but I shake my head. *There's no way I'm making him lie on the floor.*

"You're fine. It's just the noise. You'd think, after almost a decade and a half of listening to this crap, it'd get easier, but it never does."

He contemplates something then slowly scoots toward me and lowers his forehead against mine, resting his hand on my hip. "Close your eyes. I'll make sure you stay safe."

I suck in a trembling breath but don't move back, obeying him and shutting my eyes. My heartbeat soars to hummingbird speed, my adrenaline spiraling. I'm so wired I don't know how I'll ever fall asleep. Yet, moments later, my heart quiets, and I sink into wonderful dreams filled with stuff I'd never dare do in reality.

Chapter Six

Beck

I set an alarm in case I doze off before I lie back down on Willow's bed. Her lips are parted, and her eyelashes flutter every once in a while, as if she's about to wake up. I'm wondering what she's dreaming about, if her dreams are good or bad, when her leg suddenly hitches over my hip, and her palm rests against my bare chest.

I freeze as her fingers drift down, and my stomach muscles constrict. When her hand reaches the bottom of my waist, my heart jackhammers.

I bite down on my lip to restrain a moan, envisioning her hands traveling lower, touching me the way I've dreamt about since that goddamn fucking first kiss. I wonder if she'd let me touch her, too. Then I remember she's asleep and isn't aware of what she's doing.

Even though it about kills me, I move my hand to stop her, and her fingers abruptly stiffen.

"Beck," she whispers, her eyelids lifting.

Our gazes collide, and then her gaze darts down. I expect her to yank back, but instead, she stares at her fingers splayed across my abdomen, her chest heaving with each gasping breath.

The breathy noises send desire pulsating throughout my body. I don't know what overcomes me, whether all this pent-up sexual tension makes me lose my damn mind, but I delve my fingers into her hip and grind against her.

She groans, tipping her head back as her eyes squeeze shut.

I damn near fucking explode.

I'm about to repeat the movement when she jerks back as if I bit her, which I kind of want to.

"I'm s-so sorry," she sputters, her eyes huge. "I don't know why I did that ... I was just having this dream ... and then I ..." She trails off, and I know without seeing her face that her cheeks are flushed.

I don't want her to be sorry. At all. I want her to put her leg back over my hip so we can continue. But she looks so horrified. I'm afraid this moment will end up being another list fiasco if I don't smooth over the situation.

"You're fine." My voice comes out more strained than I want. If I had my way, her clothes would be off by now, and my tongue would be inside her mouth and my fingers sliding up her thighs. "Let's just forget it happened. I'm sure you were probably half-asleep, anyway."

She unsteadily swallows, holding her hands against her, as if fearing she might touch me again. "You should be mad at me for … for violating you in my sleep like that. And for almost breaking our rule."

I mentally roll my eyes. She can violate me anytime she wants. Telling her that is a whole other story.

"We're good. And you didn't break the rule. Our lips didn't touch once. Now go back to sleep so you can rest those pretty eyes."

She worriedly nods. "Thank you. And again, I'm so sorry."

She closes her eyes but doesn't fall asleep right away, her body tense. After about fifteen minutes, her soft breathing fills the silence.

Me, I remain wired, hard as a fucking rock. I seriously want to reach down and touch myself so I can calm the fuck down. Doing that with her sleeping beside me doesn't feel right, though, so I force my hands to stay put.

About a half an hour later, I finally cool down. Another hour ticks by, and the house grows quiet. I wonder if the fading noises mean people are leaving. I hope so since I have to leave soon, and the idea of leaving Willow with anyone in the house makes me feel sick.

God, I never want to leave her.

I have to meet with a guy for work at six o'clock, so when my alarm goes off at five o'clock, I untangle my legs and arms from Willow's and drag my ass out of bed. I put my shoes, shirt, and belt back on, making sure to move quietly so I won't wake her. By the time I'm dressed and ready to go, she's still sound asleep with her hand under her cheek. She looks so peaceful, so beautiful. I can't help myself.

I lean over the bed and place a tender kiss on her cheek, convincing myself the move is okay because, technically, it's not lip-to-lip contact.

Her eyelashes flutter from the contact.

"Beck," she murmurs.

I take a deep breath, loving the sound of my name leaving her sleepy lips.

"Go back to sleep, princess," I whisper in her ear. "I have to go, but I'll be back later to tow your car."

I'm not even sure if she's awake enough to understand me, but she bobs her head up and down.

Before I leave, I check to make sure her door is locked. Then I slide open the window and slip out.

The chilly morning air encases me as I inch the window closed. I hesitate for another second or two, wanting to return to her room, but I can't blow off work.

Sighing, I turn around and hike across the gravel parking lot to my car while checking my messages. My dad has called five times and left a voicemail. I don't have to listen to it to know why he's calling. It's the same reason he's been calling me for the last month: he wants me to come work for him. Well, wanting might not be a strong enough word. More like demanding.

I stuff my phone into my pocket without listening to the message, noting the Mercedes is parked beside my BMW. When I near my car, I curiously glance at the man sitting in the driver's seat, texting on his phone.

As if noting my stare, he glances up and his eyes widen.

"What the hell?" I mutter. "Why the hell are you looking at me like that?"

He has his window rolled down, so I know he heard me. He doesn't answer, though, simply starting up his engine and driving off like a bat out of hell.

Scratching my head, I climb into my car and let the engine idle for a few minutes to defrost the windows. I stay in the parking lot for longer than necessary, watching the entrance to the parking lot, making sure the Mercedes doesn't come back.

Maybe I'm overreacting, but the guy looked at me like he knew me, or maybe he knew I was friends with Willow. And in a place like this, people knowing you isn't a good thing.

Chapter Seven

Willow

Sunlight shines across my face as I open my eyes and roll over, stretching my arms above my head. My bed is empty, causing a cold emptiness to seep into my bones. But I feel refreshed, probably more than I have in a long time.

Then it all comes rushing back to me: my hands on Beck's chest, my leg over his hip, the way he grinded against me. For a split, mind-losing second, I wanted him to do it again until I remembered the rule and why it exists.

Technically, I didn't have a hip-to-hip contact rule. Still, that didn't mean I felt any better about what occurred between us. That's what I tell myself. Sometimes, I wonder if I lie to myself as much as I do to everyone else.

Thankfully, Beck shrugged off the incident. I feel so bad. After handing him a rule that we could never kiss, I violated him. Talk about mixed signals.

He probably thinks I'm crazy. Honestly, maybe I am. I don't even know why I did it. Okay, that's a lie. I did it because I couldn't get the sight of his chest out of my mind.

When I closed my eyes, I fell into a dream of Beck and

me kissing, my hands all over his bare chest, and my hips grinding against his. So, apparently, my body decided to act out the dream in real life.

Stupid, traitorous body.

God, I suck.

Sighing, I roll over and focus on if my mom and her friends are gone. The place is silent except for a dog howling from outside. It'd be a peaceful way to wake up if I hadn't just sleep-fooled around with my best friend. Plus, my bedroom reeks of pot.

Knock. Knock. Knock.

I look at the clock and grimace. Six o'clock in the morning and not everyone has left yet.

"Hey, mini-Paula, why don't you open the door, get your sweet ass out here, and put on a little show for us," a guy says from the other side of the door. "Isn't that what you do? Dance, right?"

I fuse my lips together and close my eyes. *Go away. Go away. Go away.*

"That uniform you were wearing … That's what it means … You're a dancer at Crazy Morelliesin's. How come I've never seen you there before?"

Because I'm not a dancer.

But what you do might not be any better.

"Does your mama know where you work?" he asks. "I bet she does … She used to do work there herself when she

105

was younger."

I swallow the shameful lump clogging my airway. While I knew my mom had dabbled in stripping for money, I never knew she worked at the same place as me.

I really am like her.

No! I'm not! I haven't even dated anyone and will never date anyone. Plus, I'm going to college. One day, I will be better than her.

Well, that's what I tell myself as the guy hammers on my door for the next half-hour.

When he gives up, I try to go back to sleep, but my worried mind keeps me up, and finally, I haul my behind out of bed to check out the damage in the apartment.

Before I head out into the mess, I crack the door open and peer into the hallway to make sure the house is empty. I don't spot anyone passed out anywhere, so I open the door wider and step out.

My nose promptly crinkles at the stench of weed, booze, and sweat. The mustiness in the air makes me want to run to the bathroom and take a shower. Needing to check on the place first, I put one foot in front of the other as I endeavor into the living room. The sofa is tipped upside down, the coffee table is pressed sideways against the patched wall, and a pile of beer cans is stacked in the middle of the room. My initial instinct is to clean up the mess ASAP, but I need to go peek in on my mom first.

Turning my back on the mess, I walk back to her bedroom and find her bed empty. I check the bathroom, the closets, and then the kitchen. There's no sign of her anywhere. She must have never come home from the bar.

I grow worried at the thought of all the places she could be: whoring herself on the corner, shooting up in some sleazy hotel, or lying dead in a ditch somewhere. All except the latter has happened.

I slouch onto the table and lower my head into my hands, debating whether or not I should track her down. Usually, I do, but Beck is supposed to be coming over today to tow my car. Although, after what happened last night, I question if I should let Beck off the hook and call Ari to come help me.

Backtracking to my bedroom, I pick up my phone either to call Beck or Ari—I haven't decided yet. Then I note the missed call from Wynter. I decide to call her, procrastinating my car ordeal.

"Hey, lazy butt," Wynter greets me after I yawn a hello.

"That's a first." I flop down on my bed and stare at the water stained ceiling. "Usually, you call me a crackhead."

"Yeah, well, I figured I'd mix it up a bit. Make life a little more interesting," she teases. "Seriously, though, why do you sound tired? Usually, you're up at the butt crack of dawn."

"I had a rough night."

"Because your car broke down?"

"Yeah. And there was a party going on and some guy woke me up at, like, six o'clock in the morning." I don't bother mentioning the party was being thrown by my mom. While Wynter knows I don't have a fantastic home life, she doesn't know all the details like Beck does. I also don't bring up Beck staying in my bed or that I rubbed myself against him for various reasons, one being that Wynter will look way too much into it.

"I don't know why you still live there," she says. "It'd be so much easier if you just moved to Fairs Hollow. And it's not like you love living with your mom."

"It's more complicated than just that," I mutter, massaging my temple to reduce the pressure pushing against my skull.

"Why? I mean, you're almost nineteen. You shouldn't have to live with your mom anymore if you don't want to."

"Yeah, but she needs help paying rent and stuff." *And making sure she doesn't die in her sleep.*

"Why's that your job? Isn't it supposed to be the other way around?"

"Not always."

"Still ... That really isn't fair," she says, sounding deeply perplexed. "My parents aren't that great at all, but they'd never make me pay their rent for them. And they shouldn't. No parent should do that."

"I know that." I really do. And I've tried to talk to my mom about this many, many times, about her stepping up and taking care of herself. She always says she will, but after years of being the sole provider, I've given up on her ever changing.

"You could always move in with me," she suggests. "I'm going to need a roommate, anyway, when Luna moves out."

As shouting echoes from outside, I push from the bed and pad over to the window. "Since when is Luna moving out?"

"Well, it's not official. But she and Grey have been talking pretty seriously about moving in together."

I pull back the curtain and peer out the window. "Really?" I scan the parking lot and spot a younger couple who lives three doors down standing near a trunk. They're screaming in each other's faces, the girl enraged because she thinks the guy cheated on her. I have flashbacks to the many times my mom was involved in a similar scene. "Isn't that moving a little quickly? And they're so young."

"Yeah, but they've been dating for over a year, so I don't think it's that weird. Besides, they pretty much live together, anyway, either here or at Grey's. At least when they get their own place, they can have some alone time. And I won't walk in on them doing it on the couch again."

109

I snort a laugh. "Holy shit. You walked in on them?"

"Yeah. Didn't I tell you about that?"

"No."

"Oh, my God, it was so awful. Although, I think Luna was more embarrassed than anyone."

"She gets embarrassed pretty easily, doesn't she?"

"So do you," she accuses. "In fact, sometimes, you're worse than her."

My pulse accelerates as the couple starts shoving each other. "I am not. I rarely get embarrassed."

"With normal stuff, yeah. But when anything sexual gets mentioned or implied, you totally start blushing."

"You're so full of shit."

I contemplate whether or not to go outside and break up the fight. They're just pushing each other right now, but that's how fights usually start, and things can quickly escalate, something I've seen happen a hundred times.

Before I can arrive at a decision, they abruptly stop shoving each other, and their lips collide in a deep, passionate kiss.

Yep, I've seen that happen before, too.

As the guy pulls back to peel the girl's shirt off, right there in the middle of the parking lot, I look away, my cheeks warming.

Okay, maybe Wynter is right about me. Maybe I do get embarrassed by sexual stuff. I mean, look how I reacted last night. How I manage to work where I work is beyond me. Then again, I know what the alternative is if I don't.

"It's okay, though," Wynter says with a laugh. "Once you start having sex, I'm sure you'll grow up a bit."

"Oh, whatever," I retort. "Don't act like that."

"Like what?"

"Like you've had sex."

"I've come closer than you."

"So what? That doesn't make you more grown up than me." I move to let the curtain fall forward then pause as a figure standing in front of the abandoned motel across the way catches my attention.

At first, I assume it's a random junkie waiting to buy drugs since that's what the motel is notorious for, but the person is decked out in all black with a hoodie over their head and sporting boots that look too pricey for a crackhead to afford. At least the ones that live around here. Plus, a shiny Mercedes is parked behind them, like the car I saw last night that seemed completely out of place.

An uneasy feeling churns in the pit of my stomach as I note the person's gaze is aimed at the front door of my apartment. *Shit, Mom, what did you do this time? Sell drugs? Prostitute? Screw some rich guy over?*

The person suddenly turns toward my window, and I instinctively crouch down. Maybe I'm overacting, but over the years, my mom has gotten herself into quite a few predicaments when she pissed the wrong person off. I can't count how many times she's warned me to lay low for a while and not answer the door.

I wish I could call her and find out if this has anything to do with her, but after losing three phones in less than a month, I couldn't, and didn't really want to, buy her another one.

"Oh, Willow," Wynter singsongs through the receiver. "Whatcha thinkin' about?"

I put the phone up to my ear. "Finals," I lie.

"You sure?" Amusement laces her tone. "Because I was thinking maybe you were thinking about sex."

I sit down on the floor and stretch out my legs. "Why would you think that? Especially after you implied that I get embarrassed over anything that has to do with sex, you know, because I'm a virgin and all."

She chuckles. "So what if you get embarrassed? That doesn't mean you don't ever think of having sex. I know you have before."

"Maybe a couple of times," I admit, refusing to tell her the details.

"And I bet I can guess who was around you those couple of times." Her insinuating tone makes me frown.

"No one, in particular, was around." I recline against the wall and cross my legs. "But please, by all means, explain who you think has me all hot and bothered, because

I'm ninety-nine percent sure that's what you're getting at."

"Well, he's tall with messy blond hair, likes soccer, and is kind of rebellious when he wants to be, at least to his parents and the teachers and telling the man to go fuck himself. He prefers getting high at parties instead of shit-faced, but he's not a pothead, just a dabbler for relaxation purposes. He loves playing the hero, although he'll never admit it, at least to a certain girl he's known since grade school. Everyone else he couldn't care less about. He also can be a pain in the ass sometimes, but you'll never agree with me." She gives a lengthy pause. "Hmmm … What else am I forgetting …? Oh, yeah, and his name rhymes with Shmeckett."

"That's not funny." I squirm uncomfortably as images of last night wash over me and my skin tingles all over. "Beck doesn't make me think about sex."

"Yeah, right. You're such a liar," she states amusedly. "I can see it in your eyes every time we're around him— well, that's how you've been for the last year or so. But you'll never admit it, so I don't even know why I brought it up."

I fidget with the sleeve of my shirt. "Beck is just my friend—my best friend. No offense."

"None taken. He's a way, *way* better friend than I am, anyway."

"What's that supposed to mean?"

113

"It means he'd do anything for you, which is exactly what he does every chance you give him." A splash of bitterness creeps into her tone and makes me question the underlying reason for why we're having this conversation.

Does Wynter like Beck and is jealous of our relationship? It's not the first time the thought has crossed my mind, and Ari suggested once that he thinks Beck and Wynter bicker all the time because of sexual tension. Them getting together would make sense. They both come from wealthy, well-respected families, and they share a lot of common interests, are very social, and don't spend their nights with their ass hanging out to make extra cash.

Yep, perfect together.

And I should be happy for them, yet my stomach burns with nausea, or maybe that's jealousy.

"Because he's a good friend." I force the unwanted thought from my head. "And if you were, too, you wouldn't be talking about this."

"Well, I think we already established that I wasn't the best friend, so I'm going to go ahead and say what I've been dying to say for the last few months." The humor dies in her tone, shifting to seriousness. "I think Beck—"

"Wynter," I warn.

"—is in love with you!" she shouts over me.

I want to open the window and chuck the phone outside to escape this conversation. But I can't afford to replace my phone.

"He does not. At least, not like that." *Does he? Do I want him to?*

I shake my head. What the hell is wrong with me?

"What do you mean, *like that*?" The humor has returned. She's totally enjoying my discomfort.

"Like … like love …" I push to my feet and pace the short length of my room.

Love? I don't even know what love is … do I?

Beck's face appears in my head: his smile, the way he touches my nose to get me to smile, the way I always seem to be able to smile around him.

Safe.

"Beck and I are just friends," I announce stupidly, knowing my very lame argument will never win against Wynter's mad skills. Seriously, the girl can get her way by snapping her fingers.

"If that's what you have to tell yourself, then go ahead. But one day, it'll catch up with you."

"*Catch up*? How can something like that catch up with me?" I feign annoyance when really, I'm freaking out.

Maybe it has already caught up with us. Ever since that kiss, our friendship has been bumpy, off balance, and flaming with heat. Awkward moments keep occurring, like when he grazed his knuckles across my thigh last night or every time I stare stupidly at his lips. Or when we lay in bed together, grinding against each other …

"You really want to hear my theory?" Wynter's cautious tone should scare me since she normally doesn't give a crap about what she says.

"Um … I don't know …" I bite on my thumbnail, uncertain how to respond.

"Well, I'm going to tell you, anyway." She gives another drawn out pause, either to build dramatic effect or offer me a chance to back out. "I think that one of these days, the sexual tension is going to become too much, and you guys are going to end up screwing each other's brains out."

I stop at the foot of my bed and sink down on the mattress. "Trust me; that'll never happen."

"If you say so."

"I have self-control, you know."

"Ha! Implying that you have self-control means you've thought about it."

"I have not," I gripe. "So stop saying this shit."

"Liar."

"Drama queen."

"Girl who wants to screw Beck."

"Wynter—"

"Oh, my God, I think I'm going to pierce my belly button," she cries out through her laughter.

I roll my eyes. "You so are not. You just didn't want to

argue with me anymore."

"Maybe, but maybe not," she teases. "Maybe I'm going to change my whole preppy girl image and become you. I'll even get a tattoo."

"What do you mean, *like me*? I don't have any tattoos."

"But you have a lot of piercings."

I trace my finger along the multiple earrings lining my ear. "Just in my ears."

"And in your belly button."

"Yeah, only because of you."

"Hey, you didn't have to accept the dare," she points out. "And you could've taken it out."

"I didn't really want to," I admit, lifting the bottom of my shirt to peek at the diamond glistening above my belly button, "after going through all that pain."

She laughs mockingly. "That's so not the only reason you kept it in."

"What are you getting at? I'm sure you're getting at something." I lower my shirt then rest back on my elbows. "You always are."

"Of course I am. What's the point of life if you're not getting at anything?" she asks with a seemingly out of place sigh. "But, anyway, all I was suggesting is that maybe, like our dear, sweet Beck, you have a bit of a rebellious side."

"I do not," I protest, probably sounding more offended

117

than I should. "I've never done anything rebellious in my entire life." Then again, my mom has never cared about what I did, so how would I ever rebel?

"Maybe you have a secret dark side, and the piercing is just a subtle way of showing it."

Anxiety stirs in my chest like a sleeping beast ready to awake and attack me. Beck said something similar last night about going to the dark side. Am I that obvious? If so, I worry over what else they've noticed about me lately.

"So, quick question. When are you coming back from New York?"

"Why? Are you planning on throwing me a welcome home party?" she jokes. "Or do you just miss me that much?"

"Of course I miss you," I say, relieved she didn't re-mark at my very noticeable subject change. "Even if you are a pain in my ass."

"Aw, I love you, too, Wills," she replies dryly. "And FYI, you're a pain in the ass, too, which is why we're such good friends."

"Yeah, maybe … But seriously, when are you coming back?"

"I fly back Saturday afternoon. Why? What's up?"

"It's nothing." I blow out a loud exhale. "Beck's just having a party on Friday and is making me go. And I hate the idea of going alone."

"Well, you won't be alone. Beck will be there." Again, a hint of bitterness enters her tone. "And Ari and Luna and probably Grey since the two of them are attached at the freakin' hip 24/7."

"They'll be back from their road trip by then?" I tense when I hear a knock on the front door.

"They should be," she says. "You can always call them and find out."

"Okay, I might do that." I push up from my bed as the knocking grows louder and tiptoe out of my room and to the front door.

"Or you could just go solo," she continues, "so you and Beck can finally hook up."

A nervous exhale trembles from my lips as I lean in to peer out the peephole. "Don't start again." A relieved sigh gushes out of me at the sight of Beck standing outside. "Hey, I have to go. Beck just showed up."

"Of course he did," she says. "He can barely stand to be away from you for more than a day."

"He's just here to help me."

"Oh, I bet he is. Just make sure to call me after it happens."

"First off, I'll never call you right after the first time I have sex." I wrap my fingers around the doorknob. "And second, Beck and I are never going to have sex. Trust me; he doesn't even want to have sex with me."

119

A voice in the back of my mind cackles with laughter.

"What if he did, though? Would you do it?"

"No."

"You totally just hesitated—"

"No, I didn't." *Did I?* "And why are you so obsessed with this?"

"I'm not. I'm just having fun."

"Well, can we please drop it?"

"Fine," she surrenders. "I'll let you off the hook … for now."

"Gee, thanks. How very kind of you."

"You're welcome," she quips. "Talk to you later."

"Bye." I hang up and open the door with a smile on my lips. My relief instantly shifts to confusion, though, as Beck rubs his hand across his mouth, attempting to conceal a grin. "What's up with all the smiling?"

He rolls his tongue in his mouth. "Why is that weird? I smile all the time. In fact, it's kind of my MO."

"True, but still …" I eye him over warily. "You think something's funny, but I can't figure out what."

"Yeah, maybe, but trust me; it's probably better you don't know." He bites down on his lip hard and stuffs his hands into the back pockets. "So, are you ready to tow your car back?" His gaze scrolls across the plaid pajama shorts and long-sleeved top I'm wearing, leaving a trail of heat across my skin that warms *every* part of my body. "You're still wearing your pajamas."

"Yeah, I've been lazy this morning, probably because someone spoiled me last night and made me sleep so well." I bite down on my lip. Maybe I shouldn't have said that.

A pleased smile lights up his face. "Good. I'm glad I could help. And you should do that more often."

"Be lazy?" I suddenly become very aware of how trashed the place is and that he can probably see the mess.

He nods, giving me that look I can't quite figure out. "You need more rest, princess. You're always so tired because you overwork yourself."

"I'm fine," I lie. "It's nothing I haven't had to handle before."

His gaze fastens on mine. "That's what I'm afraid of. And sometimes, when you handle too much, you eventually break."

I know what break he's referring to: the nervous breakdown I had my senior year when I was trying to juggle three jobs, school work, taking care of my drug-addict mom, all while applying to colleges.

"I'm fine. I promise." I cast a glance across the street, not knowing whether to be relieved or unnerved the person is no longer there.

Beck inches toward me and leans in, lowering his voice. "No, you're not." He gestures at the trashed living room behind me. "You shouldn't have to handle this. You never should've had to handle it."

He smells so good, like cologne and soap and everything that calms me, and I nearly lean into him, grasp his shirt, hold on for dear life, and never let go …

"I know," I say, making myself stay put. "But there's not much I can do about it."

He stares me down with determination. "Except walk away."

I fiddle with the bottom of my shorts. "I can't just bail out on her … Could you imagine what would happen if I did? She barely survived my dad walking out."

He hooks a finger underneath my chin, forcing me to look at him. "I know you worry about your mom, but you can't spend the rest of your life taking care of her and letting her drag you down. There has to be a point when you say enough is enough, or she's going to destroy your life."

"I'll be fine." Won't I?

Sometimes, I wonder how fine I'll be three years from now … if I'll graduate from college like I plan to or if something will show up and ruin that plan. That's one of the things I learned growing up in such an unstable home life: anything can happen in a heartbeat and dropkick the stability out of the ballpark, like when my dad left or when my mom decided to try heroin for the first time a year ago. She's never been the same since, and the chaotic madness in our life increased.

Maybe Beck's right. Perhaps it's time to say enough is enough.

Then what? I walk out on my mom and hope she'll clean up her act? After all, in the end, as crappy as she is, my mom is the only family I have left. And I'm the only person she has who cares enough to worry about her.

Chapter Eight

Beck

After spending the morning worrying about Willow, I was glad to be at her place again, even if it was just to tow her car home.

As I stood at her front door, I drummed my fingers against the sides of my legs, restless. The neighborhood made me uneasy; people were always selling drugs and sometimes their bodies, and a couple was screwing each other on the front porch of their apartment … At least, I think it was their apartment.

My nerves died, however, when I heard Willow talking to someone through the door, saying my name and sex a couple of times. I wasn't exactly sure what was being discussed, but listening to Willow talk about me and sex had me grinning like a dumbass.

When she opened the door, I tried to hide my elation and failed epically. Honestly, I didn't really give a shit. After all, Willow was talking about me and sex. Sex and me.

I couldn't stop grinning idiotically as I thought about last night.

Then I noticed the disarray in the living room, and my good mood went *poof* as I was painfully reminded of another thing I have to do today: have a talk with her.

Ari is supposed to meet us on the highway in about an hour, which leaves me about thirty minutes to persuade her to move away from this fucking hellhole in the middle of town, and not just move away, but move in with me. Knowing Willow, she isn't going to take what I have to say very well. She'll be stubborn, try to refuse. I've had this conversation enough times with her to know. But I'm not ready to give up.

I have nightmares of the stuff that goes on here, stuff I've heard Willow whisper about when she's really frightened. I know she holds back all the details … all the time.

"So, what happened to your mom this time that set her off?" I ask after Willow signals for me to come inside. I turn in a circle in the kitchen, glass crunching underneath my boots. Then I tip my head up and frown at the broken light above. "Someone broke your light."

"I know." She heaves a weight-of-the-world-on-my-shoulders sigh before crossing the kitchen and opening the fridge. "And I'm not sure what set her off. I think she's just rebounding."

I walk up behind her as she lowers her head and peers inside the empty fridge. "Did anyone bother you after I left? The house seemed empty."

125

"A guy knocked on my room, but that's it."

"*That's it?* You say that like it's no big deal."

"It's not. Not really. And at least he didn't come inside my room."

I take a deep breath as my frustration rises, reminding myself that I'm going to talk to her about this, get her out of here.

She extends her arm across the empty top shelf, slips her fingers behind it, and wiggles out a small box of pre-cooked bacon.

"Did you hide that back there?" I lean against the wall beside the fridge, observing her: the way strands of her long, brown hair hang in her big eyes; the arch of her back; the way her ass peeks out of her pajama bottoms … If I walked up behind her, it'd be the perfect position…

"Yeah, I did." She steps back and closes the fridge, thrusting me out of my dirty thoughts. "I have to because my mom's friends usually eat everything when they come over …" She trails off as she looks at me with her head angled to the side. "What's that look on your face about?"

"What look?" *The look where I think about fucking you from behind? Do I have a look for that, too?*

"You just look … I don't know"—she scratches at the back of her neck—"pensive or something."

"Pensive, huh?" I choke back a laugh. *Huh, so that's the look I have on my face when I get dirty thoughts of her.*

"Interesting word choice."

"Well, it's what you look like." She tears open the box of bacon. "But the question is, why?" She heads toward the microwave then reels back around with an amused look on her face. "I'm thinking either you're high or you got some this morning."

"You know I don't drive when I'm high." I pause, assessing her reaction. "And as for the getting some this morning, I actually haven't gotten any for a really long time."

"What's a really long time?" Her teeth sink into her bottom lip, her gaze flickering to my lips. "Never mind. That's none of my business."

"Why not?" I cock a brow. "I told you when I lost my virginity."

She scratches her neck again. "Yeah, and I felt pretty uncomfortable when you did."

I should drop this, but I can't. She's acting so shifty, and I want to know why, if it has anything to do with me.

"Why?"

She picks at the corner of the box of bacon. "Why what?"

I straighten from the wall and cross the tiny kitchen, eliminating the space between us. "Why does it bother you when I talk about sex?"

She studies me then frowns. "Have you been talking to

Wynter?"

Okay, not what I was expecting, but I'm definitely curious.

"No … Why?"

"Nothing." She hurriedly waves me off, facing the microwave.

I snag her by the hip, spin her around, and back her up against the counter, causing her to part her lips in shock.

"No way. You can't just ask something like that and not explain." I put a hand on each side of her, pinning her between my arms, then lean in until our bodies are flush.

Her chest heaves against mine as she sucks in panicked breaths. I expect her to shove me away, but she elevates her chin, maintaining eye contact, her bottom lip trembling.

"Why is it weird that I asked if you've talked to Wynter? You two talk all the time."

"Yeah, but clearly, you two had a conversation." I lower my head closer to her, our lips inches apart. So. Fucking. Close. "I'm guessing it was about me and sex."

Her cheeks flush, and it's probably the most adorable thing I've ever seen.

"Why would we talk about your sex life?"

"That's what I'm wondering." I slant back slightly to search her eyes. "There's not really much to talk about."

She averts her gaze from mine. "There's some stuff, though."

I lean to the side, forcing her to look at me. "What's that supposed to mean?"

"Nothing." Her blush deepens. "Can we please stop talking about this? Wynter already made me have a very uncomfortable conversation with her today."

"About sex?" I pause, tension rippling through my body as something occurs to me. "Wait. Did you … have sex with someone?"

"I'm so not talking to you about this." She places her hand against my chest and gently pushes me away, but I trap her hand and hold it right above my heart.

The fact that she didn't give me a direct answer makes my pulse race with nervous energy, which I'm sure she can feel. I don't care. I'm panicking a little. I mean, sure, I've had sex before, but not for a while, not since I realized how much I like her. As far as I know, Willow is still a virgin. If that's changed, it's been recent.

Did she meet someone?

"Why can't you talk to me about this?" I struggle to keep my voice even. "We've talked about this kind of stuff before."

She shakes her head. "We have not."

I hold up a finger. "Last year, after we played beer pong at one of my parties, we went up to my bedroom, and you admitted to me that you were still a virgin. And I admitted to you that I slept with two people."

129

"You don't need to remind me about that. I have a pretty good memory of it." Her cheeks flame bright red, and she wiggles her hand away from my chest. "I also remember that I couldn't look you in the eye for, like, two weeks because you …" She looks everywhere except at me. "But if you really need to know, the answer is no. I haven't had … sex with anyone."

There are a million things I want to say to her right now, most of them involving the words sex and touch and kiss, but I back off, remembering the last time I kissed her. Our friendship was like a shaky tightrope afterward until she created that no kissing rule. That's when I realized how fragile she is, how easily I could lose her.

I don't ever want to lose her.

I don't know how much longer I can follow the no kissing rule, either … especially after last night.

"All right, enough with the awkwardness." I snatch the box of bacon from her hand and toss it onto the table. "Go get your pretty ass dressed so we can tow your car home and then get you something decent to eat."

She offers me a thankful smile. "Sounds good. But you don't need to feed me. I can eat the bacon." She steps toward the table to pick up the box, but I sidestep, blocking her path.

"You need to eat more than that." I trail my knuckles down her side, repressing a groan when she shivers. God fucking dammit, I love it when she does that. Why can't we just do it all the time? "You're already too skinny as it is." Because her damn mom lets her friends eat all their food.

"Beck, you really don't have to take care of me," she insists, but I can see her willpower cracking.

I just wish she'd let it down completely, let me in completely. Stop fighting perfection.

"I know I don't have to, but I want to," I tell her. "And last night, we both agreed that we should let me do what I want."

"We never agreed to that."

"Well, then we should because it sounds like a pretty good agreement."

She fights back a smile. "For *you*."

"No way." I press my hand to my chest. "You totally benefit from this agreement."

She elevates her brows. "How do you figure?"

I grin. "Because everything that I want to do involves you."

She grows quiet, looking at me with worry, guilt, and a bit of shame. I hate that she feels ashamed over accepting my help. I hate that she thinks she has to take care of her problems herself. I hate that her mom has fucked with her head.

God, I hate her fucking mother. The only good thing she's ever done is bring Willow into this world.

"Fine, I'll go get dressed," she relents. "And then we can stop at a burger place on our way where *I'll* buy myself a burger. And I want to give you gas for having to drive out here twice."

"Sounds good." *Not.* If she tries to give me money, I'll sneak it back in her purse when she's not looking, something I've done before.

"I mean it." She backs away with her finger aimed at me. "One day, I'm going to pay you back for everything you've done."

"Okay." What I don't say is that she's already paid me back by letting me into her life… by always telling me how great I am … by never letting my father's negativity bring me down … by sticking up for me … by letting me hug her … by lying to get me out of trouble all those times.

By … everything.

After Willow leaves the room, I grab a garbage bag out of a drawer and begin picking up the seemingly endless amount of garbage. I've never really cleaned before since I have a maid, something I'm extremely grateful for when I find a used condom and an old pair of underwear wedged between the wall and the fridge.

Fucking, yuck. I really need to convince her to leave this shithole.

Once most of the beer bottles and cigarette butts are cleaned up, I head into the living room to put the furniture upright, but I veer toward the door as someone knocks.

I glance out the peephole to see who it is, and confusion sets in.

"What the hell?" I open the door and step out onto the empty front porch. "I know I heard a knock." My gaze roves over the cars in the parking lot, a group of people lounging around on rusty patio furniture a few doors down, and then lands on the motel across the street where a Mercedes is parked. It's the same one I saw last night.

What the hell is going on with that?

"What're you doing?" Willow's worried voice sails over my shoulder.

I twist back around and eye her over. She's changed into a pair of fitted jeans, a tight black shirt that shows off a sliver of skin, and clunky boots that lace up to her knees. Her hair is damp, her skin bare and flawless, and her glossy lips are begging to be licked.

I tear my gaze off her mouth and focus on her eyes. "I thought I heard someone knock, but I guess I'm losing my mind or something because no one was out here." When her shoulders slump, I immediately grow concerned. "What's wrong?"

"It's nothing." She ravels a strand of her hair around her finger, nibbling on her bottom lip.

"Clearly, something's bothering you." I inch toward her and lightly tap her nose. "Or else you wouldn't look so worried."

"You know me too well." She untangles her hair from her finger. "Right before you showed up, I noticed this person standing across the street, and it looked like they were staring at my house."

Tension pours through my veins. "Do you know who it was?"

"They had a hoodie over their head, so I couldn't see what they looked like." She slants against the doorframe, releasing a stressed exhale. "I'm probably just overreacting … I just get so stressed out when my mom starts partying and doing so many," she lowers her voice to an embarrassed whisper, "drugs … They make her do a lot of sketchy shit and piss a lot of people off." Her eyes flash with fear as she swallows hard. "Sometimes, the wrong people."

"Something's happened before, hasn't it?" I ask. "I can tell by the look in your eyes."

She rubs her finger below her eye as if attempting to erase the look. "There've been a couple of times when she's screwed over some drug dealers, and they've come banging on our door, demanding money."

"What!" I exclaim way too loudly, drawing attention from the neighbors. Fuck them. This isn't about them. This is about Willow putting herself in danger by being here. "Why haven't you told me about this?"

She becomes deeply engrossed with inspecting her fingernails. "Because I knew you'd worry, and I don't like worrying you … This isn't even your problem. You shouldn't have to be here, cleaning up my house and being a taxi for me … You don't even get anything in return." She lowers her hand to her side, but keeps her gaze glued to the ground. "It's not right. And I really need to stop relying on you so much."

I fix my finger under her chin and angle her head up. "First of all, I do all these things because I *want* to, because you're my best friend. Not because I have to. And second, I do get something out of it."

Her brows knit, again proving how clueless she can be sometimes. "What do you get?"

"*You*," I say boldly. Before she can react, I say, "And as your best friend, I can't let you stay here anymore. Not when I found out you've got pissed off drug dealers coming around. It's not safe, Wills."

"Nothing in my life is safe anymore," she mumbles, staring down at her feet.

"Then it's time to fix that. Move in with me."

Her eyes pop wide open, and she swiftly shakes her head "I can't do that … It's too much."

"For me or you?"

"For … for both of us."

"Don't include me in the us, because I'm perfectly fine

135

with the idea. In fact, I like it a lot."

"You say that now," she mutters, "but you'd get sick of me eventually."

"That's not true, and I think you know it," I say, softening my tone. "I think there's another reason, one you're not telling me."

"I just don't want to be a charity case." Her voice cracks.

"You're not a charity case. You're my friend … a friend who needs to get the fuck away from a life that's dragging her down."

"Moving into your house isn't going to save me from that."

"It's a start."

She smashes her lips together, peering up at me with her sad eyes. I can tell she wants to agree to move in with me, but beneath the want is fear.

What're you so afraid of? Moving out? Me? Or is it someone else?

"Will you just promise me you'll think about it?" I ask in a pleading tone. "Even if you don't move in with me … Maybe you could move in with Wynter."

She considers this, biting on her fingernail. "Maybe I could do that … She did say she might need a roommate …" Her shoulders unwind a smidgen, and my heart dies a little.

So, it's me.

"I don't think I could afford half of her rent, though," she adds. "Not when I'm paying rent on this place."

I gape at her. "Then stop paying rent on this fucking place. It's not your job to pay for your mom's apartment."

"Yes, it is." Guilt fills her eyes. "If I don't, then my mom will end up on the streets."

I mold my palm to her cheek and wipe the tears away with my thumb. "I know you may not want to hear this, but that might be a good thing. Helping her out … It's enabling her."

She sniffles then surprises me as a faint laugh slips from her lips. "Where the hell did you learn that?"

"A psychology class," I admit. "It was briefly covered when we discussed drug addiction. I've heard it enough that I know it's true."

"It is," she says. When I give her a questioning look, she adds, "I had to talk to a therapist a couple of times after I had that meltdown during our senior year." She winces at the memory of the time she broke down in English class because she got a B on an assignment.

The panic attack wasn't really about the grade, though. She'd been barely sleeping, overworking herself with two jobs, studying, filling out college applications, and taking care of her mom. No one else knew that about her, and they started mocking her for freaking out over a grade. A good grade, at that. I knew, though. I knew everything, and I hate that I did because I felt so helpless.

"But, anyway." She shifts her weight. "I let some of the details about my home life slip out, particularly the details about my mom doing drugs and me taking care of her, and the therapist said that sometimes, helping a drug addict by giving them money or paying their bills actually does more harm than good."

"Then you should definitely move out, right?" *Please, for the love of God, just say yes.*

"I don't know if I can … just leave her like that. I mean, what happens if she gets really drunk one night and no one is here to take her to the hospital to get her stomach pumped?"

I rack my brain for a persuasive enough answer. "Maybe you could come check on her every day. You could drive out here before or after work."

Her skin pales. "Yeah … maybe …"

"You could borrow my car, too." Disregarding her frown, I add, "It'd be safer that way, which is kind of the point of getting you out of here."

She thrums her fingers against the side of her legs. "Maybe I could borrow Wynter's car or take the bus."

My jaw clenches. "Why are you okay with borrowing Wynter's car, but not mine?"

"I'm not okay with borrowing anything, but with

Wynter …"—her gaze collides with mine, and an ocean of fear pours from her eyes—"it's just less complicated."

My heart stings a bit, and I massage my chest. "Wynter is anything but uncomplicated," I tell her, trying not to sound like a wounded pussy, yet I do just a little bit. "But if that's what it'll take to get you out of the house, then okay."

She nods, but I'm not letting out my breath yet. No, I won't breathe freely again until she's far, far away from her mother and a life that's never been good enough for her.

The revising of the list....

Chapter Nine

Willow

The next few days are a routine of driving to work, returning to a bare house, and hours of studying. Work. Study. Alone. Work. Study. Alone. The pattern is starting to drive me insane. I can't relax, either, not when bills are piling up, and I'm drowning in a stack of assignments up to my elbows. I also haven't figured out where my mom took off to, which makes me extremely nervous since she was in a terrible condition the last time I saw her. Plus, the person I saw across the street has me on edge.

While no one has flat-out knocked on the door and demanded money, I did notice someone lurking around my car last night. I don't know what their deal is or if it's the same person or not, but I feel like I'm playing a waiting game and will eventually lose.

I really need to talk to my mom and find out if she owes someone money.

I've searched the local bars and clubs for her and tracked down some of her friends, who aren't the most reliable sources. The only real lead I have is from a bar owner who informed me that my mom was there Monday night, flirting with a guy, and the two of them were chatting about driving to Vegas to elope. So now, not only do I have to worry about my mom going on a bender, but she may have gone on a bender with her new hubby, whom I've never met before.

Needless to say, by the time Friday night rolls around, I could really use a break from a sucky little thing called the stress of life.

Beck has been bugging me to hit up his party, and while I'm not much of a partier, I decide to go and attempt to let my hair down for a few hours.

At work, I count down the hours until I'm off while trying to decide what to wear since Beck insisted that the party was definitely a strict black-dress dress code. I cracked a joke when he reminded me of that, telling him I was excited to see what dress he was going to wear. Beck, being the goofball that he is, replied with a, "Just you wait. It's really sexy. Probably even sexier than yours." I laughed, already feeling better and growing even more eager to get away from the soul-draining apartment.

My eagerness takes a nosedive when Van, my thirty-year-old manager, informs me that we need to talk.

"Come back into my office for a second, Willow," he tells me as I'm passing by the bar, carrying an empty tray.

He's behind the bar with his long-sleeved shirt rolled up, a cigarette tucked behind his ear, and a contemplative look on his face.

"Okay." I set the tray down on the countertop, wrestling back my anxiety.

I'm sure it's nothing. You haven't done anything wrong.

Part of me wishes I've messed up, that he'll fire me or force me to quit. But it's the only job I've been able to get over the last six months that can pay all the bills, my tuition, and support my mom.

I follow Van past the stage, the neon pink lights flickering as the song switches and a set of new dancers enter. A group of guys catcall and make obscene gestures while waving money in the air. The girls onstage don't seem too bothered. Me? My stomach constricts to the point that I feel sick. In fact, for the last month of working here, I've had a constant stomachache, either from the environment or from my guilt.

When Van and I reach the back hallway, he motions for me to follow him into his office. Then he closes the door.

"Have a seat," he says, plopping down into the chair behind his cluttered desk.

I sit down, resisting the urge to tug on the bottom of my shorts as his eyes sweep over me. He's silent as he lights up a cigarette and takes a long drag.

"So," he starts, a cloud of smoke puffing from his lips, "you're probably wondering why I asked you back here."

I nervously nod. "I didn't do anything wrong, did I?"

He ashes the cigarette into a dark green ashtray, causing flakes of ash to circle the smoky air. "No, not at all. You're doing a great job, sweetheart."

I cringe at the sweetheart reference then hold my breath, sensing a *but* coming.

"*But* I'd really like to move you on stage. You're a beautiful girl." His eyes drink in the cleavage peeking out of my top. "It's such a waste to have you down on the floor. You deserve to be in the spotlight."

Deserve. As if it's a reward.

"I'm not sure I'd be very good up there." I wipe my damp palms on the tops of my legs. *Stay calm, Willow.* "I don't even know how to dance."

He sucks in another long drag from the cigarette. "It's not really about the dancing. All you need to do is show some skin and work the pole. I can have the girls teach you a few moves if that makes you feel more comfortable."

More comfortable? Yeah, like that'd ever happen.

"I appreciate the offer, Van." I will my voice steady. "But I really would just prefer to stay on as a waitress."

He grazes his thumb along the end of the cigarette. "You'd probably make triple what you're bringing in now."

For an insanely stupid moment, I consider his offer. *Triple* what I'm making? That'd be enough to pay for my mom's rent and get my own place. Then I picture getting up on stage, wearing pretty much nothing, and vomit burns at the back of my throat.

I cross my arms and legs, feeling too exposed. "I think I'll just stay on as a waitress if that's okay."

He puts out the cigarette and leans forward. "Look, Willow, you seem like a sweet girl, which is why I think you'd be so great on stage. Guys love the whole innocent, tortured act you've got going on."

That's how he sees me?

"But, when I hire my waitresses," he continues, overlapping his hands on his desk, "it's a trial to see how they'll handle the environment. If you do well, then you get moved to the stage."

My heart thrashes. "So, you're saying that I either have to get on stage or I'm fired?"

"Not so much fired as let go." He swivels back and forth in the chair. "Don't worry, though. I'll give you a couple of weeks to get used to the idea before I put you up there."

He acts like I've already agreed, and I wonder if anyone has ever told him no. Possibly not since working in a place like this requires a certain kind of desperation, a desperation I'm way too familiar with.

147

Nodding, I leave the office with a strange sense of numbness. When I enter the table area, my attention drifts toward the stage where two girls around my age are dancing on the poles, wearing nothing but a thong.

Bile burns at the back of my throat. I can't go up there. I shouldn't be working in this place to begin with.

Two weeks, Willow. You have two weeks to figure something out.

***

The rest of my shift drizzles by in a blur of serving drinks, ignoring crude remarks, and dodging advances. By the time I exit the club and head out to my car, the sky is pitch black, the air chilly, and I don't have a clue how to solve my problems.

You could always just accept Beck's offer.

I shake my head. *No. You already let him do too much this week, not only towing your car home, but buying a part so he and Ari could fix the thermostat.*

Gravel crunches underneath my boots as I weave around vehicles, heading for mine. Music drifts through the air, and a few guys are smoking near a lifted truck. When their eyes dart to me, I zip up my jacket, feeling naked in my jeans and plaid shirt.

My legs shake as I quicken my strides, one foot in front of the other. I hug my arms around myself, keeping my head low, trying to become invisible. Still, I can feel their eyes on me, tracking my every move. Their attention has me so distracted I don't notice the Mustang parked beside my car until I'm only a few steps away.

I grind to a stop immediately, an icky chill slithering up my spine as the driver's side door swings open.

Dane hops out with a huge smile on his face, like we're long-lost besties. "Hey, it's the girl from the street." He rounds the front of the car, walking toward me. "I was hoping I'd run into you again."

I force down my nerves the best that I can. "Why?"

"Because you made quite the impression on me." He stops in front of me, his gaze deliberately skimming up and down my body. "Although, you looked way better in the uniform." He fixes his dark eyes on mine. "Did you just get off?"

"I was just leaving." I move to sidestep around him, but he matches my move, blocking my path.

"Why don't you stay for a little while?" He lowers his voice, putting his face inches from mine. His breath reeks of beer, and his pungent cologne makes me want to puke. "Come into my car. Let's have some fun." He seizes hold of my hip, stabbing his fingernails into my skin as he jerks me closer. "I promise I'll make it worth your while."

My heart hammers as I lift my leg, preparing to knee him in the balls and run like hell. Then footsteps sound from behind me and cause me to freeze.

149

"Is this guy bothering you?" One of the guys who was smoking by the trunk steps up beside me. He looks around my age with sandy brown hair and kind eyes that seem oddly out of place.

"She's fine." Dane glances at me with a threat in his eyes. "We were just talking. We're old friends, actually."

The stranger turns to me. "Is that true?"

Swallowing hard, I shake my head. "No. I don't even know him."

The stranger's gaze locks on Dane. "You have three seconds to walk away."

Dane smirks, turning to face the stranger. "And then what? You're going to beat me up?"

The stranger folds his heavily tattooed arms across his solid chest. "Yeah, pretty much," he replies simply.

Dane's eyes fleetingly snap wide before he hastily composes himself. "Whatever, man. You don't look that tough, but I'm going to walk away, anyway, because I have shit to do." Dane shoots me a nasty look that causes a zap of fear to shoot up my spine. Then he stomps off toward the windowless entrance doors to the club.

Once he's gone, the stranger turns to me. "Are you okay?"

I nod with a tremulous breath. "Yeah, I think so."

"You really shouldn't walk out to your car alone. It's not safe. You should have one of the other girls walk out with you."

"I will from now on," I assure him. "And thanks for doing that. Most people wouldn't have intervened."

"It wasn't that big of a deal. The guy was just a rich punk who needed to be put in his place." His forehead creases as a pair of headlights sweep across us, giving me a better view of his face. "Hey, I think I know you from somewhere."

"I don't think so," I say, inching away from him.

He points a finger at me. "I think we have chemistry together. Professor Bralifington on Fridays, right?"

My insides fizzle as I become painfully aware that we go to the same university.

His name is Everette. We have a couple of classes together. While I don't know him very well, he could easily tell the wrong person my dirty, little work secret. People around the university do love to gossip. What if word gets back to my friends? What if word gets back to Beck?

Why have I never thought about this before?

"I have to go." I whirl around and jog for my car.

"Wait," he calls out.

I don't stop, hopping into the torn seat and peeling out of the parking lot. Anxiety chokes me as I drive away from the club, wishing I never had to return.

Find a way to fix this, Willow. You're good at solving problems. It's time for you to start figuring it out.

151

Chapter Ten

Willow

Instead of driving home, I go to Luna and Wynter's place to get ready. As I dig through Wynter's closet with Luna, searching for a dress to wear, I contemplate telling her about my job, confessing everything before this Everette guy blabs my dirty secret and word spreads like a wildfire.

Could I do that? Would she understand?

"Is everything okay?" Luna asks, sifting through Wynter's trendy designer shirts, dresses, and skirts. Her brown hair is pulled into a messy bun, and she's wearing yoga pants and a tank top. Like me, she doesn't own many dresses, so we're both looking for an outfit to wear tonight.

I open my mouth to spill the truth to her, but the words get caught in my throat. How can I tell her? Luna, who's never gotten into trouble? She's sweet and kind and innocent and thinks I am, too.

"Yeah, I'm fine," I chicken out. "I'm just stuck in my own head today."

"A couple of shots of tequila and a hell of a lot of

dancing should cure that." Her boyfriend, Grey, appears in the doorway, wearing a long-sleeved black shirt with the sleeves rolled up, jeans, and sneakers.

"You're breaking the dress code," I tease. "Where's your pretty, little dress?"

"Guys are supposed to wear a black shirt," Grey explains, checking out Luna's ass as she bends over to grab a pair of strappy heels off the floor.

"Well, that's just sexist," I reply, pulling a face at the short, fitted dress hanging up in front of me. "Maybe I should wear a suit to protest."

"You could." Grey braces his hands on the doorframe. "But I think you might break poor Beck's heart if you did."

"I doubt Beck's heart will get broken if I don't wear a dress," I say, debating whether or not to go through with my suit threat.

He rolls his eyes. "Yeah, right. Everything you do breaks his heart, and yet, he keeps coming back. He seriously is a glutton for punishment."

Luna's attention whips up, and she mouths, "*shut up.*"

"What's going on?" I glance back and forth between the two of them. "What did you mean by that?"

Grey backs out of the closet with his hands out in front of him. "Just ignore me. I think it's the tequila talking." Then he bails out like a guy who's about to get his ass handed to him by his girlfriend.

I face Luna with my hands on my hips. "Okay, spill."

She diverts her gaze from me and focuses on a knee-length pencil skirt. "This looks nice. I think I'll wear it."

"Luna …" I warn.

She hightails it out of the closet, and I chase her as she races past the bed and makes a beeline for the bathroom.

"Come on; just tell me what he meant."

She dives into the bathroom and slams the door. "He didn't mean anything. I think he's just drunk."

I check the doorknob. Locked. Of course.

I rest my forehead against the door. "I know he meant something, or he wouldn't have brought it up and then run off. And I know Grey and Beck are friends and talk … Does it hurt Beck … when I ask him for favors? Does he feel obligated?"

The lock clicks, and I move back as the door opens. Luna steps into the doorway, her expression masked with wariness.

"Helping you doesn't hurt him," she says. "It's when you don't let him help you that hurts him."

I rub my chest. My heart hurts. *I never want to hurt Beck.*

"Did Beck tell you that?"

"Not me, but he said something to Grey." She leans against the doorframe with her arms folded. "To give him credit, I think they were both high when the conversation went on, so I'm not sure if Beck actually meant to tell him some of the stuff."

"What other stuff did he tell him?"

"Not too much. Just that sometimes, it hurts him when he can't help you."

"But he helps me all the time. Too much, probably."

She hesitates. "I'm not sure if someone can help someone they love too much."

My heart sputters into a mad frenzy. "*Love?*"

Love.

Love.

Love.

Just like Wynter said.

"Like a friend," she sputters. Then an off-pitch laugh bursts from her lips. "You know what? Please forget everything I just said. Grey talked me into doing a shot after dinner, and you know how I get when I drink. I talk before I think. I definitely think it's time to sober up." With that, she scurries back into the bathroom and closes the door.

I stand there, stunned, unsure of what to do.

Unsure. Unsure. Unsure. When did my life become so full of uncertainties?

I need to get back on track, stick to my plan, and fix the problems in my life, starting with Beck's and my friendship. I need to make sure we're on the same page— the friend's page. A page I might not want to be on, but have to be.

Will he even want to be on that page when he finds out the truth about me?

Chapter Eleven

Beck

I haven't seen Willow since I towed her car back to her place, and the space is driving me insane. We've both been so busy and haven't had time to see each other. That's changing tonight, because she agreed to come to my party, surprisingly with very little persuasion. And, if I play my cards right, I can convince her to crash at my place for the night and get her away from that house for a bit.

I've talked to her a few times on the phone, and she mentioned how her mom hasn't been home in days. I don't know which is worse: her mom and her sketchy-ass friends being at the apartment or her being at the sketchy-ass apartment alone.

I asked a couple of times if she had made a decision to move out, and she still seems pretty undecided. Tonight, my mission is to change that. I don't know how yet, but I'll figure it out.

"Why the hell haven't you called me back?" my father's roaring voice shatters through my thoughts of Willow.

I spin around from my dresser as he storms into my bedroom. "Who let you in?"

Fury blazes in his eyes as he stops in front of me. "*Let me in?* Don't forget who paid for this house."

My jaw muscle spasms as I glide the dresser drawer shut. "You paid about ten percent of it, not all of it. And I thought this was supposed to be my graduation present, not some sort of collateral you could hang over my head."

"It was a present, but my name is still on the deed with yours," he says with a my-shit-don't-stink smirk, "which means I can take away some of the house if I want to."

I mentally roll my eyes at the image of him cutting the house into pieces and dragging some of it away.

"Sorry," I manage to get out. "I'm just confused why you're here. I thought you were in Vail with mom."

"I had to stay behind because of work, something you clearly know nothing about." He loosens the tie around his neck.

I pick up a leather-banded watch from my dresser and fasten it around my wrist. "So, you just let mom go off by herself again."

"She didn't have to go," he snaps, the vein in his neck bulging. "But she wanted to."

I don't blame her. Why would she want to stay behind and exchange mountains, snow, and ski slopes for an empty house and my dad's grumpy temperament?

I check the time. *Shit. The party starts in less than an hour. He needs to leave.*

"Are you heading to or from work?"

"I just took a break to get some dinner and thought I'd stop by to check up on you since you never called me back, even after I left you countless messages." He stares me down accusingly. "I thought maybe it was because you were too busy with school, but I should've guessed it was because of a party. It always is."

At first, I'm confused how he knows about the party. Then I remember the food and alcohol bottles set up in the kitchen.

"This is the first party I've had in a month." I take a clean long-sleeved shirt out of my dresser and tug it over my T-shirt. "And it's for Thanksgiving."

"Thanksgiving was yesterday," he says like that somehow proves a point. "You should be doing something better with your life than throwing pointless parties."

"I don't just throw parties." I try to keep my tone neutral, yet irritation creeps in. "I have a job, go to school, play soccer." *You'd know that if you knew anything about me.*

"A job?" He laughs disdainfully. "Loaning out money and trading stuff off isn't a job unless you're planning on working at a pawn shop for the rest of your life."

I don't know why he can't be happy with who I am. Sure, I do some stuff he doesn't agree with, like throw parties, but I get decent grades, haven't done anything too crazy like end up in jail, and while he doesn't think much of it, I do own a business. I help people who need cash fast by letting them trade valuable belongings for money, and then I sell their stuff online for a profit. It beats working in a stuffy office with my dad.

"Maybe I do want to work at a pawn shop," I tell him, though I really don't. "It's a decent job with an income."

His face reddens. "You need to stop messing around and focus on your career."

"*My* career?" I ask flatly. "Or the one you have planned for me?"

"Law is a good career to get into. You're lucky to have the opportunity to work with me." He inches toward me, a move he used to do when I was younger to intimidate me. Now, I'm five inches taller than him, so the effect is lost. "Do you know how many interns apply to work at my firm … for free?"

"You should probably hire them, then, and save yourself the money of having to pay me."

If I thought his face couldn't get any redder, I was wrong.

"Watch how you speak to me. You may be living on your own now, but don't forget my name is on the deed, too," he warns. "And if I want to, I can sell this house."

I pierce my fingernail into my palms. "I'm pretty sure

that's not how it works since both of our names are on the deed."

"Take me to court and find out." An eerie grin rises on his face. He knows he has me right where he wants me. "Now, I'd like you to stop by my office on Monday so we can talk about the hours you'll put in and what your plans are for getting into law school."

I open my mouth to tell him to go to hell, but his threat echoes in my head. My dad is one of the highest paid law-yers in the country for a reason. If he took me to court, he'd win in a heartbeat, like he wins all of his cases.

He grins smugly. "I'll see you on Monday. Have fun at your party. It'll be your last," he calls over his shoulder before leaving.

I don't move until I hear the front door shut. Then I unglue my feet from the floor and head downstairs to get a much-needed drink.

I'm throwing back a shot of Bacardi when the doorbell rings. Wiping my lips with the back of my hand, I walk to the foyer and throw open the front door.

And just like that, I feel twenty times better.

Grey and Luna are standing on my front porch, holding hands. That's not what stills the restlessness piercing inside me, though.

Will is right behind them, wearing a leather jacket, clunky red boots, and a tight black dress that shows off her

161

sexy as hell body. Her brown hair cascades over her shoulders, she doesn't have a drop of makeup on, and she's chewing on her glossy lip as her gaze wanders all over me.

God, she looks fucking beautiful. I just want to take her up to my room and keep her there forever ... The things I'd do to her ... over and over and over again ...

"We brought a present," Grey says, and for a dumbass second, I think he means Willow. Then I manage to pull my head out my lustful thoughts and realize he's holding a bottle of whiskey.

"Thanks, man." I take the bottle, step back, and motion for them to come inside.

As Luna passes, she shoots me a worried glance before Grey snatches her hand and hauls her toward the kitchen.

What the heck was that about?

Shoving the concern from my head, I turn to Willow, my lips tugging into a grin. "Hey, princess. Long time no see."

She smiles effortlessly, throwing me off guard. "I know. We need to stop doing that."

"Doing what?" I ask, confused by her happiness. I mean, don't get me wrong. I'm glad she looks happy instead of stressed, but I wonder why.

Perhaps she decided to move out.

That thought makes my smile return.

"You seem to be in a good mood," I say as she stumbles past me and into the foyer.

"I'm really not." She wrestles off her jacket and chucks it toward the coat hanger but misses by about ten feet. "Or I wasn't until about an hour ago."

"What happened an hour ago?" As soon as the words leave my mouth, the light from the chandelier above casts across her face, highlighting her glazed over eyes. "You're drunk."

She holds her finger and thumb an inch apart. "Maybe a little bit."

Willow isn't much of a drinker and definitely not a pre-gamer, so why did she start tonight?

"Is everything okay?" I tilt my head closer to her and lower my voice. "You usually don't drink."

"I know. But I was having a rough night and was about to have a panic attack, so when Grey brought out this bottle of whiskey, I ..." She lifts her shoulders then lets them fall in a lazy shrug. "I guess I'm a drinker. But I'm not that surprised. I mean, I already do a ton of bad stuff, anyway, just like my mom, so what's one more thing?"

"First off, you're nothing like your mom," I say, wishing she'd stop saying stuff like that. "And second, why were you having a panic attack?"

She lifts a shoulder, the look on her face heart-wrenching. "Lots of stuff ... I can't tell you about this stuff, or else you'll be disappointed in me."

"Princess"—I sweep her hair out of her eyes—"I could never be disappointed in you. No one could."

"You say that now, but only because you don't know everything."

"Then tell me everything."

She clumsily shakes her head, jutting her lip out. "I can't."

I leave my hand resting on her cheek. "But I thought we told each other everything."

"Not everything." She leans into my touch, her eye-lashes fluttering.

Good God, kill me now and I'd die a happy man.

"And I know it's that way for you, too," she whispers. "I know you talk to Grey about stuff you don't tell me."

My attention darts toward the kitchen, and I scowl at Grey. *"What did you tell her?"* I mouth, sure I already know.

While Grey and I aren't close, about a month ago, we got high together, and I decide to solve my Willow problems by chatting his ear off.

Grey pauses, mid-pour. "I'm sorry. I was drunk." Then he grabs Luna's hand and bails out the back door, spilling his drink along the way.

Huffing out a breath, I return my attention to Willow. "What did he tell you?"

She squints one eye, thinking. "I don't really remember … something about breaking your heart, maybe?" The confusion in her eyes gives me hope that she won't remember any of this in the morning.

I'm starting to relax when she abruptly throws her arms around me and presses her chest against mine.

"Can we do something tonight?" she asks, peering up at me through her eyelashes.

"We can do anything you want." *Especially when you're looking at me like that.* "Just name it, and it's yours."

She smiles contently. "I want to relax and have fun with you."

"Well, you're in luck because relaxation and fun just happen to be my specialty."

Smiling, she kisses my cheek. "Thank you, Beck. You're the best. And if you need anything at all, I'm here for you, too."

I shut my eyes and take a calm-the-fuck-down breath. The last time she was so affectionate toward me, I tried to kiss her. I can't do that again. I can't lose control. I need to stay sober and keep my hands to myself until I can get to the bottom of what's bothering her.

Well, that's what I try to convince myself.

As she laces our fingers and pulls me toward the kitchen to get a drink, I easily follow, wondering if maybe I lost control a long time ago.

Chapter Twelve

Willow

I used to believe I was allergic to parties. Every time I went to one, my body physically reacted. My muscles tightened, stomach churned, and my blood pressure went up, like a gazillion notches.

Okay, maybe I didn't really believe I was allergic. Rowdy crowds, loud noises, and drunken stupidity just make me edgy. Tonight, though, I've turned into a hypocrite. Tonight, I'm at Beck's party, and I've had enough to drink that the loud music isn't horrible, the drunken stupidity is more funny than annoying, and the crowd ... Well, all the people crammed into the spacious living room are still kind of overwhelming yet not enough to make me want to leave.

I blame my relaxed state of mind on the whiskey I drank before I left Luna's place. I hadn't planned on drinking, but as the weight of life began to splinter my chest apart, I decided I needed to calm down. So, I took a few drinks, or three or four or ten, and then I headed off to my favorite place in the world—Beck's.

Beck has stuck to my side the entire night, adding to my relaxed state of euphoria.

Beck and whiskey equal forgetting all of my shitty choices.

Beck and Beck equal happy drunk Willow.

Beck. And Beck. And Beck. He's a stream through my mind, my favorite song stuck on repeat.

Shit, I'm so drunk.

Every so often, worry creeps up in my drunken stupidity, warning me I'm playing with fire and am about to get burned. Right now, that probably sounds more appealing than it should.

"Relax, Princess," Beck breathes into my ear as the bass of the song throbs through my chest. He moves up behind me, aligning his chest with my back, folding his fingertips into my hips. "Dancing's supposed to be fun." He grins at me from over my shoulder, his hips pressed against my ass.

Sober, I might panic the hell out with the intimate move. Drunk …? Well, it feels kind of good.

Okay, really, *really* good.

"I am having fun," I announce, which is the partial truth. I'm not having a shitty time or anything. It's just, every time too many people get all up in my business, I have flashbacks of being at work or at the apartment during one of my mom's parties.

"No, you're not. You're all worked up." He molds his palms around my hips, and I slump against his chest, my head bobbing back. "Stop worrying so much about whatever everyone else is doing and dance with me." He draws me even closer, if that's possible, and slips his arm around my waist, splaying his fingers across my abdomen.

Soberness attempts to press through my numbed mind, and my voice of reason attempts to make a grand appearance. We're too close. Way, way, I-can-feel *everything* close. *Beck is touching me. Beck is grinding against my ass. Beck is enjoying this dancing thing a little too much. I'm enjoying this dirty dancing a little too much. Remember what happened the last time we both enjoyed dancing too much.*

I should probably stop this, right? Suddenly, my voice of reason sounds drunk, too.

I sneak a glance at Ari, Luna, and Grey to see what they think of this dirty dancing going on between Beck and me.

Ari is too distracted, busting out disco moves, and Luna is too busy gazing lustfully into her boyfriend's eyes. If Wynter were here, she'd totally notice the one-step-away-from-a-porn-show dancing going on. Wynter misses nothing.

Even though only Beck and I seem to be aware of how much we're touching each other, I still feel as if I'm secretly doing something naughty. If I were sober, I'd bail out now. But I'm not sober. I'm drunk and dizzy and confused about what I want and what I don't want. Who I am and who I'm not. Where I belong and where I don't.

Up until a couple of months ago, I was a plan-everything, play-by-the-book kind of girl, even if my decisions weren't always the best. So, this reckless, dancing with confusion thing is foreign, wild, crazy, out-of-control territory.

What the hell do I want? To stop dancing with Beck? For him to stop touching me?

I shake my head a few times to clear the fogginess in my mind. All that does is make the room spin.

"Stop overthinking," Beck playfully scolds, softly pinching my hip. When I freeze, he sighs. "You said you wanted to have fun tonight, *remember?*"

I bob my head up and down.

"Well, in order to have fun, you have to relax. Trust me, I know. I'm all about the fun." He massages my hips with his fingertips. "You're too tense. You need to loosen up. And not just tonight, but every damn day. I think I'm going to make that my goal ... to make you loosen up every single day."

I giggle because he's drunk and babbling, and it's hilarious.

"Oh, yeah?"

"Yeah." He puts his lips to my ear, grazing his teeth along my earlobe. "You must be really drunk since you're not arguing with me."

I shiver in the best way ever. "I probably should … You're too good to me."

"No way. I'm not good enough. I'll never be until I find a way for you to live a stress-free life."

"I don't know if that's possible … I'm always tense. Life is tense. If life weren't tense, then maybe I could chillax. I don't think I'll ever be able to do that," I murmur, reaching back to run my fingers through his hair. I don't even know why I do it other than I've lost complete control of my obsessive need to harness my feelings.

My hand and fingers develop a mind of their own, needing to feel how soft his hair is, something I've thought about a time or two over the years if I'm being totally honest with myself.

"I've been like this since the day you met me, so you shouldn't be so surprised."

He chuckles softly in my ear. "That's not true at all."

"Is so."

"Is not."

"Is—"

"Shh …" he whispers hotly against my ear. "Less arguing, more sexy dancing."

I giggle again for probably the umpteenth time. Then

we start to move to the beat, a soft, sultry tempo. Slowly, I unwind, matching his rhythm effortlessly. As the song quickens, we grind faster, our bodies in sync. His hands explore up and down my sides, around the curve of my hips, along my arm, over my breasts. Goose bumps sprout across my flesh with each brush of his fingers.

I try to fight back another shiver unsuccessfully. Honestly, I don't care.

More time passes, and more people cram into the living room to grind up against each other. At some point, Luna, Grey, and Ari wander off. I barely notice, lost in dancing, relaxing, and *forgetting*.

As the music switches to an upbeat, energized song, Beck circles his fingers around my wrists then moves my arms above my head, making me do this dorky clapping thing. I snort like a pig, and he chuckles before placing a kiss on my temple.

My legs quiver, and I nearly buckle to the ground, but he catches me in his arms and holds me closer. I smile, feeling so content. After the shitty night I had at work, I didn't think a good mood was going to be attainable. But Beck always seems to know how to turn me from overworked, exhausted Willow into a silly, giggling girl.

"See? Fun, right?" he asks, still holding my hands above my head.

I shiver as if I'm cold, although my skin is damp with

171

sweat, and his fingers tense around my wrists.

"You okay?" he asks, sounding in pain.

I manage a head bob, but my body betrays me with another shiver.

Jesus, get a grip on yourself. He's just whispering in your ear. There's nothing sexual about it. I nearly laugh at my thought. *Yeah, like I could even recognize a sexual moment if it came up and grinded against my ass.*

Just like Beck is.

"What's so funny?" Beck asks as another giggle escapes my lips.

"Nothing." I shut my eyes as the music and heat absorb into me. "You were right … This is pretty fun. I feel so relaxed I could probably fall asleep."

"Well, don't do that. I want to spend more time with you. I feel like I haven't seen you in weeks."

"You just saw me a couple of days ago. I wish we could hang out more, but with work and school and my mom …" I trail off, my mood starting to dive at the mention of my mom.

"Have you heard anything from her?" he asks tensely.

I shake my head. "No. The last I heard, she went to Vegas to elope."

"You really think she'd do that?"

"Yeah. And I'm nervous, when she comes back from Vegas, she'll try to let her new boyfriend move in … if he sticks around for that long."

His chest puffs with a deep breath. "I want you to stay the night with me and take a break from that house."

I don't know what to say. I've stayed the night before, and right now, I really, really want to. What happens if I try to do naughty things to him while I'm sleeping again? Or worse, when I'm awake?

He remains quiet through the entire chorus. "Have you thought any more about moving in with Wynter?"

"I've thought about it a little," I admit. "I really want to talk to Wynter before I make any decisions. I'm sure she won't care if I move in … but I need to find out how much rent is and if I can afford it." And I need to find a new job and find out how much my paycheck is going to be.

"You could always just move in with me." He delicately kisses the side of my neck, causing my eyes to roll into the back of my head and my back to arch. He lets out the faintest groan. "Let me take care of you."

I open my mouth to protest, to remind him we're too close to breaking the rule, but I end up yawning.

Wait. What were we talking about?

"I'm tired. I think I'm ready to crash."

"Stay awake a little longer." He brushes his lips against the side of my neck again, right along my soaring pulse. "I want to spend some time with you and talk for a little bit."

Normally, I'd argue, but he sounds so desperate. "I'll try to stay awake and hang out for a bit. I might need some coffee, though."

He lowers my hands to my sides, returning his palms to my waist. "What about if we take a break and go outside? Get some fresh air? Look up at the stars? I think there's supposed to be an eclipse tonight."

I nod through another yawn. Fresh air. Outside. Away from people. Sounds great. "Let's do it."

The throng of people dwindles as Beck threads his fingers through mine and abandons his party with me in tow. I'm eager to get outside, but when we reach the large, recently remodeled kitchen, a couple of guys and a girl stop to chat with Beck, yammering about school, what's going on at the local clubs, and giving updates on the latest gossip going around the east side of Ridgefield, aka the posh, fancy-schmancy side of town. Beck keeps giving me sidelong looks and eye rolls, and I have to bite down on my lip to stop from giggling.

The longer we stand there, the more soberness creeps up on me and the more I'm reminded of who I am and where I come from.

"I heard you were thinking about trading in your car for a Bentley," a dude with curly blond hair and a thick neck tells Beck.

"I don't know about that." Beck takes a sip from his

drink. "Bentley's aren't really my style. I like things a lot less flashy."

Thick neck's brows pucker, and the blonde standing beside him wearing too much eyeshadow and too little of a dress rolls her eyes.

"Oh, Beckett, you're so living in denial." She bites her lips, twisting a strand of hair around her finger. "You're a rich, spoiled brat just like the rest of us, who loves expensive, flashy things. You might as well just own it."

I crinkle my nose at the use of his full name. Beck hates when people refer to him as Beckett because that's what his dad calls him. These people aren't in our group of friends. They're his friends, and it's strange to be standing here, watching the exchange. I mean, I knew Beck had other friends outside of our group, but I didn't imagine them as rich snobs.

"I'm not living in denial," Beck insists. "I was just pointing out that I don't need pricey, flashy things. That's all. So chill out."

"You mean, like your car. Or your house." Blondie gives an insinuating look around the spacious kitchen and the high arched ceilings. "Even the girls you date are high-end." Her gaze skates to me. "Well, usually."

"And on that note." I turn to the back door and walk out, letting their voices fade away as I down another gulp of my Jack and coke.

I should've known better and walked away from the beginning. I know how rich people can get. The club I work at is filled with rich men who like flashy things and like to brag about being wealthy and make others feel bad that they're not. The fact that I work there, what I do … what Van wants me to do … just might justify the girl's look.

I think about where I was tonight, what I was wearing, what I was doing. How, when I look in the mirror, I see my mom staring back at me.

Blondie's right. I'm definitely not high-end.

I'm at the bottom. The very, very bottom.

Chapter Thirteen

Willow

I don't know how long I stand outside, waiting for Beck. It could be seconds, minutes, hours—I'm too drunk to have a grasp on time. I know enough time passes that I finish my drink and return to drunken and comfortably numb land.

A light breeze blows strands of my long brown hair into my face as I stumble up to the railing on the back porch and stare out at the field just beyond Beck's backyard. I'm not sure what to do, if I should go back inside or wander to my car and pass out for a few hours until I sober up. I could go find a room to pass out in, but I doubt finding an empty one is possible, considering how many people are here.

Maybe I should just lie down on the porch and go to sleep. That kind of sounds nice ...

The back door creaks open.

"Hey, sorry about Titzi," Beck says. It's unnerving what a calming effect his voice has on me. "She can be a bitch sometimes. Don't worry; I reminded her of that."

"Her name is Titzi?" I glance at him as he walks up

beside me.

He bites down on his bottom lip, fighting back a smile. "What's wrong with Titzi?"

"I don't know. It just sounds an awful lot like ditzy." I rest my arms on the railing. "And tits." It feels like I should be embarrassed for saying that, but I can't summon up the will to care enough.

Thanks, Mr. Jack Daniels, for saving me from embarrassment.

Beck busts up with laughter. "Oh, my God, did my sweet, little Willow just say tits?" He turns around, putting his elbows on the railing, and squints at me. "How much have you had to drink?"

"Not too much," I lie. "And I've said tits before."

He stifles a laugh. "No, you haven't. You never say dirty words unless you're talking about your anatomy class or something, and that's scientific."

"I say fuck, which isn't scientific," I point out, offended. Why does everyone think I'm such a prude? Why do I suddenly care? *Because you're druuuuunk.* "And dick."

"That's not the same."

"How do you figure?"

"Because of how you use those words."

Puzzlement tap dances against my intoxicated brain. "I don't really get what you're saying. I'm not as innocent as you're trying to make me sound." *Not even close.*

178

"That's not what I'm trying to say." He chews on his bottom lip, and all of my attention focuses on his mouth. "When you use words like prick and fuck and dick, it's because you're pissed off, right?"

I nod, ripping my gaze off his mouth. "That's normal. A lot of people do that."

"Yeah, but other people also use the words in different ways besides to express anger." The porch light casts a glow across his face, highlighting the amused sparkle in his eyes. "Like, for example, saying, *'Hey, let's go fuck all night long in my room. We'll have hot, sweaty sex as I put my dick in your—'* "

"Oh, my God, I get your point!" I throw my hand over his mouth, my cheeks erupting with heat.

His breath dusts across my palm as he chuckles, and I narrow my eyes despite my stomach somersaulting.

"Maybe I should be asking you how much you've had to drink tonight."

"Maybe a few too many," he admits, his lips tickling my palm. "All I was trying to say is that there's a difference between using dirty words to curse and using dirty words to turn someone on."

"You didn't turn me on." I squirm at the way my stomach coils.

He cocks a brow. "You sure about that?"

"Y-yes." I remove my hand from his mouth. "You

179

probably should stop talking."

He arches a brow. "Why?"

"Because you're saying stuff … and I …" I shift my weight. "You're just saying this stuff because we're drunk."

"How do you know I'm drunk? Maybe I'm just finally saying what I've always wanted to say to you." When I gape at him, he sighs. "I may have drunk a little too much."

I hold up four fingers, I think. "Quick, how many fingers am I holding up?"

He squints one eye, leaning in. "Seven, ten, twenty-nine." His forehead bumps into mine, and we both giggle as he stumbles back. "Relax, princess, I'm not *that* drunk. I just like watching you blush. It's adorable." He skims his knuckles across my cheekbone, causing me to blush and shiver. Then he sinks his teeth into his bottom lip, totally aware of how he's affecting me.

"I shouldn't have worn a dress," I announce, wrapping my arms around myself, trying to downplay the shiver.

"I was a little surprised you did. I think I've only seen you wear a dress, like, maybe three times."

"I only did it because you told me I had to."

"I'm glad you did … Although, I was kind of hoping you'd wear those shorts you had on the other night." His gaze drops to my legs. "God, your legs are so fucking hot."

Tingles tickle my skin, and I shiver uncontrollably.

The last time I acted this way, we ended up kissing.

I nervously glance at the back door, feeling like I should bolt to my car. Through the door's window, I see Titzi laughing at something with thick neck dude. I recall what she said about me and frown.

"I don't know why you say those things to me," I mutter. "I know I'm not your type."

"Hey." He turns me by the shoulders, forcing me to face him. "You are ten times prettier than Titzi. You're ten times prettier than every single girl in my house. In Ridgefield. In America. In the world. All of the universe and beyond."

Prettier wasn't really what I was getting at, but I crack a tiny smile. "You took it one step too far with the 'and beyond.' Up until then, you had me."

He frowns, looking kind of sad and very unlike Beck. Usually, he's all about the smiles unless his dad's being a dick.

"Are you okay? You seem sad suddenly."

"I'm fine. It's just that …" He unexpectedly laces his fingers through mine and yanks me down the porch and across the backyard. "Come on. I promised you a fun night, and I'm ruining it by being mopey."

I want to ask him why he suddenly went from rainbows and sunshine to depressing rain cloud, but I get distracted as he lets go of my hand and hops over the fence.

181

"Where are we going again?" I ask as I hoist myself over the fence and land in the field beside him.

He glances up at the glittering stars and the moon. Then he snags my hand and takes off across the field. "I'm not sure yet. Somewhere quiet … where we can talk and watch the eclipse without any interruptions."

I peek back at his two-story house. The lights are like fireflies sparkling in the darkness, and the music is nothing more than a murmur. Peace. I feel so at peace right now, something I never expected to happen tonight. Maybe ever.

"What about Ari, Luna, and Grey?" I return my attention to Beck. "Maybe we should text them to see if they want to come out here. Ari's really into astronomy. He'll probably want to see it."

"Ari already knows about the eclipse," he replies, looking up at the sky. "He's the one who told me about it."

"Okay." I peer up at the sky, smiling as the stars dance in circles. Then I look at Beck and remember what happened the last time we wandered off alone at a party. "Still, maybe we should text him to see if he wants to come out here. The view is amazing. He'd love it."

"It looks the same anywhere else." He glances over his shoulder at me. "I want to hang out with just you for a little while, okay?"

Nerves bubble inside me as I think about the last time Beck and I wandered off like this. His lips touched mine, a butterfly kiss that made me completely, blissfully happy and entirely terrified. The day after was when I decided to limit our time together, to stop relying on him so much, to not set myself up for heartbreak.

Yet here we are again. Alone. Together.

It always comes back to him. Why is that?

Despite my apprehension, I allow him to guide me across the grassy field, our final destination unknown. Knowing Beck, we could end up anywhere. Vegas. Mexico. Locked in a closed theater for an entire night, which yes, actually happened once and was as fun as it sounds.

"Where's your head at, Wills?" Beck asks, tightening his hold on my hand.

"I was just thinking about stuff." *You. Us.*

"What kind of stuff?" He hikes deeper into the field, and I follow him without a second thought. "You're not worrying about money and school and shit, are you? I told you that you weren't allowed to do that tonight." He turns, walking backward, and gestures at the sky. "This is a worry-free night. No stress allowed. In fact, you're only allowed to appreciate everything that is peaceful and beautiful."

"I'm trying to, but it's hard not to worry sometimes." *About you. Us.*

He tsks at me, swaying from side to side.

I try not to laugh. *He's so drunk.*

Seconds later, I stumble over a rock and nearly fall on my face.

Okay, maybe I'm so drunk.

He giggles at my clumsiness, and a very unattractive snort erupts from my lips, which only causes him to giggle like a hyena.

"See? Fun, right?" he asks after his laughter dies down.

I nod, grasping his hand. "Yep. But probably only because you're here."

He smiles, stopping in the field. The movement is so unexpected I crash into him, which leads to another fit of giggles from both of us.

After we stop acting like ditzy girls, the air quiets, and stillness settles over us.

Beck angles his head up to gaze at the stars, pulling me closer to his side and draping his arm across my shoulders. "How can you worry about anything when you have a view like this?" He kisses the side of my head for the second time tonight and calmness blankets over me, yet my heart contracts with a terrified sputter. "It's like someone painted this just for us. Wouldn't that be so cool? If someone actually painted the entire sky … What if that's why the sky exists? What if someone just decided to paint it one day, and we're just living in a canvas?"

I snort a laugh. "Dude, are you high? You sound so high right now."

He draws me even closer until the sides of our bodies collide. "Nah. I'm just buzzed. And really, really happy."

The happiness in his voice brings a smile to my face. "Well, I don't want to ruin your dream of living in a canvas, but there's a ton of proof that completely discounts your theory."

He dips his mouth toward my ear. "Oh, come on; where's your dreamer side?"

I shiver from the feeling of his breath and mentally curse myself. What's the deal tonight? I've done that, like, five gazillion times!

"I don't think I have a dreamer side," I admit. "I've always been more of a realistic kind of girl."

"No way. You have a dreamer inside you. I know you do."

"Nah, I don't really think I do—"

He turns, bringing me with him, and wraps his arms around my waist. "Yes, you do. And I'm going to prove it to you." Then he begins to sway us around, dancing to music only he can hear.

I have no clue what he's doing, but I dance with him, anyway, because I'm relaxed and calm and desperate to latch on to the feelings.

"Can you hear it?" he whispers in my ear.

Another shiver. Another confusing skip of my heart. "I don't know …"

185

"Are you cold?" he asks, his breath feathering across my skin.

I manage not to shiver this time, but goose bumps and tingles sprout across my skin. "I'm not cold … I'm just …." Confused. Lost. Weirded out. Clearing my throat, I loop my arms around his neck and shift the conversation elsewhere. "So, what am I supposed to be hearing? All I hear are crickets." *And my heart beating like a freakin' lunatic.*

His hands find the small of my back, and he urges me closer to him. "The music, silly."

"You can hear it all the way from the house?"

"No, not that music. *Our* music."

"Our music?" Huh?

Instead of answering, he starts to hum. And just like that, it clicks.

Our music. Our song. The first song we ever danced to back in seventh grade. We were at a dance and Beck, being his popular, outgoing self, had a line of girls waiting to dance with him. And I, being the shy, awkward girl I still am, spent most of the night hanging out near the punch bowl, watching my friends have fun until Beck took matters into his own hands.

"All right, no more of this." He snatched the cup of punch from my hand and tossed it in the trash.

"Hey, I was drinking that," I stupidly argued. The

186

punch tasted like shit.

"No more standing around and being boring, Wills." He grabbed my hand and guided me to the center of the dance floor.

"I'm not really a dancer." I fiddled with my secondhand dress, trying not to freak the hell out as he dragged me into the crowd.

Hardly anyone was paying attention to us, but a few were, and that was enough to make me feel uncomfortable and worried. I had only danced behind closed doors. I'd probably look like a spaz.

"Sure you are." He placed a hand on my back and guided me toward him until the tips of his boots clipped mine. Then he started moving, keeping up with the fast tempo of the pop song playing. "Everyone's a dancer, even if they don't know it."

"Try telling that to that guy." I nodded at a guy from our school who was flapping his arms like a crazed-out chicken.

Beck studied chicken-dancing dude with his head cocked to the side. "I think he's pretty awesome."

"You would because you could pull off those dance moves," I said. "But I'd look like a freak if I tried something like that."

"You never look like a freak," he insisted, redirecting his attention to me. The music switched to a softer song,

187

and we slowed down to match the beat. "I wish you wouldn't be so hard on yourself all the time."

"I'm not hard on myself all the time." Was I?

"Sorry, but you are, and it makes me sad." He jutted out his lip. "See? So, so sad."

I giggled, and he smiled proudly.

"There we go," he said. "Don't you feel better now that you've smiled?"

I nodded and inched closer to him, letting him lead us through the song. When it ended, I expected him to go back to his line of girls, but he danced us right into the next song. And the next. And the next.

I blink out of memory lane as Beck starts singing the lyrics of the song in a very off-key pitch.

I seal my lips together, suppressing a laugh. "You're so tone deaf."

"No way," he argues then chuckles when his voice cracks on a high note. "Okay, maybe you're kind of right."

"*Kind of right?*" I question, and he playfully pinches my side. I laugh, but the way my stomach somersaults causes me to panic. I play it off, cool, calm, collected. At least, I think I do. "But at least you gave it a good effort like you do with everything." I yammer nonsense as my eyelids grow heavy. "That's one of my favorite things about you. You're not afraid to do anything. And you always do what you want. Sometimes, I wish I could be more like you." I yawn and, unable to keep my head up, rest my cheek on his shoulder. My eyelids start to lower. I seriously could fall asleep right now.

"I don't always do what I want," he whispers, breaking the silence.

The uncertainty in his tone makes me step back to get a better look at him.

"What's wrong?" I search his face through the darkness. "You sound … I don't know. Worried?" And vulnerable.

"Nothing's wrong," he mutters. "I don't even know why I said that."

"Don't lie to me. I know when something's bothering you." I pause to give him a chance to answer then press, "Is your dad being a dick again? Do I need to do some ass kicking?"

"He did stop by tonight, but that's not what's bothering me right now." He tucks a strand of hair behind my ear. "I appreciate the offer to kick his ass, though. That might be funny to watch. And I'm pretty sure you'd win." He laughs, but it sounds wrong. Forced.

I frown. "Then what's wrong? I can tell something's bothering you."

"I'm okay. I promise. I'm just …" He studies me again. Then he moves back and sinks to the ground without letting go of my hand. "Sit down with me, and let's stargaze."

I open my mouth to press, but another yawn leaves my lips. Between the shots I took earlier and the late hours I've been up studying and working, I'm crashing hard.

Beck gently tugs on my hand. "Sit down, sleepy head, before you collapse."

I glance down at the dress I'm wearing. "This is Wynter's dress. I'm not sure if I should get it dirty. You know how she can get about clothes."

"Who gives a shit if it gets ruined? Besides, she's always mad at something. Come sit down with me and watch the stars. Live in the moment instead of in the future. And fuck Wynter and her stupid tantrums."

Oh, Beck, if only life were that easy. Maybe if my future was set, I could stop stressing out so much. But I have no idea where I'll be in three years, where I hope to be, which are two entirely different things.

Hope is so uncertain. My future is so uncertain. The only thing that isn't uncertain is Beck's and my friendship. Well, it used to be. Lately, there's been a shift, a confusing, dangerous, against my rule shift.

I probably should leave. I can feel that shift hovering in the air right now. In fact, I know I should walk away. But I find myself dropping down onto the ground in front of him.

He immediately circles his arms around my waist and

lures me back against him. Then he slips a leg on each side of me, surrounding me.

Ignoring the thundering of my heart, I rest back against his chest. "Can I ask you a question?"

He strokes his fingers up and down my side. "You can always ask me anything."

"You and Wynter … You guys haven't ever …?" I pause, thinking about what Ari said to me about their arguing being sexual tension. Then I think about what Titzi said, about Beck liking high-end girls, something Wynter definitely is. "Have you guys ever hooked up?"

What is wrong with me? Why the hell did I ask that?

"*What*? God, no," he says, sounding appalled. "Why the hell would you even ask that?"

"I don't know." I shrug. Apparently, I'm drunk, and that makes me act like a jealous idiot. "I was just curious, I guess. I'm not the only one who thinks that. Ari thinks you guys fight all the time because you secretly like each other. And you did have a crush on her once. You even kissed her."

His arms tense. "That stupid kiss was just a silly, middle school thing. And yeah, I may have had a crush on her in elementary school, but that was a long-ass time ago and lasted about two fucking seconds. I don't look at her that way anymore. And I would never, *ever* hook up with her. She's not even my type."

191

His words cause a small smile to grace my lips. I don't even know why other than I'm an idiot, which I think I already mentioned.

"You're such a liar," I tell him. "Wynter's gorgeous. She loves to have fun and is totally a people person. That's exactly your type. She's basically the female version of you."

Silence encases us. I feel so stupid for having this conversation.

I sound jealous.

"Gorgeous, huh?" he remarks with amusement. "Personally, I've always thought of myself as dashingly handsome, but I'll take gorgeous, I guess."

Perplexed, I replay what I said. *Gorgeous? I called him gorgeous? Why would I do that?* I mean, yeah, he is gorgeous with his blond hair that always sticks up perfectly chaotic. Plus, he has perfectly shaped lips, his lean body is ridiculously sexy, and his eyes … Don't even get me started on those. They might be the most perfect eyes I've ever …

Wait. Where was I going with this?

"*Dashingly handsome?*" I attempt to joke, my voice sounding squeaky. "What are you? Prince Charming or something?"

"I could be. I'm definitely *gorgeous* enough to be," he says cockily. "Besides, since you're my princess, it would make sense."

"So cheesy." I make a gagging sound, and he chuckles. "And I didn't mean it like that. Well, I did, but I didn't. I was just trying to say that you're gorgeous like Wynter." I grow flustered and confused. Dizzy. Lost. Drunk. Exhausted. "You know what? Never mind. I'm just going to stop talking because I can't even keep track of what I'm saying."

He drags his thumb down my side. "Relax. I'm just messing with you. You're so damn cute when you're flustered."

I roll my eyes, more at myself. "No, I'm not. I'm dorky. And I'm only flustered because I'm drunk."

"I completely disagree." His fingers delve into my hips, and then he draws me back, pulling me onto his lap and resting his chin on my shoulder. "I like this … you and me under the stars. The flirting. The conversation. It's been a while since I've been this relaxed. I've missed you."

I gulp. *He thinks we're flirting?*

I replay through my foggy memories of tonight and eventually figure out why: the dancing, the touching, the dirty comments, the cute and gorgeous comments, the jealousy in my tone when I asked him about Wynter.

Yep, we've been flirting all night.

Every goddamn time we drink, this shit happens.

I'm never drinking again.

193

I'm never flirting again.

Ha, you're such an idiot!

My thoughts laugh at me.

"You're getting tense again." He slides his hand up my arm to massage my shoulder. "Relax. The eclipse is about to start, and then we can go back inside and eat some cake."

"You know the way to my heart." I smile, but worry tiptoes inside me.

Flirt. I flirted with Beck. It's going to be senior year all over again.

Maybe it's for the best. You wanted to stop relying on him so much. Maybe this will force you to.

That thought makes me sick.

Tearing my attention from my stupid, idiotic thoughts, I focus on the moon. We stay that way for minutes, maybe hours, staring up at the stars, watching the sparkle, waiting for something magical to happen in the sky.

"You're wrong," he whispers out of nowhere, causing me to jump.

"About what?" I ask, sounding a little breathless.

"About Wynter being my type."

"You're still thinking about that?"

"Of course. I want—no, need—to make sure you know I don't like her. Not like that, anyway." He sweeps my hair to the side then leans over my shoulder to catch my gaze. "Wynter and I ... We may act similarly sometimes, and a lot of people may think she's gorgeous or whatever, but I'm definitely not into her. In fact, I like someone else. I have for a while."

Beck's always been such a flirt, which has led to him getting into some dramatic and awkward situations. Usually, he's charming enough to smooth the situation over pretty well. On the other hand, he has asked me a few times to talk to a girl who's developed a crush on him and won't back off.

I used to be okay with that, yet toward the end of our senior year, I started avoiding getting involved in his love life. Partly because I was busy working to get into a good college and partly because ... Well, I didn't like hearing about him and other girls.

I still don't if I'm being really honest with myself. And right now, I feel like Miss Honesty. However, I play the part of a good best friend, owing him that much.

"So, who is it this time?"

"Wow, Wills. I'm hurt." Oddly enough, he does sound hurt. "You act like my crushes are fleeting and insignificant."

"They're not insignificant, but they're definitely fleeting," I say apologetically.

"That's not true." He combs his fingers through my hair then places a kiss on my bare shoulder. "I've liked the same girl for a couple of years. I just haven't said anything because we're really close, and I know she'll freak out because she has this no-dating rule with every guy and has a no-kissing rule with me."

My heart beats wildly in my chest as I think back to what Grey said earlier. A slow, painful realization punches me.

Beck likes me? Like *that*?

No. I have to be wrong. Have to be.

Please, please say that I am.

Deep down, I think I might have known for a while. I've just been too afraid to admit it.

"Aren't you going to ask me who I'm talking about?" he whispers with unfamiliar nervousness in his tone.

Beck is nervous.

This is so bad.

I swallow, willing the word "no" to leave my lips. No sound comes out.

"If you don't ask, I won't say it." His tone carries an underlying meaning.

He's giving me a choice: keep my lips sealed and let our friendship be or ask and then … Well, I don't know what will happen.

Asking Beck is going against my plan. If I ask, I'll ruin the beautifulness we have together. I don't want that. I want to stay right here in his arms as friends and hold on to the calmness he's always given me.

I find my lips parting, anyway. Later, I blame my reaction on the alcohol, stress, and sleep deprivation.

Later, not right now.

Right now, I can only think about one thing.

Asking.

"Who is it?" I blurt out.

His chest crashes against my back as he frees a trapped breath. "Oh, my God, I can't believe you asked … I didn't think you would."

Cupping my cheek, he tilts my head to look me in the eyes. His fingers are quivering as badly as my heart.

One, two, three seconds tick by, and then he grazes his lips against mine.

Oh. My. God. I can barely breathe as his lips brush mine once, twice, three times. My eyelids slip shut, and the air gets ripped from my lungs.

Beck is kissing me. My best friend in the universe is kissing me. Like, really freaking kissing me. Holy freakin' what-the-shit? I need to stop this. Now!

But when he gently nibbles on my bottom lip, every single one of my worries goes good-bye, see you later, I'm-taking-a-visit-to-the-stars.

I latch on to the bottom of his shirt, desperate to hold something, steady myself, grasp onto rationality. I can't seem to think about anything other than his comforting palm on my cheek, his warm body against mine, the softness of his lips. And when he angles my head back and slips his tongue inside my mouth, kissing me with so much intensity, I swear my heart explodes out of my chest.

This wasn't part of my plan. This kiss is so unplanned. This kiss isn't supposed to be happening …

Stop this, Willow. Stop it now before things get out of hand.

He groans against my lips, deepening the kiss, pulling me closer, and making me feel so safe.

No … I think I'm wrong … This kiss might be …

Everything.

Our tongues tangle together, and I almost fall blindly into the kiss. But the voice of reason whispers to me, begs me to stop this. I should … before things get too out of hand. My body has other ideas, and instead of breaking the kiss, my hands slide up Beck's chest as I rotate around to straddle his lap.

He groans, his fingers leaving my cheeks to tangle through my hair while his other hand wanders to the small of my back. He urges my body closer, pressing my chest against his.

Another throaty, begging groan. I don't even know which one of us does it, but something about the sound sends us into a frenzy.

The slow kiss turns reckless, as if he has absolutely no control over what he's doing and doesn't give a shit. Apparently, I don't either because I kiss him back, grasping on to him and grinding my hips against his over and over again like I did that night in my bed. Only, I'm wide awake now and completely aware of his hardness pressed against me as he pulls me closer, closer, closer, moving with me, groaning, gasping, wanting, needing. This is only the second time I've ever kissed a guy, but seriously, it could be my last because I don't think anything could be better.

Nothing could ever be any more perfect than this ...

As I kiss him back eagerly, I let him slip his hands underneath my dress. His fingers tremble as he cups my ass and rocks his hips against mine. Tingles erupt everywhere, and I bite down on his lip hard.

A throaty groan leaves his lips then he slides his tongue deeper into my mouth. Our tongues tangle. My fingernails dig into his shoulder blades. I feel out of control, tumbling into the unknown. Nothing else matters. Nothing else exists except Beck and me and the way our lips move together, the way he holds me like he's afraid I'm going to fall. It sure as hell feels like I'm falling into a place I've never been before where nothing makes sense ... where I'm lost ... where I'm veering off my path ... where I have no idea what I want or who I am anymore. And at the moment, I don't care.

Perfect. This moment is perfect. Beck is perfect.

"God, I've wanted this for so long," he whispers

199

against my lips, diving in for another kiss as he rocks his hips against mine again.

I clutch on to him, my knees pressing into his sides as I let out a gasp. He does the movement again and again until my thoughts become foggier. I feel like I'm drifting away to the stars, and for a second, I wish I never had to leave.

Then Beck whispers, "You're so amazing and beautiful. Fucking perfect."

And just like that, reality washes over me like ice cold water.

I jerk back, gasping for air. "H-holy s-shit."

"Please don't panic," he begs without missing a beat. "It's just a kiss. Nothing has to change if you don't want it to."

I struggle to get my erratic breathing under control.

He knows me too well. How does he do that? How does he read me when he can't even see my face through the darkness? How can he be so perfect?

Perfect.

You're fucking perfect, he said.

No, Beck, I'm not.

And we can't be perfect together.

Because I'm not perfect. And when you realize that, you'll leave me, and I'll be broken like my mom.

"I have to go." I stumble to my feet, tugging the hem of the dress down over my butt.

He springs to his feet and reaches for my arm. "Wait. Can we talk about this?"

"I can't talk right now." Not about this. Not when he's this close. Not with the vivid memory of the perfect kiss still branded onto my lips and the way my body felt as he was grinding against me.

Holy shit, I think I just had my first orgasm … with Beck.

Holy shit. Holy shit. Holy shit.

I don't look at him as I take off across the field toward his house.

"Goddammit, will you please just stop panicking." He matches my strides. "You can't run off yet. It'll fuck up our friendship, and I need us to at least be friends."

At least be friends? As opposed to what? A *couple*? And then what? We just date until he discovers how much I'm like my mom then dumps my sorry ass? Then I'll go back to my trashy life, feeling like shit and turning into a bitter woman who can't thrive without a man?

No, I can't turn into that.

My pulse speeds up as I continue to clumsily jog toward the house, only slowing down when I reach the fence to his backyard. I catch my breath then, daring a glance at him.

Worry fills his eyes as he approaches me with caution, which makes me worry I broke him.

What have I done?

"Please don't run," he pleads, stopping beside me. "I know you. And if you run off before we figure this out, you'll stress out about it all weekend and come up with all sorts of crazy ideas in that pretty little head of yours. And then I'll have to worry about you worrying, and we both know how much I hate worrying." He rolls his eyes and heaves a dramatic sigh. "It's so exhausting and time-consuming." I don't know whether he's joking for my benefit or for his.

Not wanting to worry him anymore, I try to offer him a reassuring smile, but the look only makes him frown.

"I won't spend the weekend worrying," I say quickly. "I know we were just being silly or drunk or … something." Honestly, I don't know what we were being. That's part of the problem. The unknown hovers over my head like a storm cloud threatening to rain down.

Starting to panic again, I reach for the fence to hoist myself over it. "I have to go. Luna said I could crash at her place tonight, and I have to get up really early to go back home and check on things." *Liar. All you have to check on is an empty apartment.*

He stares at me, his expression unreadable. "Okay … But promise me you'll call me tomorrow." He extends his arm toward me with his pinkie hitched. "Pinkie swear you will."

I link my pinkie with his, hoping he can't tell how badly I'm shaking. "I promise."

Without saying anything else, I jerk my hand away and drag my drunk ass over the fence. Then I run inside to find Luna and get the hell out of here. Well, that's what I convince myself.

Really, I'm running away from something I'm not sure can be outrun.

Chapter Fourteen

Beck

I try not to take it personally as I watch Willow run away from me like I'm the carrier of some deadly disease. But I do a fucking lot. It's my own damn fault for kissing her. I knew how she'd react, yet my drunken mind rationalized that the timing was right.

I'm starting to wonder if the timing will ever be right.

Huffing a frustrated breath, I haul my ass over the fence and dive into my backyard. I consider heading to the beer pong table to play a game or two to distract myself, but I'm no longer in a partying mood. A first for me.

Willow got under my skin in the best fucking way possible. I can still taste her cherry lip gloss, smell her perfume, feel her hips as she was grinding against me, feel her firm ass as I pressed her closer. I've wanted to kiss her for so long, and now that I have, I want more.

So much more.

More than she might be willing to give.

I push my way through the throng of people, making my way up to the back porch. I don't know where I'm going, what I'm doing, or what I'm going to do when I get there, but since all of my thoughts are centered on Willow, I have a feeling I might chase her down like a needy guy and scare her off even more.

Thankfully, Ari cuts me off at the back door and saves me from doing something stupid. He has a cup in his hand and the sleeves of his shirt rolled up.

"Why do you look pissed off?"

"Do I?" I play dumb, my thoughts wandering back to the field, to the kiss.

God, she tasted good. Really, really fucking good. And the way she shivered as I traced my hands over her body, tangled my fingers through her long brown hair, ran my palms up her thighs all the way to the bottom of her dress, the way she let out a moan as she came apart …. I think, during all those years of dirty dreams, my imagination might have failed me, because that kiss was better than my wildest fantasies. Hands down, the best kiss ever, and I've done my fair share of kissing and then some.

What I didn't realize until tonight, is that there's a different level of kissing I hadn't even tapped into. Good kissing, bad kissing, and perfect kissing.

Yeah, I know I sound like a fucking sap, but I'm too far gone to give a shit.

Ari squints at me through his glasses. "Does this have anything to do with Willow running out of the house like it was on fire?"

My jaw tightens as my wounded ego stings. "Perhaps."

"You didn't …" He narrows his eyes. "You fucking kissed her, didn't you?"

"So what if I did?" I reply defensively, not liking how pissed off he looks.

"Fuck, I thought you said you weren't going to try that shit again. Last time, everything was so awkward between you two, and it made things complicated between every-one."

"I didn't try that shit again. I *did* it again," I state pointlessly. "And me and Willow kissing has nothing to do with you or Luna or Wynter. This is between me and her."

He rolls his eyes. "You're an idiot if you believe that because, in the end, Wynter and Luna are going to side with Willow, which means Grey is, too. That leaves me siding with you, and that just fucking sucks."

"No one's siding with anyone," I assure him. "I'll fix this."

"Please do," he says then takes a long sip of his drink. "I don't want everyone fighting."

I shake my head, annoyed he's turning my kiss with Willow into a group issue. "I'm going up to my room. You can crash in one of the guestrooms if you need to."

I don't wait for him to respond before walking into my house. I plan on going to my room so I can alleviate some of the sexual tension jumbled inside me, but I end up getting suckered into playing a game of quarters on my way there. By the time I finally drag my drunk ass upstairs, Willow has consumed my every thought, and I'm so worked up I can barely think straight.

I wrestle to get my phone out of my pocket as I stumble into my bedroom. I don't bother turning on the light—I probably couldn't find the light switch if I tried—and flop down on my bed. It takes me a few tries before I manage to open a new text. After giving myself a pat on the back for being so awesome, I deliberate what I want to type. The longer I think about it, though, the more I realize thinking is overrated. So, I type the first thing that pops into my head. Then I roll onto my back and shut my eyes, drifting off into my fantasies.

Chapter Fifteen

Willow

I wake up the next morning to the sunlight streaming through Wynter's bedroom window and the alarm on my phone screeching like a wild banshee.

"Gah." I reach over and swat the thing with unnecessary force, causing it to fall onto the floor. At least the stupid alarm shuts off.

I yank the blanket over my head and teeter back and forth between sleep and being awake. I've never been a morning person, even after years of working a morning shift at a café. My hangover isn't helping the situation, either. I should just go to sleep, get a full night's rest for once. But I need to get home, take a shower, check on things, and then get dressed for work.

I cringe at the reminder of work and the ultimatum Van gave me. Now that I've had a day to think about it, I know I won't be able to go through with dancing on stage, which means I'm going to have to get another job. Maybe even two or three.

Grimacing, I pry myself out of my sleepy state, lean

over the edge of the bed, and pick up my phone from the hardwood floor. I quickly examine it to make sure it didn't break. The back popped off, but other than that, it seems fine. Thank God. The last thing I need is to have to pay for a new phone.

My relief is short-lived, though, when I note I have a missed message.

From Beck.

Images of last night creep back to me: stars ... dizziness ... giggling ...

What the heck did I do last night?

My puzzlement only magnifies as I read his message aloud, struggling to translate the wonky wordage going on. "*Heeeeyyyyy, so I'm lying here in bed after playing too many games of quarters. I'm seriously drunk off my ass...*" Huh? So that's why almost every letter in nearly all the words is duplicated. "*But, anyway, I'm going to get straight to the point. I meant what I said in the field, Wills. I've liked you forever. You're seriously the most beautiful, determined, smart, amazing girl I've ever met. And that kiss ... I know you probably want me to say I regret it, but I can't. I can't lie and say I wished I never experienced the most amazing kiss ever. It was so fucking hot. I can't stop thinking about it.*

"*And touching your ass ... God, you have a fine fucking ass. And I just wanted you to know that. All of that ... to*

209

know how much you mean to me—always have. Ever since the day I had Theo drive me to your place to pick you up, and you were standing on the side of the street. I was so worried and just wanted to hold you ... But even before that, I liked you. All the way back when I gave you that snow globe ... God, you'd gotten so beautiful over the summer, and it drove me crazy that I wasn't the only one who noticed. I just wish you could see yourself how I see you ...

"I know you think you're like your mother, but you're the opposite. You're sweet and kind and caring and put everyone else before yourself. And you work so hard for everything. You're so perfect ... But, anyway, I'm going to go to sleep now because I'm super drunk and can't really see the keys anymore. Hopefully, you can read this message and don't freak out when you do."

My heart thunders maddeningly in my chest as the pieces of last night connect and collide.

I flop down on my bed and stare up at the ceiling. "Fuck. This is bad. Worse than last time. I didn't even just kiss him, I—"

"Kissed who?"

The sound of Luna's voice startles me, and I nearly fall off the bed as my head whips in the direction of the doorway.

She's standing there in her pajamas, looking so dang

happy about something.

"What? No, I didn't kiss anyone." I can't even conjure up a good lie.

She gets all giddy as she crosses the room and climbs onto the bed beside me. "When did this happen? Last night?"

"No."

"Then when?" She keeps on smiling, as if knowing a secret I haven't shared yet.

"I don't know." *Think, Willow, think. You can't tell her the truth. Then it all becomes real. And then you're going to have to deal with the consequences.*

"Oh, come on." She grabs my hand and yanks on my arm, pulling me upright. "You're supposed to tell me these things. That's what girls do. At least, that's what Wynter says, and she is the best at being a girl."

"Yeah, she is." I huff out a breath, sending strands of hair out of my face. "Fine, I'll tell you, but only if you promise not to ask any questions."

She drags her fingers across her lips, as if zipping up a zipper. Then she sits there with a goofy grin on her face, practically bouncing. I swear to God, she already knows.

How can she know?

Wait. Did Beck tell her?

"Last night, I kissed someone," I mutter.

Holy crap. Shit just got real.

"Okay … Who was it? And where did it happen?"

"Don't you already know that?" I ask, assessing her reaction.

Her forehead crinkles. "How would I know?"

I can't tell if she's lying or not. Luna isn't much of a liar. Still, she seems to *know* something, or perhaps paranoia is kicking in.

"I kissed someone in a field last night," I divulge, pulling my knees up to my chest. "That's all I'm going to tell you because the rest is too complicated."

She frowns. "At least tell me who it is."

Now I frown. "You really don't know?"

She shakes her head. "I really don't, but I have an idea."

"How could you have an idea? I don't even like anyone. Not enough to kiss them, anyway."

"You might say that, but I don't think it's true. I think you're just afraid to like someone, particularly this someone, because you two would be perfect together, which means if you broke up, things would be un-perfect."

My lips part in shock. Holy mind reader.

"If you really don't want to tell me, then you don't have to," she adds, kneeling on the bed to face me. "I understand needing to keep stuff to yourself sometimes."

Thump, thump. Thump, thump. Thump, thump. My heart is a ticking time bomb in my chest, ready to go off at any moment and destroy me. My mom's heart was the same way … before my dad left. I remember him saying that to her.

"You think too much with your heart, Paula, and not with your head," he said. "And hearts aren't good decision-makers."

"You're wrong," my mom replied. "I mean, my heart made me decide on you, didn't it?"

My father frowned while I smiled. Looking back, my father probably knew he was leaving my mom and was trying to warn her, but my mom was too busy living in lovey-dovey land to understand. Or maybe she did know and wasn't ready to accept the truth.

I won't be like that. I'll accept and then find a way to move on. I won't become my mom.

"I kissed Beck," I say flatly while my heart leaps with enthusiasm.

Shut up, heart. Just shut up.

Luna's cheeriness goes kerplunk. "You don't seem very happy about it."

"That's because it was a mistake." The words nearly split my heart in two.

Die, heart, die.

Luna looks like she might have died a little, too. "What do you mean, 'it was a mistake'?"

I shrug nonchalantly, ignoring the tearing sensation in

the center of my chest. "That it shouldn't have happened. That I wish it didn't." *Lies. Lies. Lies. All lies! When did you turn into such a dirty liar?*

"Willow …" Luna says with pity in her eyes.

"Look, I was drunk," I cut her off before she can try to convince me that the kiss did mean something. "We both were … Beck probably regrets it, too." *Ha! Look at you, lying to yourself, too. Just read his text again.*

"I doubt that," she says. "I'm actually surprised you two didn't kiss a lot sooner."

I blink at her. "Huh?"

A knowing smile crosses her face. "Don't act so surprised. You two have almost kissed, like, a hundred times."

"Because we were *drunk*."

"Yeah, so what? For some people, being drunk helps them do stuff they want to do but are too afraid to do sober."

My heart races at the truth her words carry.

I can't deal with this.

I push to my feet and grab my jacket off the floor. "I have to get home. Can we talk about this later?"

She frowns, obviously hurt, and I feel like the biggest bitch ever. But fear keeps me moving forward, one foot in front of the other.

"Thank you for letting me stay here," I say, bolting out the door like a coward.

I pass by Grey on my way through the living. He turns to say something, but I throw a wave over my shoulder, run out the door, and jump into my car.

The tires spin as I skid out onto the road, driving toward Ridgefield. My adrenaline is soaring, my legs are shaking, and my mind is wired, centered on Beck, my mom, and my dad as I fly through town. I don't even notice that the light turned red until I'm halfway through the intersection.

Horns fire off, and I jolt out of my trance, swerving my car off to the side of the road after I make it through the light.

Shoving the shifter into park, I bash my hand against the top of the wheel. "Shit! Fuck! Dick! This is what happens when you get consumed by guys! You almost get yourself killed!" I let my head slump against the steering wheel. "What am I going to do? This thing with Beck can't happen. But we need to stay friends, or else I'll lose my damn mind."

Take a deep breath, Willow. Fix the problem. You can do this.

I rack my mind for an answer, and the memory of the last time Beck and I kissed surfaces. I freaked out then, too, but I fixed the … problem by laying out a rule that we were never allowed to kiss again. That worked for a while … until it didn't.

215

Rules normally work for me. Maybe I just need better rules.

Leaning over the console, I open the glovebox and dig out a pen and the paper with the rule written on it. Then I sit back, strike a line over the rule, and write a new set of rules, growing calmer with every stroke of the pen.

Rule #1: No wandering off into fields together to go stargazing.

Rule #2: Absolutely no lip-to-lip contact.

Rule #3: No falling in love.

Once I finish, I set the list and pen down. Then I drive toward Beck's, crossing my fingers he'll be my best friend instead of the guy I made out with last night.

Chapter Sixteen

Beck

I rub my hand across my throbbing forehead as I open my eyes to the blinding sunlight spilling into my bedroom. My phone is buzzing on my nightstand, and I literally have no idea what the hell happened for the last ten hours, how I got into bed, or what I did before I got there. Definitely not a first for me. I hate the gaping-hole-in-my-mind feeling.

Rolling over, I fumble around until I find my phone then swipe my finger across the screen.

Ari: Hey, man, what's up with the weird text you sent me last night? I couldn't make sense of it.

I scroll back to what I sent and shake my head. I seriously have issues with drunk texting.

Me: Sorry, man. I was drunk texting again.

Ari: You really need to stop doing that. One day, you're going to text the wrong thing to the wrong person.

Me: Maybe. Haven't done it yet, though.

Ari: Just want to give you a head's up that you texted Luna last night, too. And Wynter. I'm not sure

what you said, but they seemed pretty amused by the whole ordeal.

Me: I'm sure they were … Where are you? I think I might come chill for a while. It might be the last chance before I'm no longer a free man.

Ari: Why? You getting married or something. Lol!

Me: Yeah. Didn't your sister tell you?

Ari: I might've fallen for that if my sister didn't hate your guts. Seriously, why is this your last chance to hang?

Me: Because, come Monday, I'm officially working for my father.

Ari: What the fuck? I thought you weren't going to let him push you into doing that.

Me: Yeah, well, I wasn't until he threatened to sell my house.

Ari: I thought you bought that.

Me: He paid for a small part as my graduation present. I'm realizing how stupid of a move it was to let him.

Ari: Shit. That sucks. What're you going to do?

Me: Work for him until I can figure something out.

Ari: Sorry, man. I'm at Luna's right now if you want to come over. Grey's here, too, and Wynter should be here later. Willow was here earlier, but she took off before I got here. I think she has to work, so I doubt

**she'll make it back. Then again, are you two even talk-
ing?**

Willow … Willow … Willow?

Memories rush back to me, and I bolt upright in my
bed.

Kissing her until my lips ached. Touching her all over.
The little moans escaping her mouth. Wanting her so much
I could barely breathe.

And then I sent a text message.

Me: Gotta go. I'll try to come over later.

Ari: Okay. Sounds good.

I close up the message and switch to the text I sent
Wynter last night, knowing that one will be easier to handle.

Me: Heeeeyyyy didmnaltihtbjwihe!

I scratch my head. "What the hell was I even trying to
type?"

Next, I open the message I sent Luna, avoiding the
thing I don't want to handle. The text I sent her is equally
as confusing and funny as Wynter's, but my humor flat
lines as I read what I sent Willow.

My eyes skim over the freakin' long-ass text, or should
I say, my soul.

"Goddammit." Blood roars in my eardrums. If the kiss
didn't ruin our friendship, this message sure as hell did.

Dropping my phone onto the bed, I lower my head and

massage my temples. "I really fucked up this time."

The truth is that beneath the worry lies a bit of relief that I finally got the truth out. I just wish I didn't know Willow so well. But I do. And she might not ever speak to me again after this.

No, you can fix this. Just think of a way. Call and tell her you were wasted. Assure her it'll never happen again.

Lie.

I'm opening the dial pad, debating whether to call her, when my doorbell rings.

Throwing the blankets off me, I don't bother putting a shirt on as I drag my hungover ass down the stairs and throw open the front door. Then I blink. And blink. And blink again.

"Wait, am I dreaming?" I rub my eyes with the heels of my hands. "Or am I still drunk?"

She stares at my bare chest with her lips smashed together, clutching a piece of paper. She has on the dress she was wearing last night, her hair is down and tangled, and her eyes are bloodshot, either because she's hungover or has been crying. The thought that those pretty eyes were recently shedding tears makes me want to hug her, but I'm not sure the gesture would be welcomed at the moment.

"Hey," I say, instead. Then I shake my head at myself. *Nice one, dumbass.* "Do you want to come in?"

She tears her eyes off my chest and eyeballs the

threshold as if it's the devil about to grab her and drag her into the fiery pits of hell. "I don't know. Is it safe?"

Her question throws me off.

She doesn't feel safe with me?

"Of course it's safe. I'd never hurt you, Wills."

"I know that." She frowns at the ground, scuffing the tip of her boot against the concrete. "I'm just wondering if it's a good idea for us to be in the same room together."

Okay, fuck this. I'm not letting us go where she wants us to go.

Fixing my finger under her chin, I angle her head up. "Let's not do this, princess. We kissed." *And then some.* "So what? We don't need to act awkward because of it."

"So, you agree with me?" she asks with hope in her eyes. "That what happened was a mistake?"

I want to tell her yes, give her what she wants, alleviate her stress. But the lie won't leave my lips.

"No, that's not what I was saying," I tell her, fighting the compulsion to stare at her lips. If I do, I'll lean in. And if I lean in, I'll want more. I'll want all of her. "I was just saying that we don't need to let things get awkward."

"But I feel awkward," she whispers, her eyes wide, her chest heaving with shallow breaths.

"Well, let me fix that." *By kissing you until you can no longer think straight. By making you moan again. Over and over ...*

221

She nibbles on her bottom lip, and my gaze centers on her lips. I start to lean in, consumed with the need to kiss her, expecting her to move back. Instead, she remains motionless, staring at my mouth.

I move closer, testing her. We're so close. Wanting, wanting, wanting …

Our lips crash together. I don't even know who eliminates the inch of space between us. I don't even give a shit. All that matters is that she's kissing me back with so much passion I swear to God our lips are going to bruise.

My body floods with need. I need her closer. My hand skims down her body to her waist, my fingers pressing into her thighs as I lift her up. She gasps then hitches her legs around me, throwing me off balance a bit, and I stumble to the side. Her back hits the doorjamb, but she only deepens the kiss and bites down on my bottom lip.

I groan, my body pulsating with desire as I rock my hips against her. Her legs tighten around my hips as a gasp escapes her mouth. I grind against her again, and her fingernails stab into my shoulder blades as she clutches me, her dress bunching up to her waist, completely opened to me.

Slipping my palms up her smooth skin, I turn to get us into the house and away from any gawking. When I get there, I fully plan on peeling that dress off her.

But as quickly as the kiss started, she's jumping out of

my arms and shoving the piece of paper at me.

"R-read this." Her voice trembles, and her legs shake as she tries to get her balance.

I can't even breathe, let alone process what she's trying to say. "What?"

She sucks in an uneven breath and then steps toward me with her hand out. "I need y-you to read this."

I glance at the paper then at her. "How did we go from us kissing to me needing to read a piece of paper?" A piece of paper that I'm pretty sure has another goddamn rule on it.

"Please, just read it," she begs, her fingers trembling.

Frustrated, I take the paper from her, purposefully grazing my fingers against hers. When she shivers, I have to fight back a grin. Then any amount of optimism gets squashed as I read the list scribbled on the piece of paper aloud.

"Rule number one: no wandering off into fields together to go stargazing."

"Because it's what started this whole thing to begin with," she explains, smoothing her hands over her hair, frazzled.

Yeah, like that's going to solve anything.

"Rule number two: absolutely no lip-to-lip contact." I glance up with my brow arched. "We've had that one before."

"Yeah, I know." She scratches at the back of her neck. "I think it's pretty self-explanatory why I kept it."

"But is it doable?" I give a pressing glance at her lips, which are still swollen from our kiss, and then at her wrinkled dress and tangled hair. "Because it didn't work."

She smooths her hands over her hair and dress, staring at a rosebush beside the front door. "Yeah, I know. That's why I added the other rules to help this one work."

I bite back the need to point out that she can't even look me in the eye when she says it and read the last line. "Rule number three: no falling in love."

Yeah, it might be a little too late for that. At least for me. I can't tell her that yet. This list proves that.

A stupid list that I want to shred to pieces.

"I just want us to have some boundaries," she says, finally looking at me. "That way, we can still stay friends without any more incidents."

There are a thousand things I want to say to her right now. Usually, I bite my tongue and bury down my feelings, desperate to hold on to her. At the moment, I'm either too hungover to care, or that kiss shattered any ounce of willpower I have left.

"Incidents?" I cross my arms and lean against the doorjamb. "Is that what you call the hottest kiss of your life? Well, it was for me."

"Beck ..." She trails off, her massive eyes reflecting

her fear. She looked the same way after we kissed during our senior year, and our friendship nearly shattered to unfixable pieces.

I decide to back off for now. Not because I'm agreeing to her stupid rules, but because I need time to figure out a way to prove to her that we belong together, that a relationship with me won't destroy her. I'd never destroy her.

"Fine, I'll obey the rules." *For now.*

Her muscles unravel as she releases a deafening breath. "Thank you. I so needed to hear that." She hesitates then carefully wraps her arms around me. "I can never lose you."

"You won't," I promise her, hugging her closer, my heart pounding. "And you want to know why?"

She pulls back, nodding.

"Because I can never lose you, either."

She smiles, but nervousness resides in her eyes. "You won't lose me," she assures me. "You and I are going to be friends until we're seventy, remember?"

"Yeah, I remember." I think I changed my mind.

I don't want to be friends anymore. I want more.

I want all of her.

She glances down at her watch. "Shit. I have to be at work soon." She looks back at me. "We're good, right? I mean, what happened just barely … We can just forget about—"

"We're good," I say. As for forgetting, that's never going to happen. I don't want it to.

She offers me one final smile before jogging back to her car.

I watch her drive away then step back into my house and into the kitchen. Evidence of a party lies everywhere, from the empty glass bottles on the marble counter to plastic cups piled in the trash can.

My thoughts drift back to when I cleaned up Willow's place after her mom threw the party; only, the apartment was trashed with way more than just alcohol bottles.

I need to get her out of there somehow, something I've known for a while. Yet now I'm holding a stupid list that pretty much forbids me to get closer to her.

What Willow doesn't realize, though, is a damn piece of paper and some ink can't change how I feel.

Grabbing a magnet and a pen from a drawer, I stick the list on the fridge. Then I draw a line through each one of her rules and replace them with a task.

Task #1: Get Willow out of that house.

Task #2: Prove to her that I'm not going to destroy her.

Task #3: Tell her I love her.

I step back, looking at my plan, unsure if it's going to work. Still, I have to try. Avoiding how I feel about her isn't an option anymore.

Those   kisses   made   sure   of   that.

While Rules #1, #2, and #3—aka the

new list—are in play...

Chapter Seventeen

Willow

The next week drifts by slowly. I spend most of my time doing homework, working at the club, and applying for new jobs. I haven't heard from my mom yet, which makes me worry about her nonstop. Plus, the emptiness of the apartment is wearing on me. Between the loud music playing every night, the constant shouting—someone is always shouting—and the random knocks on the door that I never answer, I feel like I'm going to lose my mind. If she doesn't return home soon, I might move out. Rent's due next month; perhaps I won't pay it. Could I just not pay a bill? Do I even have it in me?

I did a search for some apartments to rent near the university, but everything within a fifteen-mile radius is currently full or out of my price range. I consider calling Wynter, but she lives in a nicer place than all the other apartments I checked, so I doubt I'll be able to afford the rent, especially when my job situation is so iffy.

Money isn't the only reason behind my moving hesitancy. I'm still struggling with letting go of the fear that my mom may come back and need me, and I'll be gone. I don't know how to fix that problem. What choice is right? Is there is a right choice, or is there even a choice?

Having a choice, though, rapidly dissipates when, early Thursday morning, I'm woken up by a loud voice coming from somewhere close by. Maybe even from inside the apartment.

Fumbling for my phone, I call the first person that pops into my mind, hoping he's awake this early.

"Hey, I was just thinking about you." The sound of Beck's voice slightly settles my racing pulse.

I exhale, releasing a breath I swear I've had trapped in my chest for days. I haven't talked to him since I handed him the list and that wonderfully amazing kiss that can never happen again. I didn't realize how much I missed hearing him until now.

"You sound very awake for it being so early," I say, climbing out of bed.

"I had some stuff to do," he replies with a weighted sigh.

"What stuff?"

"Just some stuff for my dad."

"Really? Since when do you do stuff for your dad?"

He sighs again. "It's a long story, one I can't really get into now."

"Okay, but you'll tell me later, right?" I ask as I tiptoe over to my door to see if I can tell if the voice is coming from inside the house or outside.

"Sure." His evasiveness throws me off. "Anyway, enough about me. Let's talk about my favorite person."

"Okay. Well, I talked to Wynter the other day, and she said New York was great." I make a joke when really, I'm freaking out. Not just because I'm talking to Beck after we kissed and fooled around, but because I'm worried someone might be in the house.

"So not funny," he scolds playfully. "Seriously, how are you, Wills? I haven't talked you since ... well, you know. And you looked a little freaked out when you left my house."

I chew on my thumbnail. "I'm fine. I've been meaning to call you, but ... I just wasn't sure if you wanted to talk to me." Or if I could handle it.

"I always want to talk to you," he assures me. "I've wanted to call you, too, but I've been busy figuring out some stuff."

"What kind of stuff?"

"Stuff I'll tell you about later when I've got everything figured out."

"Okay." I want to press, but the voice grows louder. *Shit.* I lock the door and back up. "Beck, as much as I love talking to you, I actually called for a reason."

"What's wrong?" he asks worriedly.

"I think someone might be in my house," I say, stopping when the back of my legs bump against my bed. "I don't know who it would be. I mean, it could be my mom, but the door was locked, and I'm pretty sure she lost the key a long time ago."

"Hang up and call the police," he orders, his voice laced with fear.

"It could just be coming from outside. Sometimes, it's hard to tell. The walls are so thin."

"I don't give a shit if you think it's from outside," he growls. "Call the police. Right now. Or I will."

"O-okay," I stammer, more as a reaction to how angry he sounds. I don't think I've ever heard him sound this angry. "I'll call you back in a second."

"Just switch over to a different line," he tells me firmly. "I don't want to hang up."

"Okay." I'm moving the phone away to do what he says when my door jostles.

"Willow, hon, why's the door locked?" my mom asks, knocking on the door.

I feel like I should be more relieved to hear her voice, and that probably makes me a terrible person. More than I already am, anyway.

I put the phone back to my ear. "Everything's okay. It's just my mom."

"Are you sure?" he asks, not seeming too relieved, either. "If you're not one hundred percent sure, you still need to call the police."

"I'm sure. She just spoke to me through the door." I walk back across the room and open the door. "I'm sorry I worried you. I've just been so jumpy being here by myself."

"You don't need to be sorry for worrying me. I want to help you every chance I get, no matter what. I don't like you being there by yourself."

"I know. And I really am considering moving out." I grip the doorknob as my mom knocks again. "I'm kind of glad my mom is here. Now I can talk to her about the idea."

"Do you really think that's a good idea?"

"I don't know, but I have to at least let her know."

"Why? She'll just try to talk you out of it."

"I doubt that. She doesn't really care if I'm around or not. I only stuck around this long because I worry about her, not the other way around."

"That's not the reason I think she's going to talk you out of it," he says quietly. "I think she's going to try to talk you out of it because you've been taking care of her for years. You pay her bills, buy her food, clean the house, clean up after her. And if you leave, she's going to lose all of that."

I smash my lips together, breathing in and out of my nose as the truth of his words pierces my heart. "I know," I whisper. "I've already thought about all of that." Hearing

233

him say it makes my heart ache, makes the brutal truth real. Very, very painfully, aching, can barely breathe real. "I still need to say something to her. And I can't move out until I find a new job." I realize my slip up a second too late.

"What's wrong with the one you have at the library?"

"It just doesn't pay very well." Each lie I utter makes me loathe myself even more.

My mom bangs on the door so violently I jump back. "Okay, Willow. It's time to open the door."

"I have to go," I tell Beck. "I'll call you later."

"You better," he says worriedly. "Or else I'll drive over there and make sure you're okay."

Part of me wants to never call him back so he'll make due on his threat. That wouldn't be right, though. Instead, I agree, and then we both utter a reluctant good-bye before hanging up.

I let out a gradual exhale. I was worried about talking to him again, but now that I have, I feel better. It wasn't as awkward as I thought it was going to be.

This might work.

Hopefully.

Then my good mood splatters against the cracked linoleum when I open the door.

"Took you long enough." Her bulging eyes are blood-shot, her clothes are stained with dirt, and her greasy hair is pulled back into a messy bun. "You got any cash on you?"

234

"Um, hello to you, too," I say, stumbling backward as she pushes past me.

"Hello," she grumbles, striding straight for my dresser. "Where do you keep the cash again? I can't remember."

I nervously watch her as she throws the top drawer open "What cash?"

"The stash of cash you keep hidden." She dumps the contents of the drawer onto the floor, scattering my clothes everywhere.

"Yeah, I don't have a stash of cash." I cross the room and grab her hand as she's about to yank out another drawer. "I spend almost every penny I make on bills and paying your stupid debts."

She jerks her arm back. "That's such bullshit! I know you have extra money! How else could you afford all that stuff?"

"What stuff?" I ask with honest confusion. I don't have much of anything.

"Your car, those school books you have." She drags her fingers down her face so roughly she leaves red marks on her skin. "Better yet, where's all that money you were saving up for tuition? Let me have some of that."

"That money's gone," I say, annoyed she has the audacity to ask for it.

"Gone where?" She scans the room in a panic.

"To pay my tuition. And since I've been going to

school for a few months now, you should know that."

"You go to school? Since when?"

I bite my tongue and just stare at her, hating that she's like this, hating that she's my mother, maybe even hating her, which only makes me hate myself.

Her eyes land on me, and the panic in her expression fizzles as she inches toward me. "You know what we haven't done in a while?" Her smile looks all sorts of wrong.

"Everything," I say, unable to stop myself.

"That's not true. We do stuff all the time."

I want to point out all the reasons she's wrong, but she's probably strung out, which pretty much makes her a ticking time bomb that could destroy what little life I have left in an instant.

"Like that time we went to the park." Her chapped lips twist into a forced smile.

"The last time we went to the park, I was five." And Dad was still here.

"Oh, that's not true." She wraps her arms around me and begins rocking me back and forth like she did when I was a kid. "I love you. You know that, right?"

When I was younger, I loved when she said this. That feeling died around the time I turned twelve and realized she only threw those words out there when she was in trouble and needed my help bailing her out of whatever problem she'd gotten herself into.

"Where's your new husband?" I ask, concerned he might be in the house somewhere.

She slants back to look me in the eye, having a hard time focusing on one spot. "Who told you I got married?"

I shrug. "Some bar owner overheard you talking about it."

"Oh." She frowns. "Well, that was a mistake."

"So you didn't get married?"

"No, I did. But it didn't work out."

"It's only been, like, a week." That might be a new record for her.

She waves me off with a flick of her wrist. "Most Vegas marriages only last until the alcohol and drugs wear off."

I note her bloodshot eyes. "So, why did you decide not to stay married to him?"

"Because he was boring and annoying and kept checking out other women." She grinds her teeth over and over again as if she can somehow grind the memory of her short-lived marriage away. "But that's okay. I've got better things to do."

"Really?" I doubt it. Usually, when she gets dumped, she has a bawl fest on the bathroom floor.

She nods, her jaw still grinding, her eyes practically bulging out of her head. "I just need another fix, and I'll be good." She looks at me, pleading. "But I can't do that unless I have some money."

I shuffle back from her. "I'm not giving you money to buy drugs."

"Why not?" She itches her arm repeatedly, leaving scratch marks. "You've done it before."

"Unknowingly."

"But that doesn't make it any different."

"Yes, it does. It makes me an enabler."

"What the hell does that mean?" she snaps, the rage in her eyes making me shrink back. When she notices my edginess, the anger erases, and she offers me a plastic smile. "Come on, Willow. Just help your mom out. I promise it'll be my last time asking you for help."

"N-no, it won't." I stand firm, crossing my arms, refusing to back down.

Her lip twitches and her fingers curl into fists. "You're such an ungrateful brat who only cares about herself."

I shake my head, loathing the tears pooling in my eyes. "Do you even know what I was doing for the last week while you've been MIA? I've been hanging around the apartment as much as I can because I've been worried about you."

"Why would you worry about me?" She gapes at me like I'm an idiot. "I was having the time of my life."

"I didn't know that," I bite out. "You didn't tell me where you were going."

"How is that my fault? It's not like I have a phone so I can call you."

"You could've stopped by before you took off and at least let me know where you were," I tell her. "But that doesn't even matter. The point is, I shouldn't have ever been here, because I shouldn't be living here anymore. This place is shitty, the neighbors are shitty, and you treat me shitty, yet I stay here because I worry you're going to come home one day with too many drugs or alcohol in your system, and no one will be here to take you to the hospital."

She rolls her eyes. "I wouldn't die if that's what you're getting at. I know my limits."

"Says every drug addict ever." The words roll off my tongue without any forethought, shocking myself as much as I do her.

"Shut the fuck up!" she shouts then whirls around and slides her hand across my dresser, sending all of my snow globes to the floor. Glass shatters. Water spills everywhere.

Broken. Everything is broken.

"See what you made me do!" my mom screams, wild-eyed. "If you would've just given me the damn money!"

"You broke them all," I whisper, tears pooling in my eyes. "Dad gave me those. It was the only thing I had from him."

"Your dad?" Her sharp laugh makes more tears fill my eyes. "Newsflash, Willow. Your dad doesn't care about you, so I don't know why you'd care about anything he gave you. No one cares about you! And the sooner you learn that, the better off you'll be!" With that, she storms out of the room, slamming the door behind her.

I don't chase after her. I remain frozen in place, staring at the broken snow globes, the only items I had left from my father.

He doesn't care about you.

He doesn't care about me.

No one cares about you.

Maybe I should be glad they're broken. Perhaps I should've never kept them to begin with. That thought doesn't make it any easier as I unglue my feet from the floor and head to get a trash bag to clean up the mess.

My mom is gone by the time I make it into the kitchen, and while I'm scared of where she might be and what she may be doing, I don't want her here.

When I return to my room, I begin picking up the broken glass. With each piece I throw away, a tear slips from my eye. By the time I finish, I'm bawling.

I sink to the floor and hug my legs against my chest, allowing myself to cry for a minute or two until I'm on the verge of losing it. Then I put the floodgates back up, trapping the pain and worry inside.

As I stumble to my feet to go get my phone, I notice a single snow globe beside the back of the dresser. I crawl over to see which one survived and don't know whether to smile or frown at the Eiffel Tower inside the glass ball.

I don't know what that means or if it means anything, but I pick up the snow globe Beck gave me and tuck it safely in my dresser drawer. Then I collect my phone off my bed to call Wynter and do something completely out of the ordinary for me: ask her if I can move in with her without a new job lined up, without having a plan. I don't want to do it. I don't want to jump into something without knowing I can handle the entire situation. But staying here isn't an option anymore. Not after this.

I dial her number, sitting on my bed, holding my breath.

"Hey," Wynter answers the phone cheerfully. "I was actually just about to call you and see if you want to go shopping with me. I need a dress for this stupid party my parents are having."

"I'd love to go, but I have to work," I say, biting my fingernails.

"All right, what's up? I know something has to be up when you say stuff like you'd love to go shopping with me."

"I need a favor." Only four words, but it takes all of my strength to get them to leave my lips.

"Of course." She sounds surprised. "What's up?"

"I need a place to live." Shame strangles me. "I know

you said that Luna might be moving out, and I thought maybe I could rent her room for a bit."

She doesn't answer right away, making my anxiety skyrocket.

"I really wish you would've called a few days ago." Her tone conveys remorse. "I just leased out the room to someone else. I even had her sign a contract."

My chest tightens, squeezing every ounce of oxygen out of me. "That's okay." I force a fake, even tone. "I'm sure I can find another place to rent."

"What me to go apartment hunting with you?" she asks. "We can start by checking the places around campus."

"That's okay," I lie, knowing all those places are full. "I think I'll just go after class tomorrow."

"Are you sure? I really don't mind going with you."

"It's fine." I'm fine. Fine. Fine. Fine. The word is really starting to lose all meaning.

"Okay, well let me know if you change your mind." She pauses. "Although, I might know someone who would rent a room to you for dirt cheap."

A glint of hope sparkles inside the sea of despair I'm drowning in. "Really? Who?"

She hesitates. "Beck."

The glint of hope simmers into a thin trail of smoke. "I think I'll check around the apartments first and see how that goes."

She sighs. "Okay, but just so you know, I doubt there will be many to rent during the middle of the year. It would be a lot easier if you just stayed with him. You could always move out at the end of the year when places start opening up."

I want to explain to her why I can't live with Beck, but I fear I'll be opening Pandora's box.

"I'll think about it."

"Good." She seems to relax. "Let me know what you decide."

"I will."

We say good-bye then hang up. I lie down in my bed and curl up into a ball, wishing life was easier, simple, less complicated.

Wishing I didn't feel like I was drowning and about to be forced to take my final breath.

243

Chapter Eighteen

Beck

I'm working in my dad's office, sorting files on his computer, trying not to worry that Willow hasn't called me back, when my phone rings.

I lean back in the chair to retrieve it from my pocket, expecting the call to be from Willow since she told me she'd call me back. But Wynter flashes across the screen, and I hesitate, unsure if I want to answer. Yeah, Wynter's my friend and everything, but she can be a real pain in the ass sometimes, at least to me. But ignoring her seems like kind of a douchey move, so I press talk and put the phone up to my ear.

"What?" I answer, balancing the phone between my shoulder and my ear so I can continue working and not prolong my time here.

"Wow, way to greet your friend," she replies. "God, Beck, what did I ever do to piss you off?"

I click a few keys. "Do you really want me to answer that question?"

"Probably not," she replies then sighs. "Hey, have you

talked to Willow today?"

"Yeah, she called me this morning." I pause as I stumble across a file labeled "Personal Business," a file my dad mentioned I didn't need to mess around with. Curious, I double-click and open the contents. Then my jaw drops. Holy shit. "She's supposed to be calling me back later today. If she doesn't, I'm going to call her back when I get off work."

"Well, I think you should call her soon." The urgency in her tone causes me to straighten in the chair.

I move my hands off the keyboard and slant back in the chair. "What happened?"

"I'm not really sure. She called me out of the blue about twenty minutes ago, sounding upset and asking if she could rent my spare room. When I told her I just leased it out to someone, she got even more upset, although she was trying to hide it. I don't know why she always tries to pretend everything's okay when it's not. It's why she ends up having nervous breakdowns."

"Yeah, I know," I mutter, thrumming my fingers against the desk. "She didn't say why she was upset, though?"

"No, but I could tell it didn't just have to do with me not being able to rent her a room. She was upset before that."

"You should've told her she could crash on your

couch. She hates asking for help, and if she went to you
…"—I swallow hard—"something must have happened."

"Shit. I didn't even think about the couch thing. I did
tell her she should move in with you, though."

"I bet that went well."

"Yeah, she didn't seem too thrilled about it. Why is
that?"

"None of your business."

"Ha, if you really believe that, then you don't know me
at all."

"No, I do know you," I say exhaustedly. "But I had to
try."

"Well, stop trying and fess up." She pauses. "Did you
two do something again?"

I wait a second too long to respond.

"You did!" she cries. "Oh, my God, I told Willow this
was going to happen. That sooner or later you two would
screw each other's brains out."

"We didn't fuck. We just … kissed." And touch. And
grinded. And fucking kissed again.

"Oh, my God, you sound so turned on right now," she
whines. "It's so disgusting."

"So what?" I don't even bother trying to deny it. "It
was a hot fucking kiss."

"TMI, Beck."

"You're the one who brought it up."

She puffs out an exasperated exhale. "You know what? I think I'll get the details from Willow. Your details come with too many noises I'd rather not hear."

"Why do you need details at all? It's not really any of your business."

"Why do you do that?" she snaps. "Why do you act like I'm such a bad person?"

"I don't act like you're a bad person," I retort. "I just don't know why you need to know everything. Plus, if you ask Willow about the kiss, she's going to get more upset."

"Why?" she asks. "She didn't like it?"

"No … I think she did." I drag my fingers through my hair, slumping back in the chair. "You know about her no-dating rule, right?"

"Yeah, she mentioned it once, but I didn't think she was being serious."

"Well, she was, and now that we kissed …" I'm one step away from touching myself as images of Willow and me kissing flood my thoughts. "Well, let's just say she's trying everything she can to make sure it doesn't happen again."

"But you want it to happen again?"

"Um, yeah. I thought that was pretty obvious with the noises I was making."

"God, you're so gross," she mutters. "Anyway, we're getting off the subject. I called to tell you about Willow be-

247

ing upset because I knew you'd want to take care of her."

"I've been trying to." I lean forward and lower my head into my hand. "I've offered to let her move in with me over and over again, but she's so stubborn. So, if you have any ideas at all, please share. I'd really like to get her out of that shithole she's living in now. That place is sketchy as fuck."

"Just do what you always do," she replies in a sugary sweet tone. "Bat your baby blue eyes to get your way."

"I so do not fucking do that."

"You do that all the damn time, and I think you know you do."

"Whatever." I raise my head from my hand and sit up straight. "I'm going to hang up so I can call Willow."

"Let me know how it goes. I worry about her."

"So do I." More than anything.

After I hang up, I dial Willow's number. The call goes straight to voicemail, and seconds later, I receive a text.

Willow: Hey, I'm at work, so I can't talk. I don't get off until late so can I call you tomorrow?

Me: Actually, can we hang out tomorrow? I really need to talk to you.

Willow: Sure. Is everything all right? You sounded a little irked on the phone.

I shake my head. Leave it to her to worry about me when she's buried up to her chin in stress.

Me: I'm fine. I swear. I just really want to see you.

Then, as an afterthought, I add: **I miss you.**

She doesn't reply right away, and I start to worry I spooked her. Then my phone buzzes with an incoming text.

Willow: I miss you, too. I have class tomorrow. I get out at two if you want to stop by. I have work later. Maybe we can grab something to eat or something.

The restlessness in my chest relaxes since she's being cooperative. Then again, she doesn't know what I want to talk about.

Me: Sounds good. If you want to call me when you get off work, too, you can. In fact, I wish you would.

Willow: If it's not too late.

I sigh, knowing she won't yet grateful she's at least hanging with me tomorrow.

Me: You can always call me. Whenever. Wherever. Any time you want.

I end the messages at that then try to shove my worries of Willow aside for the moment and plug my phone into the computer. Then I copy the files in my father's personal business folder, files that I'm pretty sure prove he's committed tax fraud. I'm not positive yet, but I know a very smart girl who might be able to help me understand them better. And while I don't know what I'll do if I find out the information is true, it doesn't hurt to have some blackmail material handy in case he refuses to quit blackmailing me into working for him.

Once I get all the files downloaded, I put my phone away and reach for a piece of paper to work on solving a problem that desperately needs solving: convincing Willow to move in with me.

While I don't think getting her to agree is going to be easy, I might have an idea to help her see why living with me is better than living with her mom. A way to help her understand. A way she understands.

I press the pen to the paper and start writing a list.

Chapter Nineteen

Willow

Work sucks big time. Van keeps reminding me that I'll soon be up on stage, even going as far as discussing what outfit I should wear. By the time I leave, I'm exhausted and worried and scared and feel so dirty. My fear only doubles when I notice the Mustang in the parking lot. Thank God I'm not alone and have Rowan, one of the dancers, walking with me to the car.

"When you start up onstage, you'll really want to be careful coming out here," she tells me as she puffs on a cigarette. She's wearing a leather jacket over a sequined pair of shorts and a bikini top, the outfit she wears on stage. "A lot of guys will try to buy time with you, but they need to go through Van to do that."

I nearly stop dead in my tracks. "That goes on here?"

Smoke snakes from her lips as she gives me a *duh* look. "Um, yeah. What did you think the back room was for?"

"I don't know." I zip up my jacket. "I thought maybe it was storage."

She laughs, ashing her cigarette. "Van's right. You're definitely going to rock on stage with that whole innocent act."

I offer her a tight smile, not bothering to mention that I'm going to quit before that happens. I only wish I had a damn job lined up already. "Well, thanks for walking me to my car."

"Yeah, no problem." She puts her cigarette between her lips before turning and walking off.

I dare a glance at the inside of the Mustang as I slip my key into the door. Dane isn't inside, thankfully, but my nerves don't lessen as I open the door and climb in.

The second my butt hits the seat, I shut the door and push down the lock. Then I slide the key into the ignition and …

Glug. Glug. Glug …The damn engine won't turn over.

I pound my palm against the steering wheel then slip my hand into my jacket pocket to get my phone, unsure who to call since no one knows I work here. Well, except for my mom, but she wouldn't be any help even if I could get a hold of her.

"Car trouble?"

The sound of Dane's voice sends a surge of fear through my veins.

Swallowing hard, I fix my attention on my phone. "I'm fine." I open my text messages and scroll through my contacts, pretending to be calm when I'm one window knock away from peeing my pants. My heart only pounds harder when Dane tries to open the door.

"Come on; let me in," he says, jiggling the door handle. "I'll get your car to start for you. And I won't even charge you cash."

"Go away." I honk the horn, and he jolts.

He then quickly recovers, pressing his forehead to my window. "Honk all you want, sweetheart. No one can hear you out here. And if they did, they wouldn't care."

He's right. Well, mostly right except for Everette. He cared.

But he's not here, is he?

And the only other guy in your life who's ever protective of you is about thirty miles away and doesn't know about your dirty little work secret.

No, you're going to have to handle this on your own.

I reach for my pepper spray, and start to roll down my window, ready to spray him in the face. But when a Mercedes rolls up beside my car, I freeze. Terror whiplashes through me as a man in his forties wearing a button down shirt and jeans hops out and strides toward the front of my car.

Good God, I'm going to die tonight, either by the hand of Dane or this man who's clearly stalking me for reasons that probably have to do with my mom.

You're not going to die. Just fix the problem. Call Beck because it's either that or let Dane or rich dude end you.

My fingers tremble as I start to push Beck's number, ready to accept the consequences of my actions and pray I don't lose him. But I pause as the older guy storms toward Dane, slams his palms against his chest, and shoves him to the ground.

"What the fuck!" Dane shouts, scurrying to his feet.

The man puts his boot on Dane's chest, pinning him to the ground. "If you so much as come near her again, I will fucking end you. Got it?"

My jaw nearly smacks my knees. Who the freak is this badass old guy?

"Fuck you, old man," Dane spits, struggling to get up. "This isn't any of your business." His face bunches in pain as the man leans more of his weight on Dane's chest.

"I don't think you're really in a position to decide that, are you?" the man asks, rolling up his sleeves and revealing his muscular, tattooed arms. "Now, I'm going to move my foot. You have exactly five seconds to get up, get in your car, drive away, and never, ever come back here." With that, he steps back, removing his foot from Dane's chest.

Dane launches to his feet, balling his hands into fists. "You're going to regret ever doing that."

"One," the man starts counting, sounding kind of bored.

Dane spits on the ground, as if that somehow proves he's tough.

"Two," the man continues, and Dane's eyes briefly widen. "Three."

Dane spins around and barrels for his car. The man keeps counting as Dane starts up the engine. He reaches five as the Mustang flies out of the parking lot, leaving a cloud of dust behind. Once the taillights have vanished down the road, the man turns to me.

"Are you okay?" he asks cautiously.

"Um … Yeah …" I don't know what to say. Why did he do what he did? If he expects some sort of payment …

He must read my hesitancy because he says, "I just wanted to help. That's all."

"Okay … Thanks." I stare at his eyes, which look strikingly familiar under the glow of the lamppost. "Do I know you?"

Instead of answering, he walks toward the front of the car. "Pop the hood, and I'll see if I can figure out why it won't start."

The fact that he knows about my car trouble puts me right back on edge.

"I can't pay you," I say, "with money or anything else."

His eyes enlarge, and then he promptly shakes his head. "I don't want anything at all."

"Then why are you doing this?"

"To help you."

I don't know whether I should trust him, but the doors are locked and the pepper spray is in my hand if I need it.

"Fine." I pull the lever that pops the hood.

He flips the latch underneath and raises the hood, disappearing out of my sight.

I hold my breath as he works, my finger hovering over Beck's contact number, preparing to dial if I need to. Several minutes tick by before the man peers around the hood.

"Turn the key and see if it starts," he says.

I turn over the key and breathe freely again as the engine grumbles to life.

The man pushes down the hood and walks over to the driver's side window with his now greasy arms crossed. "I think you might really need to consider getting a new car. I temporarily fixed it, but the engine's about to fall apart."

"Thanks for the advice," I say, moving my foot toward the gas pedal, eager to get the heck out of here. "And thanks for temporarily fixing my car."

"Anytime." He lowers his head to level his gaze with mine, and again, I'm struck with an odd sense of familiarity. "I'd really like to help you get one."

So much for his nice-guy act.

"I already told you I'm not that kind of girl."

"What kind of girl do you think I think you are?" he

asks, a crease forming between his brows.

"The kind of girl who …" My cheeks heat, and the words won't leave my mouth. I gesture at the club. "The kind of girl who can be bought."

Shock floods his eyes as he jerks back. "That's not what this is about."

"There must be something you want," I snap. "Or else you wouldn't have just offered to help me buy a car."

He inches closer, shoving his hands into his pockets. "There actually is something I want."

I shake my head, questioning why I'm even still here. "Of course there is."

"Your time," he stresses. "That's it."

My hand on the steering wheel begins to tremble as anger burns under my skin. "And I can only guess what we'd do together while we're spending time together."

"Will you stop saying that kind of shit? That's not what this is about." He looks appalled. No, more than that. He looks utterly sickened, like he's about to puke all over the gravel.

I don't know how it clicks or why. All I know is that one moment, I'm looking at some stranger who saved my ass from Dane, and the next, I'm looking at my father. Only, he's fifteen years older than the one I remember.

"Willow, please just hear me out," he says, probably seeing the recognition on my face.

I shake my head, shoving the shifter into drive. "Stay away from me!" I shout before peeling out of the parking lot.

I drive like a mad woman back to the apartment, checking the rearview mirror every so often to make sure he doesn't follow me. He doesn't, and I don't know what that means. Will he try to talk to me again, or will he walk away? I don't know what answer scares me the most. By the time I pull up in front of the apartment, my skin is damp from an approaching panic attack.

Parking the car, I get out and stumble into the house. I head straight for my mom's room and begin digging through boxes and drawers, looking for something—anything—that will prove that man isn't my father. That he didn't just try to come back into my life after leaving me with a mother who couldn't take care of herself, let alone a child.

When I was younger, I spent nights pondering the idea that perhaps he died and that's why he never came back. It hurt to think he was dead, but it hurt just as much to think that maybe he just didn't want me anymore.

After nearly tearing the room apart, I find what I'm looking for tucked underneath the mattress. My mom said she threw everything of my dad's away, but I knew she was lying. And I was right.

I gather the few photos in my hand and then sink to the

floor as I study the man standing beside my mom and me. The tattooed arms. The familiar eyes. The man from the parking lot.

My chest throbs with an old, aching wound. But I refuse to cry anymore over my father, so I bottle up the sadness and the excruciating ache and lock it away with the rest of the problems I'm not ready to deal with.

I know I'm only biding time. Sooner or later, all of this is going to catch up with me.

Chapter Twenty

Willow

My mom doesn't come home that night, and part of me is glad. I don't want to see her or my dad yet. I'm honestly not sure I want to see any of them again, even if I do feel guilty and sick for thinking such awful things.

I consider cutting Chemistry class the next day to avoid another problem I'm not ready to deal with, but I've never been one for cutting class, so I drive to school, worried my current employment will be the topic of juicy gossip. Apparently, Everette isn't much of a gossiper, though, something I discover after class when I run into him in the hallway.

Literally.

"Oh, my God, I'm so sorry," I sputter an apology, stumbling back from him, feeling like an idiot for slamming into him while staring at my phone. I was distracted, checking my email to see if any of the jobs I applied for responded back.

A couple of places offered me a position, but they don't pay very much. Still, I might be able to get away with accepting two if I have to.

Everette offers me an understanding smile. "It's okay. I'm not very good at texting while walking, either."

"Still, I should know better after crashing into people multiple times." I smile back, nervousness bubbling in my stomach that he knows my secret.

"I'm sure everyone does it." He glances around the hallway then leans in, clutching the book he's holding. "I'm actually glad I ran into you. I wanted to make sure you're okay."

"Yeah, I'm fine," I mutter quietly, anxiety pumping through my veins.

"I don't want you to feel uncomfortable, and I promise I won't ever bring it up again," he says in a hushed tone. "But you ran off so quickly … It had me nervous that maybe that guy hurt you or something."

"That's not why I ran off." I adjust the strap of my bag higher on my shoulder and peer around the mostly vacant hallway. "I was just surprised to see someone I knew there."

He nods in understanding. "I won't say anything to anyone. We all have stuff we don't want other people to know, right?"

I nod, surprised by his sincerity. "Thanks. I really appreciate that."

Smiling, he opens his mouth to say something, but

261

Beck strolls up.

"Hey." He stops beside me, standing so close our shoulders touch. His gaze bounces between Everette and me before finally landing on Everette. "What's up, man?"

"Not much." Everette stuffs the paperback into the back pocket of his faded jeans. "You playing soccer again this weekend?"

"I was thinking about it, but I need to check on a few things first." Beck grows quiet, rubbing the back of his neck.

Everette raises his brow like *okay?* "I guess I might see you there, then." He looks at me. "See you in class next week?"

I nod, and then he heads down the hallway, digging his phone out of his pocket.

I nervously turn to Beck. I haven't seen him since I gave him the list. I honestly didn't know how I was going to feel being near him again, if I'd lose it. But his nearness seems to calm some of the clusterfuck of shittiness current-ly crammed in my chest.

I discreetly eye him over, chewing on my lip. He's wearing a long-sleeved grey shirt, jeans, and a beanie with a few strands of hair sticking out from underneath. My eyes travel to his lips, and I find myself touching my own, re-membering our kisses, how soft his lips are, how wonderful it felt to bite them, how life felt perfect for a moment.

Completely and utterly and wonderfully, smile all the time, flutters in my heart, tingles on my skin perfect. But that was only a delusion, something I was reminded of yesterday.

I quickly try to force the mental images of the kiss away, and my senses go haywire from the scent of his delicious cologne, his overpowering warmth, and my desire to touch him again.

I stab my fingernails into my palms. *Don't you dare. You already have too much to worry about.*

Beck shifts his gaze to me, question marks and uncertainty flooding his eyes. I wonder if he'll bring up the list or if we're going to just act like nothing happened, like we did after the last kiss.

"You know him?" Beck asks, nodding in the direction Everette wandered off in.

"Um, yeah. He's in my Chemistry class." *So not what I was expecting him to say.* "He seems nice."

He nods, studying me intently. "He is."

The strange, hurt look on his face has me feeling lost. "How do you know him? From soccer?"

"Yeah, he plays on one of the other city leagues, and we've chatted a few times after games." He shoves up the sleeves of his shirt, glancing up the hallway then back at me. "What were you guys talking about before I walked up?"

I shrug, loathing myself that I'm about to lie to him once again. "Nothing. Just an assignment."

A pucker forms at his brows as he studies me again, as if trying to unravel my thoughts. "It looked like you two were kind of having a pretty intense conversation."

"The assignment was for a final, and you know how I get about finals." Guilt smashes my chest, making it difficult to get air into my lungs. I can't tell Beck the truth. Not about this. What I can do is talk to him about my father. Not until we're alone, though, in case I lose control.

He glances down the hallway again then fixes his gaze on me again. "You're not … Is there something going on between you two?"

"What!" I cry out, drawing attention from people passing by. I inch closer to him and lower my voice. "Why would you think that?"

He shrugs, his jaw set tight. "Because that's how it kind of looked with how close you two were standing to each other. And you had this look on your face like you were relaxed."

Try more like relieved Everette wasn't going to tell anyone my secret.

Still, I don't want Beck thinking I'm dating anyone, especially after I made such a big deal about the kiss and us never hooking up again.

"I promise you, I'm not seeing anyone, including Everette," I tell him, and the tension in his body loosens. "You should know that, considering … well, everything." My gaze magnetizes to his lips again as images of our kisses soar through my thoughts. My skin warms like gooey melted chocolate, chocolate I want to eat … taste … and … I blink.

Oh, my God, what the hell is wrong with me? I've lost all of my self-control.

Panicking over my out of control thoughts, I hastily change the subject. "So, what have you been up to for the last week? I feel like I haven't seen you in ages." *Exactly seven days ago, since I gave you the list. But who's counting?*

"Yeah, I know. I wanted to hang out, but I've been busy."

"With school?"

His shoulders slump. "And work."

"Since when are you busy with work? I thought that was kind of the point of having your own business and doing what you do: you make your own hours."

"Not with that job." He sounds irritated, although I don't think it's toward me.

I stuff the textbook I'm holding into my bag. "You have another job? Since when? Oh, was that why you were up early when I called you yesterday?"

He nods then motions for me to follow him. "Come on.

I'll explain while we walk." He starts to walk down the hallway then pauses. "We are still hanging out, right?"

I nod. "Of course. I was just getting ready to text you when I ran into Everette."

His lip curls in annoyance at the mention of Everette, but when he notices me watching him, he forces a fake smile. "Want to go to the café on the corner? There's actually something I really need to talk to you about besides my current job position, and that place is pretty quiet."

"Sounds good to me." I smile, growing uneasy as I think of all the things he could want to talk to me about. "It's not bad, is it?"

He glances at me distractedly. "What?"

"What you want to talk to me about."

"No, not at all. At least, I don't think so."

"Can you give me just a hint, so I don't worry?" I ask as we push out the doors and step into the warmth of the sunlight.

"Now what would be the fun in that?" He chuckles at the look on my face then slings his arm around my shoulder.

I tense for a microsecond and consider pulling away. Then that safe feeling takes over, and I lean into him.

God, I needed this more than I even realized.

Need? The word sends panic and shock through my body.

Need.

Need.

Need.

The start of my mom's downfall.

I start to lean away.

"Relax." His lips pull into an adorable lopsided smile that convinces me to stay put. "The café is only about two minutes away."

"Two whole minutes," I joke. "I think you're overestimating my patience."

"You're usually pretty patient."

"Not when you tell me you need to talk to me about something."

"It's just an idea I had," he explains as we hike across the lawn underneath the shade of the trees.

"About what?"

"About me helping you with moving out of that apartment."

I slow to a stop. "Beck, I really appreciate your help, but—"

He places a finger over my lips. "No protesting until you've heard me out, okay? Just give me that."

Well, crap. How can I say no to that, especially while he's batting those baby blues at me?

I nod reluctantly. "Okay, I'll hear you out." My lips move against his finger, and his gaze flits to my mouth, his tongue slipping out to wet his lips. "But only because you're my best friend." I aim for a light tone, but I sound cringingly breathless.

Desire flames in his expression and my heart stammers from the look. Thank God he rips his attention off my mouth before I end up collapsing on the ground.

"That's the only reason, huh?" he teases. "So, what does that mean? That you never hear anyone else out?"

"Not usually," I joke in an off-pitch voice that makes me cringe. "I guess you should consider yourself very lucky."

We start walking again, stepping onto the sidewalk and heading for the corner.

"Oh, I do," he assures me, grinning from ear-to-ear, "especially right now."

My brows dip. "Why now?"

He winks at me. "I'm here with you."

I roll my eyes. "That was so cheesy."

He nudges me with his shoulder. "Don't pretend you don't like it."

I roll my eyes again, but when he smiles at me again and my heart flutters, fear lashes through me. I don't know if my nerves are from the kiss or if all the stress bearing down on me has turned me into a twitchy squirrel. But I don't like being nervous around him, not when he's the only person who calms me down.

"What are you thinking about?" he asks, suddenly seeming apprehensive, too.

"Homework," I lie. *God, I suck.*

The sunlight reflects in his eyes as he assesses me. "Are you sure? You seem ... nervous."

"You should know by now that I'm just a nervous person," I remind him as we hop off the sidewalk to cross the street.

"Yeah, but I also know that, if anyone can calm you down, it's me." He grins proudly. "So what do I need to do?"

Kiss me again.

Touch me again.

Make me go back to the stars.

What the fuck is wrong with me?

"Tell me what you want to talk to me about," I reply as we arrive at the entrance to the quaint coffee shop. "And then I have some stuff to talk to you about."

His brow rises as he looks at me. "You do?"

I nod. "A lot of shit happened yesterday." When his lips part, I place my finger over his lips like he did to me. "You get to talk first, and then I'll go."

He slowly nods with a puzzled, impish glint in his eyes. I soon find out where the look is stemming from as he nips my finger then backs away, leaving my jaw hanging to my knees.

269

Jessica Sorensen

When he reaches the door, he pulls it open and motions for me to go in first, bowing like a total weirdo. "My lady."

That gets me to laugh.

He grins. "I knew that one would win you over."

I roll my eyes, ignoring the torrid emotions funneling around inside me. "You're such a weirdo." I enter the café, breathing in the delicious scent of coffee and baked goods.

He lets the door swing shut behind us. "Like you're not."

I get in line, looking over the menu on the marquee. "No, not at all. I'm the opposite of a weirdo."

He moves closer, and I stiffen, conflicted, wanting, fearing. Want. Fear.

"Junior year at my end of the school year bash," he whispers in my ear. "You spent the entire night pretending you were a wizard and casting magic spells on everyone."

It takes me a moment to hear his words through the fogginess in my brain.

"I was drunk." My voice comes out hoarse, and I quickly clear my throat. "Normally, I don't do that kind of stuff."

"The beginning of sophomore year," he says. "You made me play dress up with all that weird steampunk shit you collect."

"Hey, I don't know why that makes me weird." A hint of a smile rises on my lips. "You're the one who played

270

dress up."

He lightly pinches my hip, and my body jolts, my back arching toward him and my ass brushing against his hips. Tension electrifies as we both freeze. Beck starts breathing loudly. Or maybe I do. It's really hard to tell when we're this close.

What the hell is happening? It's like those kisses broke my ability to think clearly.

"What can I get you?" the cashier girl asks, dousing the moment.

I jump forward, taking a breath to settle my lunatic heart.

Dammit. I should've put a no touching rule on the list. But I really didn't think things would be this bad between us. They never have been before. Then again, I've never grinded my hips against Beck until I came apart. Over and over and over again...

"Miss?" the cashier looks at me like I'm the weirdo Beck just accused me of being. "Are you going to order anything?"

I glance from the menu to her. "Um ..."

"She'll have a caramel latte." Beck steps beside me, a ghost of a smile dancing on his lips. "And I'll have a mocha cappuccino. And we'll both have ham and turkey subs."

I smile gratefully at him, and he throws me a wink before turning back to the cashier.

She smiles at Beck, twisting a strand of her highlighted hair around her finger, going all doe-eyed. "Do you want any cookies to go with that? They're two for a dollar."

Beck looks at me, seeming highly amused. "What do you think, princess? You want something sweet to nibble on?"

I battle the overwhelming urge to stare at his mouth again. "Sure."

His eyes sparkle with delight as he glances back at the cashier. "We'll take two chocolate chips."

Her gaze dances between the two of us. Then she untwists her hair from her finger and punches in the order. "That'll be nineteen fifty-seven." Her tone isn't so friendly anymore, and I smile to myself, though I have no right to.

I swing my bag around to dig my wallet out, but Beck swats my hand away.

"My treat," he says, retrieving his wallet from his jeans.

"I'm paying for mine," I tell him firmly, slipping my hand into my bag.

"Please just let me pay for this one. I'm the one who suggested we get coffee, anyway." He opens his wallet and digs out a twenty.

"So what? I'm the one who's going to be drinking it." I take my wallet out, grab a ten because that's all I have and hand him the bill. "I'm going to pay for my own beverages and food, or I'm not going to eat and drink them."

He hesitates before taking the money from me and stuffing it into his wallet. "Next time, I'm buying."

I disregard the remark. "And no trying to slip it back into my wallet when you think I'm not looking."

Shock flashes in his eyes, but he quickly shakes the look away. "I have no idea what you're talking about."

"You so do."

"Do not."

"Beck, you're so full of—"

"Oh, look, a table opened up." He hurries off toward a table near the window and takes a seat.

I give the cashier my name then make my way around the tables and sink into the chair across from him.

I slip my bag off my shoulder, set it by my feet, and rest my arms on the table. "Okay, what do you need to talk to me about my living situation for?" My tone is formal, casual, despite my crazy lunatic heart.

He chuckles, his eyes crinkling at the corners. "You're seriously the most impatient person sometimes."

I reach across the table to flick his hand, but he drops his other hand over mine, trapping my palm on the table.

"Now you're my prisoner." He grins wickedly. "And I'm never letting you go."

My heart pulsates from the contact, and not necessarily

in a bad way. I try to wiggle my hand free, but he refuses to let go.

"No way," he says. "I'm not letting you go until you hear my idea completely out."

"You're making me nervous … if you have to trap me here to say whatever it is you need to say."

"I just want to get through my entire speech without any interruptions. That's all."

"But you're afraid I'll try to bolt?"

"Not really bolt so much as wander off when I start saying things you may not want to hear."

"I don't do that," I say, flattening my hand on the table.

"You do sometimes." He traces his thumb across the back of my hand, and I shiver. "You did in the field."

A huge elephant wearing a tutu and ballet slippers appears next to us and starts twirling around as awkward silence fills the air. Part of me wants to keep my lips fused and never speak of what happened, let the elephant dance and twirl between us for the rest of my life. The other part of me knows how distracting that would be. And wanting a distraction is what led me to get drunk last Friday, which led to me making out with Beck.

"So, what's your idea that will help my living situation?" I force the elephant to sashay away.

His brows pop up, as if he half-expected me not to say

anything at all. "I want you to move in with me."

I had a feeling he was going to say that. "I don't think—"

He swiftly extends his free hand across the table and gently places it over my mouth. "Please, just listen to my entire speech before saying no, okay? It's not as bad as you're thinking. At least, I don't think so."

I hesitantly nod, despite not wanting to, but he has such a pleading look on his face.

To reduce some of the stiffness between us, I crack a joke. "Man, you must be getting desperate"—my lips move against his palm as I speak, and butterflies frolic in my stomach—"if you have to pin my hand to the table and gag me."

He withdraws his hand, his lips threatening to turn upward. "Well, desperate times call for desperate measures." He puts his other hand over mine. "You're turning me into a desperate man, Wills."

I don't know what to say to that, so I don't say anything at all. Inside, my heart reacts with a spastic flutter. Damn little weirdo. It needs to start acting normal again.

His lips quirk at my silence as he strokes the back of my hand with his fingertip. "I want you to move in with me."

It takes all of my willpower not to cut him off right there.

"And I know you don't want handouts from me—that's not what this is. I promise. In fact, I was thinking that you could pay some rent. That way, you will feel more comfortable." He sucks in a preparing breath. "Also, I know you're probably thinking about the list and how its existence is a good reason not to move in with me, but I promise you it'll only make the situation better because it gives us boundaries. It'll keep us in line so we stay ... just friends." He swallows hard at the last part.

"I love the offer." And part of me really does. "But I just don't think it's a good idea with everything going on. And besides, there's no way I could afford to rent your place."

"I know that," he says. "And that's why I want to make rent be whatever you can afford. It's not like I need the money, so it doesn't even matter. I'm only letting you pay rent because I know you won't consider this unless I do."

"I know you don't need the money, but ..." I rack my mind for an excuse. I'm scared. Scared to move. Scared to move in with a guy I kissed. Scared to move in with a guy I want to kiss. "Then why would you even want a room-mate? I mean, people usually get roommates to split the cost of rent."

"I don't want to do this because I want a roommate," he stresses. "I want to do this to take away some of the stress your mom's put on you for years. And I know you want to move out of that apartment. You even called Wynter to see if you could rent a room from her."

My head slants to the side, my brows knit. "Wynter called you and told you that?"

"Of course she did. She was worried about you. She cares about you." He cups my hand between his. "She said you sounded upset … Did something happen?"

Cares?

Cares.

Cares.

Cares.

According to my mom, no one cares about me.

I shrug. "My mom came home, asking for money to buy drugs. That's it. I don't even know why I got so upset. It's not like she's never done that before."

"Princess …" He holds my hand like it's the most precious thing in the world. "It wasn't okay any of the times she did it, and I think deep down you know that. You deserve so much better, even if you don't think so." He traces circles on the back of my hand with his thumb, watching me, as if waiting for me to say something. I know if I open my mouth, I just might fall apart. "Let me help you, please. I want to … I want to take care of you."

"I don't need anyone to take care of me. I'm fine." I choke on the lie. The truth is, I want to accept his offer because I'm terrified of not getting a good enough job, of not

being able to pay rent, of living my life while always worrying if my mom is dead. Of becoming the woman who
stood in front of me in my bedroom, begging for money
and destroying the snow globes my dad gave me just because I wouldn't. The woman who told her own daughter
no one cares about her.

I suck in a breath and another, trying to compose myself. I've been running on stress and anxiety for weeks
now, and I feel like I'm standing on a cliff, about to fall.

He traces the folds of my fingers. "You're not fine. I
know you. I know you well enough to know you're worrying about your mom. Just like how I know those bags under
your eyes are because you didn't sleep last night, probably
because you worried about your mom and bills and God
knows what else. I can help you if you'll just let me." His
voice softens. "Just say yes, move in with me, and let me
take some of the stress out of your life."

He offers too much.

I want it too much.

"You've already taken care of my sorry ass too many
times." I rub my free hand across my forehead, feeling a
headache coming on.

I wish I could fully explain to him why I can't accept
his help. Explain that I hate relying on people. I need to
take care of myself. I hate trusting people when they gener-
ally break that trust, like my stupid father who thinks he

can walk out then just come back and think everything is going to be okay. Like my mom who rips me to shreds when I don't do what she wants. I want to explain how I'm scared all the damn time of failing, of turning into my mother, of being a terrible person, getting perfection then losing it, of losing Beck, of getting my heart broken. And not just broken, but broken by him …

What the hell? When did that change? When did I stop worrying about getting my heart broken in general to just worrying about Beck smashing my heart to pieces?

Blood roars in my eardrums as all my fears and worries pour through me simultaneously. Panic strangles my throat. I'm about to fall off that cliff. A fall that I think has been coming for months now.

"Calm down and take a deep breath, Wills. Everything's okay." He squeezes my hand. "I'm going to let go of your hand. I need to get something out of my pocket."

I obey, inhaling and exhaling as he reaches into his pocket. I expect him to take out his phone, so when he sets a folded piece of paper onto the table, confusion pierces through my storm of anxiety.

"What is that?" I ask as he slides the paper across the table toward me. "Is that the list I gave you?"

He shakes his head, his eyes fixed on me. "It is a list, though, of all the reasons you should move in with me."

When I don't pick the paper up, he takes my hand and

sets it in my palm.

"I knew that talking to you probably wouldn't work," he says. "You need to have something you can really look at and think about."

I fold my fingers around the paper as tears threaten to pour out of my eyes. How can he know me so well? How can he *see* me?

What else has he seen?

I hold on to the paper, too afraid to look at the list, afraid of what's on there, of what's not on there. Afraid I want what's on there.

"Beck, I really love that you want to help me—I do," I say, trying to breathe and think straight. "And taking care of me all these years when you didn't have to … There aren't even words that can express how grateful I am. You're my hero. Seriously, I don't know where I'd be without you … if I'd even be alive. Which might sound dramatic, but I'm not kidding. There've been so many times when you've picked me up and saved me from sleeping in a car and getting harassed by drug dealers. Or that time my mom dropped me off on a street corner near a crack house because she wanted me to go buy drugs for her, and when I wouldn't, she got pissed and kicked me out of the car. You came and picked me up, and I was so scared because there were those people who kept trying to convince me to come into their houses … And I really thought they were going to kill me …" I trail off as the tears start to fall. "But you don't have to take care of me anymore. Trust me, if you knew the whole story, you'd stop trying so hard."

"You're wrong." He grabs my hand as I shake my head and start to pull away. "Maybe you should tell me the whole story and let me be the judge of that."

I can't tell him.

Won't.

I won't risk losing him.

I can't handle letting him look at me differently.

I want him to always look at me like he's looking at me now.

With compassion.

And need.

Want.

And something else that scares me half to death, something I'm pretty sure might break rule number three on the list.

But, as my lips part, all of it spills out, foul, ugly words that sum up the bad choices I've made over the last couple of months. My job. The lies I told him. How much I hate myself. My dad showing up. How much I think I might hate him and my mom. That all I am is hate anymore. And how he can't want something so ugly and messed up?

When I finish, there's only silence. No one moves.

Breathes. Even when my name is called to come get our order, neither of us budge or say anything.

Really, is there anything left to say?

"I can't breathe," I whisper, staring at the table, unable to look at him.

I want to take it all back, but I can't.

My chest splinters apart as the silence goes on.

Pressure builds inside me.

Hold it back, Willow. Do not lose your shit.

"Wills, I didn't even realize it was that—"

He gets cut off by chair legs scraping against the floor as I push to my feet.

I dash away from him like a coward and run into the bathroom, locking myself in a stall. Then I slide to the floor, clutching Beck's list while sobbing my heart out. Just. Like. My. Mom.

I don't know how long I cry, but by the time the tears stop, my eyes are swollen and my chest hurts. I think about getting up, but moving means facing Beck, and I don't think I'm ready yet. That is, if he's even still out there.

Does it matter? You have to pull yourself off the bathroom floor eventually.

Swallowing down the shame and agony, I reach for some tissue, but then I note the list clutched in my hand. I unfold my fingers from around it. Do I dare read it? Can I handle what's on it?

Does it even matter anymore?

Knowing Beck will probably never talk to me again, I take a deep breath and start reading.

*All the reasons you should
move in with me:*

1. *Because it would make
   your life a bit easier.*
2. *Because it will eliminate
   some of your stress.*
3. *Because you won't have to
   worry about trying to sleep
   through loud, obnoxious
   parties. In fact, you'll always get final say in
   whether we have a party.*
4. *My place is closer to the
   school, which means you
   won't have to drive around
   in that piece of shit car so
   much.*
5. *Because I love having you
   around.*
6. *Because we can have pillow fights at two o o'clock
   in the morning.*

283

7. *And don't forget those midnight talks we always have. Only, instead of having them over the phone, we can lie in bed together and talk.*

8. *Because I'll be the most awesome roommate ever.*

9. *Because, while you think you don't deserve someone helping you, you do.*

10. *Because I made a promise to you when we were younger, and making sure I keep that promise is absolutely the most important thing to me.*

11. *Because every single night you're at that apartment, I lie awake in bed, worrying about you.*

12. *Because your mom doesn't deserve to have you around.*

13. *Because you shouldn't be paying for your mom's rent when she treats you so*

poorly.

14. *Because I want you to live with me more than I think you realize.*

15. *Because you're my best friend, and I care about you more than anything in the world.*

16. *I have more, but I'll stop there for now. If you're stubborn about this, I'll make a list long enough that it takes you forever to read, and then you'll just be stuck with me until you're finished.*

Care.

Care.

Care.

He cares about me more than anything in the world?

By the time I reach the end, I don't know whether to cry or laugh.

"I want to take it all back," I whisper through the tears. "Not just the lies, but the decisions."

That's the thing. I can't take stuff back, no matter how much I want to.

285

I don't know how long I stay in the stall, letting tears slip from my eyes, but eventually, I manage to drag my ass off the filthy tile floor.

Unlatching the door, I open the stall and walk out and immediately grind to a halt, blinking and blinking and blinking again, wondering if stress has finally made me hallucinate. No matter how many times I blink, Beck remains leaning against the bathroom door with my bag in his hand and a look on his face like he's about to approach a skittish cat.

"What are you doing in here?" I rub my eyes, trying to wipe away all the tears. "This is the girls' bathroom."

"Really?" He mocks being shocked. "Good thing you told me. I was about to pee in one of the sinks."

I smile, but the movement aches. "You're such a little rule breaker."

"I know." His intense gaze causes me to step back.

I take another step back as he approaches me, only stopping to avoid bumping into the wall.

"Don't worry; I'm not going to break your rules," he says, stopping in front of me.

Breaking the rules was actually the last thought on my mind.

I swallow hard, begging my voice to come out semi-normal. "Why are you in here?"

"To make sure you're okay." His gaze travels across

me before coming to rest on my eyes.

I can't read him at all, so I wait for him to say something. All he does is take my hand, brings my palm to his lips, and places a soft kiss against my skin.

"Let me help you, please," he whispers. "I can't stand seeing you like this … in so much pain."

I choke on my next breath as tears flood my eyes. "How can you even want to anymore … after what I told you?"

He places another kiss on my palm. "Nothing you said changed how I feel about you. If anything, it just makes me even more determined to get you to move in with me and get you away from that shit."

"No one forced me to do it, Beck," I say, shivering from another kiss. "I chose to work at that place because the money was good, and I was tired of working three jobs and still barely being able to pay the bills. I chose to lie about it because I was too much of a coward to face up to my bad decisions."

"We all make bad decisions. You know me well enough to know how many times I've fucked up."

"Just because your dad thinks you fuck up, doesn't mean you actually do."

"That's completely untrue. And only you see it that way because you're a good person who only wants to see the good in me."

287

"I'm not a good person," I choke out.

"Yes, you are." He touches his lips to my palm again.

"No. I'm. Not." I'm losing the battle, my will, my everything.

Another kiss. Then another. "You need to stop thinking so poorly of yourself and start seeing yourself for who you are: a kind, caring, beautiful, strong girl who's survived the shitty hand she was dealt and come out on top. Who graduated, got into college, and paid for her own way. Who took care of her mom when she was way too young to be doing so. Who cares about other people so fucking much she lets herself break apart to take care of them. I just wish you'd let other people care about you … Let me care about you."

Care.

Care.

Care.

He cares about me.

My mom was wrong.

Maybe she was wrong about everything. Maybe not all guys bail.

Beck hasn't bailed, and he saw me at my worst. And I didn't break when I thought he left. I picked myself up off that bathroom floor.

I want to kiss him so badly I can barely breathe. The only way I can think of to get the air back into my lungs is to seal my lips to his.

So, I do.

His lips part in shock, and I almost pull back, fearing he doesn't want this anymore after what I told him. Then his arms loop around my waist, and he presses me so closely there's no room left to breathe. Air doesn't seem so important anymore. Just kissing him. Touching him. Feeling safe.

He always makes me feel so safe.

Tears burn my eyes as I realize why that might be.

Overwhelmed, I pull back enough to get air. Beck rests his forehead against mine, his erratic breathing caressing my cheeks.

"Are you okay?" he whispers, grasping my waist.

I shake my head then nod, so unsure of everything. "I don't really know …"

He tucks my head underneath his chin and picks me up in his arms. "Everything's going to be okay. We'll get you through this."

The *"we'll"* part breaks something inside me, because it makes me realize I'm no longer alone in this—that I'm choosing not to be. I latch on to him, holding on for dear life. And he does the same, maybe even holding on more tightly.

The end of the list...

Chapter Twenty-One

Beck

I didn't expect today to go down like it did. Sure, I knew Willow had secrets, but the weight she was carrying around was heavier than I thought. How she even managed to carry all of that shit around with her is mind-boggling. What's even more astonishing is how much she blames herself. Seeing the pain connected to her nearly tears my heart in half.

As she grasps me like I'm her lifeline with her legs and arms wrapped around me, I hold on to her with everything I have in me, afraid to ever put her down again. When a woman enters the bathroom and starts having a shitfit over me being in there, though, I know it's time to leave.

That doesn't mean I'm letting Willow go anywhere.

"Will you come back to my place with me?" I whisper in her ear.

She bobs her head up and down. "O-okay."

The woman shoots me a nasty look as I pass by her, heading for the door with Willow in my arms.

"You're lucky I don't get the manager," she sneers

with her hands on her hips. "It's so disrespectful for you to be in here."

"Oh, no, not the manager." I slip my arm underneath Willow's butt and hold her against me while I maneuver the door open.

"You little punk," the woman snaps. "What's your name so I can go report you?"

"It's go-fuck-yourself-and-leave-me-alone. I'm trying to help a friend," I retort back before stepping out and letting the door shut.

Willow chuckles with her face pressed against my shoulder. "That was kind of rude."

"No, what was rude was her making a big deal when it was clear I was in there helping out a friend who is having a really hard time." I make my way past the tables, disregarding the stares we get.

"Yeah, I guess you might be right." She lifts her head, her muscles tightening. "Maybe you should put me down. People are staring."

"Well, people need to mind their own business," I say loudly enough for everyone to hear then smile when some of them look away.

Willow rests her head on my shoulder with her face turned toward my neck. "You know, I'm always saying you're my hero, but you really do feel like one right now … carrying me out of here like this. It seems very heroish."

"That's because I am secretly a hero. A superhero, actually." As I reach the front doors, I turn around and walk through backward.

When I step outside, I head for the crosswalk. Neither of us speaks, we only hold on to each other as I cross the road and hike across the grass toward the parking lot. When I reach my car, I open the passenger door with one hand then set her in the seat and place her bag on her lap. Keeping my eyes on her, I close the door then hurry around to the other side.

Once I get in and start up the engine, I back out of the parking space and steer out onto the road. The longer we drive in silence, the more I want to say something. But I'm not sure what to say, and honestly, I want her to talk first so I know she's ready to talk.

"She broke my snow globes," she says so abruptly I jump.

Gripping the steering wheel, I let my heart settle before I speak. "Who did?"

She turns her head away from the window, her eyes glassy with tears. "My mom. When she asked me for money yesterday, she broke them ... all except the one you gave me, which was completely by accident, but I was still so glad." She rolls her eyes at herself and sighs. "I don't know why I just said that. Out of all the things I could've said,

295

that's my opening line."

"I'm glad you told me." I reach over and lace our fingers together, hoping she doesn't pull away. "What I don't like is that she broke them. I know how much they meant to you."

She stares at our interlaced fingers. "They only meant something to me because my dad was gone and I thought I'd never see him again. Now that I have … I'm kind of glad they broke." She wipes her eyes with the back of her hand, sniffling before lifting her gaze to mine. "How bad of a person does it make me that I want to forget my dad exists?"

I shake my head. "It doesn't make you a bad person at all. I want to forget my dad exists, and he didn't even walk out on me."

She angles her body toward the console. "Yeah, but he treats you so poorly. He doesn't even deserve to be in your life."

"And neither does your dad if you don't want him to," I tell her, skimming my thumb along the back of her hand. "You earned the right to hate him the second he bailed on you. You don't owe him anything, just like you don't owe your mom anything. The only person you do owe something to is yourself."

"I don't agree with you," she mutters. "I haven't done anything to deserve anything."

I think she's referring to that job again. When she told me about it, I wanted to track her mom down and scream at her for being a shitty parent and making Willow think she needed to do anything to take care of her, things that are causing her self-torment. And her dad isn't any better. He never should've left her to begin with. Although, after telling me about the creeper he chased off last night, I'm glad he decided to try to come back into Willow's life. But fuck, the fact that she was even in that situation makes me want to lock her up and keep her safe forever, even if that does make me sound like a controlling asshole.

"Can I ask you something?" I approach cautiously.

"Yeah ..." She hesitates then nods. "Go ahead. I owe you that much."

"You don't owe me anything. I want to make sure you're not planning on going back to that place."

Humiliation pours from her eyes. "You mean the club?"

I nod, grazing my finger along the back of her hand again. "After what you told me ... with what happened with that guy ... and then with your boss wanting you to ..." I take a composing breath. "I just want to make sure you don't plan on going back there."

Her fingers tighten around mine. "I was never planning on doing that ... I mean, the whole ..."—her cheeks turn bright red—"stripping thing. I can barely stand being near

297

the stage, let alone on it."

"So, you're not going back?"

"No … But I do have to go back to get my final paycheck." Her shoulders slump. "God, I'm picking up my final paycheck, and I don't even have a job lined up yet."

My lips part. "That's okay. I can—"

"No, you can't," she says.

Goddammit, she's so stubborn.

"I don't know why you can't just accept my help. I mean, I do know why since I understand you. But I really wish you'd just move in with me and let me help you like I *want* to."

She stares down at our interlaced fingers again. After a moment or two, a smile tugs at the corners of her lips. She quickly clears the look away before I can figure out what's got her smiling.

"Did you mean it?" she asks quietly.

I slow down the car to make a turn into my neighborhood. "Mean what?"

"All that stuff on the list," she says, giving me a tentative look.

I carry her gaze. "Of course I meant it. Every damn word." Her lips start to turn upward again, so I press on, wanting a full smile. "Especially the pillow fighting part. That was actually the most important part of the list, so make sure to remember that when I knock on your door at two o'clock in the morning."

Her laughter bursts through, and the wall of tension around us crumbles into dust.

"All right, I'll keep it in mind," she says. "But maybe we should make them ten o'clock pillow fights. I'd really like to start going to bed at a decent hour."

I don't want to smile just yet, but fuck, it takes a lot of willpower to hold it back. "You're saying you'll live with me?" I ask as I turn into the driveway of my two-story house.

Her chest rises and crashes as she breathes profusely. "I will, at least until I can find somewhere else to live. But I'm going to pay you." When I open my mouth to protest, she adds, "I have to pay you, Beck. It's just how I am, and I'd feel shitty if I didn't."

"Then I'm going to make the price dirt cheap."

"Make it reasonable."

I park in front of the garage and silence the engine. "Reasonable with a discount."

"Beck—"

I place my finger against her lips. "Shush. Just let me do this one thing. It'll make me happy, and you'll be less stressed out over your finances."

She remains quiet for what feels like forever before reluctantly nodding. "All right, I'll let you win this one."

I feel like I'm finally getting somewhere.

Then worry flashes across her face. "I think we need to talk about what happened in the bathroom."

"You mean when I hugged you?" I play dumb. But it's either pretend I don't know what she's talking about or watch her pull out a piece of paper to add more rules.

And I don't want any more rules. I want no rules. Nothing between her and me. Ever.

"Not the hug … the kiss …" Her eyes descend to my lips and then to her lap. "I can't do this anymore," she mutters. "God, how did our friendship get so complicated?"

"It doesn't have to be complicated," I say, knowing I'm treading on thin ice. But I don't want to fight my feelings anymore. And with how much we've been kissing lately, I know she has to feel something more than just friendship. "If you'd just stop fighting what you really want and let yourself have what you want."

She tucks a strand of her hair behind her ear and peers up at me. "That's the problem. My mother wanted something all the time, and she kept looking for it in the bartender or the next-door neighbor. Even my teacher once."

"Really? Which one?"

"Mr. Deliebufey."

I don't know what kind of face I pull, but it causes her to giggle.

She covers her mouth with her hand. "I really

shouldn't be laughing about that."

"No, you definitely should." I smile, mostly because she's smiling. "We should've laughed about it back in fifth grade when it happened. Why didn't you ever tell me about it?"

She lowers her hand from her mouth and gives a half-shrug. "Because I was embarrassed. I mean, he was our teacher, and he wore that gross toupee that looked like a dead cat."

"Oh, my God, I forgot about the toupee." I pull a face. "Okay, I'm not a fan of your mom, but she seriously sold herself short dating him."

"That was kind of my point. She always dated these sleazebags because she was desperate and didn't want to be alone. Then they would break her heart, and she'd fall apart until she met someone new and then try to clean up her act. At least, that's how she used to be. Then she started dating drug addicts and got high all the time." She sighs, her shoulders hunching inward. "I don't want to turn out like her. I really don't."

I gape at her. "Wait, you think you're going to turn out like your mom?"

She lifts a shoulder. "Sometimes, I wonder if I will. And then I started working at that place where she worked once ... and then the whole thing with you ..." She grows quiet, staring out the window.

"What whole thing with me?" I ask softly, my heart hammering in my chest.

Her shoulders rise and fall as she breathes in and out. Then she turns her head toward me. Her eyes are glossed over with tears, radiating her fear. "You've always taken care of me, and I've always loved it more than I wanted to admit. I remember that time when I was fourteen and you came and picked me up from my house. When you put your arm around me, I'd never felt safer in my entire life. And when you made that promise to me … I wanted it so much. But wanting something like that from someone else … getting so consumed by someone … It's what destroys my mom time and time again. She's never been able to handle being on her own unless she's high or drunk … I want to be able to say that I'd be okay if you left me, but even just thinking about you leaving me makes my heart ache." She's breathing fiercely at the end, as if her words have shocked her to death.

My reaction mirrors hers. Never have I imagined she feels the same way about me as I do her. I have no fucking clue how to handle her fear. And it's all because she thinks I'll break her heart, and she'll go off the deep end like her mom.

"You want to know the first time I realized I liked you more than as a friend?" I ask and then hold my breath, worried she'll say no.

She wavers for what seems like the end of all time before giving an unsteady nod.

"It was back when I came home from that trip from Paris—when I gave you the snow globe." I feel like I'm about to cut my heart out, hold it out to her, and hope she'll take it, which kind of seems really disgusting when I think about it. "You looked so different, and I remember noticing. I thought I was just being weird after not seeing you for three months and just really missed you. But then Levi, this guy I hung out with sometimes, came up and asked me if you had a boyfriend, and I got really jealous and told him you did."

"You did?" she asks, surprised.

I nod. "I totally did. Then I felt bad because you trusted me so much, and I never wanted to break that trust. So I told you at lunch. Then Wynter started teasing you about having a crush on someone else, and I thought—well, hoped—it was me. When I found out it wasn't, my heart got a little crushed."

She elevates her brows. "Your heart got crushed when you were fourteen?"

I nod, reaching out and cupping her cheek. "It did. And when I was fifteen. And sixteen. And seventeen. And eighteen. And a week ago. A day ago. Every time I'm reminded that I can't be with you the way I want to. Never have I felt my heart break so much as when I saw you

303

break apart over guilt you should never feel. It kills me to see you in so much pain. And I'd never, *ever* do anything to cause you that kind of pain, whether you think so or not." I smooth my finger along her cheekbone. "And whether you believe me or not, I know you'll never turn into your mom. You've had your heart crushed by her and your dad, and still, you took care of your mom every damn time she fell apart.

"You're so fucking strong, Wills. Everyone around you knows it. Your mom fucking knows it, although she'll never admit it. And I know you are more than everyone because, whether you think I do or not, I know you better than anyone."

"I know you do." Tears flood her eyes. "You've always been there for me. Even when I tried to push you away, you always came back."

We stare at each other, our hearts erratically pounding, and then we're both leaning in. I don't even know who moves first. It doesn't matter. All that matters is our lips meet in the middle, and she doesn't pull back.

Her fingers tangle through my hair as she draws me closer. We kiss fiercely, grabbing onto each other, gasping for air yet refusing to break the connection to breathe.

I don't know how long we stay in the car kissing, but when the sun begins to set, we break apart and head into the house. The second we step over the threshold, our lips collide again.

Grabbing her thighs, I scoop her up in my arms, and she hitches her legs around my waist. I groan, remembering the last time she did this: how I rocked against her, how she moaned.

I want more this time.

As much as she'll give me.

Carrying her blindly through the house, I stumble down the hallway and into my bedroom. When she pulls back to see where we are, I think she might panic. Instead, she seals her lips to mine and bites down on my lip. My body shudders, and I damn near collapse to the floor but manage to stumble over to the bed.

Setting her down on the mattress, I cover her body with mine and kiss her slowly, deliberately, letting her know I'll take my time.

"We don't have to do anything right now," I whisper raggedly against her lips.

"What if I want to?" she gripes, and then her eyes widen.

I almost laugh. Willow has never been good at talking about anything sexual. Listening to her talk about her past, I can understand why. God knows what she saw living in that house with her mom and countless boyfriends. She probably felt uncomfortable all the damn time.

I prop up on my elbows to look down at her. "I don't

want you to feel uncomfortable when you're with me."

She rests her palm on my chest, and my heart slams against her hand. "I don't really think I ever have." Then she cups her hand behind my head and brings me in for another kiss while arching against me.

I groan, lowering my hips against hers, eliciting a gasp from her lips. Over and over again, we move together, never breaking the kiss. Her hand wanders up and down my chest just like it did that night in her bed. When her fingers find the hem of my shirt, I push back to peel it off and toss it on the floor. Then I lower my mouth to hers again. The taste of her is driving me mad, and when she traces her fingers up and down my chest, I damn near lose all my self-control. Suddenly, the slow kiss turns reckless, our tongues tangling, our bodies moving.

"Is this okay?" I ask as I grasp the bottom of her shirt.

She bobs her head up and down, and all of my reservations crumble as I yank her shirt off. Her bra soon follows, and I push back and look down at her. Her brown hair is a halo around her head, her big eyes have never looked more beautiful, and her chest rises and crashes with every breath. When my eyes descend to the shiny diamond above her belly button, I bite back a moan.

Holy shit.

I skim my fingers across it, and my cock gets hard as hell as she shivers.

"When did you get this?" I ask, tracing a path down her stomach.

"About a year ago … Wynter talked me into it." She bites down on her bottom lip, grasping the blankets as I reach the waistband of her jeans. "Oh, my God, Beck, that feels so good."

I just about lose it right there. "Fuck, you're so beautiful." I slip my fingers down the front of her jeans and press my lips to hers.

Perfect.

That's what this moment is.

Maybe, if we never come up for air again, we can stay this   way   forever.

307

Chapter Twenty-Two

Willow

I can't believe this is happening. Okay, maybe I can. Deep down, I think I might have known all along that a piece of paper couldn't stop where Beck and I were heading. I was just procrastinating the inevitable. I could've fought this longer … Maybe. But when he said all those things—those wonderful things that made my heart pound in my chest and made that crack in my heart heal a little—I didn't want to fight it anymore. I wanted to have him. I needed to have him. The need scared me because wanting and needing are two different things. Wanting, you can live without. Needing is like air. You can't live without it.

I don't want to live a life without Beck.

I want him.

I want to feel safe.

Safe.

Safe.

Safe.

That thought races through my mind over and over again as he kisses me passionately with our chests pressed together. His fingers are inside me, pushing me to that starry place again. I've lost all control, and I don't know what to do about that except enjoy this moment. When it's over, then I'll focus on the next. And so on and so on. Sure, the uncertainty of my life scares the shit out of me, but knowing I'm not alone makes it a bit easier. I don't just have Beck. I have my friends.

I'm not alone.

People care for me.

And I care about them.

I care about Beck.

I care about him so much.

More. Than. Anything.

My pulse speeds up at the thought, but I fight back the panic and focus on those stars again. Those wonderful, blissful, goddamn amazing stars.

His fingers start to slow as I return to reality, his lips leisurely moving against mine as if we have all the time in the world. When his lips finally break away, he touches his forehead to mine with his eyes shut.

"Are you okay?" he whispers.

I trace a path up and down his spine. "I'm perfect."

His lips twitch into a smile. "It's nice you finally realize that."

Shaking my head, I lightly pinch his side. He doesn't even flinch. I do the movement again, doing a little tickling, and he remains unfazed.

"Try all you want," he says with a cocky grin, "but you won't get me."

"Wanna bet?" I ask with my brow arched.

He sits back with his hands out to his sides. "Go ahead and try."

"Fine. I will." Grinning, I sit up, push him down to the mattress, and straddle his waist. Then I tickle him everywhere. Well, almost everywhere.

He stares up at me with his hands tucked under his head and a lazy grin on his face. "You missed one spot."

He doesn't think I'll do it. I don't really want to do it … well, sort of. Okay, I kind of do. I'm just feeling a little shy about it.

I sit back, staring down at him. "You don't think I'll do it?"

He chuckles, grinning smugly. "No, I don't, but the determined look in your eyes is really fucking adorable."

I think about all those times he tickled me, especially the time he made me almost pee my pants, and suddenly, I really want to prove him wrong. I don't know what pushes me to go through with it, whether all the kissing has made me lose my sanity, or maybe Beck just makes me feel comfortable enough to do it. Somehow, though, I find enough courage to slip my hands down his pants.

"Fuuuccck." He lets out a groan, his back arching up

310

as my fingers touch him.

Definitely not a ticklish reaction, but I repeat the movement, anyway. He moans again then reaches up and draws my lips to his. I keep touching him as his tongue delves between my lips and explores my mouth until he moans out my name, until he loses complete control, his eyes shut, his hands gripping my hips.

"That's not very fair," I say, removing my hand from his jeans. "I think you enjoyed that way too much when I wanted to get you back for all those times you tickled me."

He chuckles, sounding exhausted but content. "You want me to show you the secret spot?"

"I tried everywhere." I pout.

"Not everywhere."

When my brows lower in confusion, he sits up, slides me off his lap, then leans over to unlace his boot. After he gets it off, he removes his sock, grabs my hand, and sketches my fingers up and down the bottom of his foot. Then he lets out the girliest giggle I've ever heard. I trace my fingers up the arch of his foot again and again until he begs for mercy.

After we're done messing around, he changes into his pajamas while I put on one of his shirts. Then we lie down in his bed together with his arms around me, our legs tangled.

Safe.

311

Safe.

Safe.

I keep reminding myself of this as my thoughts try to drift to my future. To my past. To the now. All of which Beck knows about.

He knows me and didn't run. He saw the ugly and still wants it.

I thought I lost him, and while it hurt, I still picked myself up.

Everything will be okay.

Once step at a time. Don't panic.

"Just breathe, princess," he whispers, his lips brushing the top of my head. "Everything's going to be fine."

"I feel like I need to get up and do something," I admit. "Fix the problems."

"We will," he says. "Tomorrow."

There he goes with the *"we"* again.

I like the sound of it.

Probably too much.

Maybe it's not so bad as long as there's still a me and him between the we.

I take a deep breath and then another. "What do we do now?"

"Now, we get some sleep," he says, pulling me closer.

I'm a little terrified to close my eyes, knowing tomorrow I'll have to face everything: moving, getting a new job, figuring out a new plan. But as I lay in his arms with him stroking his fingers up and down my back, calmness overcomes me enough that my eyes shut.

I fall asleep faster than I have in years.

Chapter Twenty-Three

Beck

I wake up the next morning with Willow's head resting on my chest, my knee tucked between her legs, and my phone ringing insanely. I make no move to answer it, not wanting to ruin this peaceful moment that managed to carry all the way from last night.

When the damn thing refuses to shut the fuck up, I give up and collect it off my nightstand. When *Dad* flashes across the screen, I grimace.

"Who is it?" Willow asks, looking up at me.

"My dad." I reject the call, toss the phone down, and pull her close until her body is flush with mine.

"What do you think he wants?" she asks through a yawn.

For me to come to the office. I hesitate to tell her, knowing she'll worry, and that's the last thing she needs right now.

Sensing my tension, she lifts her head and blinks down at me, her hair tickling my face. "What did he do?"

I slip my hands around her waist, urging her to lie back

down. "Nothing he hasn't done before."

"Beck ..." she warns. "I know when you're lying."

"Oh, you do, do you? Then tell me if I'm lying right now," I say, letting my fingers sneak under the shirt she's wearing. "I want to put my fingers inside you again and watch you moan."

Her cheeks flush, but her gaze never wavers from mine. "Don't try to distract me. Tell me what he did."

I trace my fingers back and forth across her waist, paying extra attention to that diamond in her belly button. "You really want me to tell you instead of doing this?"

Her lips part, but no words leave her mouth as I trail my fingers down between her legs. Right as I'm about to slip them inside her, she captures my hand.

"We can do that later," she says breathlessly. "Right now, I want to know what your dad's done to you. I can tell he's done something."

"Oh, fine." I sulk, hoping that will win her over, but apparently, my baby blue-eyed charm doesn't work on her. All she does is give me a tolerant look. "He blackmailed me into working at his firm."

She pushes back to look down at me. "*Blackmailed?*"

I sigh and give her a recap of what happened. I also tell her about the files I found on his computer. When she asks if she can see the files, I hand over my phone.

She slips out of the covers, giving me a great view of

her long legs as she stretches out and rests against the headboard. She starts searching through files, growing more intrigued with each one.

"I'm pretty sure he's committing some tax fraud," she remarks, examining the screen closely. "At least, he did this year."

"Really?" I ask. "I wasn't positive."

"Well, I took a few accounting classes so I could help the owner of that grocery store I worked at during senior year, and I learned enough to know that not all of these numbers are matching up on some of the documents. Plus, I'm pretty sure some of these accounts don't exist unless your dad owns a dance club in Hawaii, which I'm fairly sure he doesn't."

"He doesn't," I say, stretching out beside her.

"That's what I thought." She looks up at me and hands me my phone. "What are you going to do about it?"

"I don't know yet." I scratch my chest.

I left my shirt off last night but put on a pair of drawstring pajama bottoms. Usually, I sleep naked. But I didn't want to make her uncomfortable her first night here. I'll save the nakedness for later when she wants to strip down with me. Well, as long as she doesn't freak out again and put an end to us, something I'm still a little concerned about.

"What do you think I should do? Honestly, I want to

blackmail him back, but I'd like the opinion of a more lev-elheaded thinker."

"You think I'm a levelheaded thinker?" she questions, hugging her knees to her chest.

I tug on a strand of her hair. "You talked me out of thinking we were living in a canvas, didn't you?"

"I almost forgot about that … Still, I'm not sure if I should tell you what to do with this one." She rests her chin on her knees. "If you want my opinion, though, I'll give it to you."

I nod, moving in front of her. "I want your opinion more than anyone else's."

Another smile. Another prize I feel like I've won.

She stretches out her legs, putting one on each side of me before scooting closer to me. "Well, I think I can prob-ably give you the same speech you've been giving me for the last few months, only insert mom with dad. So here goes." She clears her throat. "You need to get away from your dad. He's never been good to you, and him trying to control what you do isn't right."

"Yeah, but what if he's right? What if I need direction in my life?"

"You bought your first house when you were eighteen. I'm pretty sure you're on the right path."

I waver. "Or I'm just another spoiled rich kid."

"Trust me; you are in no way, shape, or form like

Titzi." She slides closer until her ass is between my legs and her hands are on my shoulders. "That girl is stupid. Your father is stupid. Anyone who has ever doubted you is just plain stupid."

And there it is, the reason I fell in love with her.

I roll my tongue in my mouth. "Fine. I get what you're saying, but I just have one more question."

"Okay. What?"

"Can I keep you, like, forever?"

Her eyes widen. "Beck …"

"What?" I give her my best innocent look. "It's a reasonable question, especially when you're so damn valuable. Why would I ever want to give you up?"

She rolls her eyes. "Now you're just being cheesy."

"Admit it. You like my cheesiness."

"Maybe just a little."

We're both smiling like idiots, but I put a stop to the goofiness as I go in for a kiss, dragging her into my lap.

By the time our lips part again, my dad has tried to call me seventeen times.

"Do you want to do the honors?" I ask Willow with my phone in my hand. "Or should I?"

"I think this is something you should do. It'll be therapeutic after all those years he's beaten you down."

I feel restless as I stare at my dad's name in my contact list.

"You'll be okay," she insists, kneeling on the bed in front of me. "Just call him up and tell him you have some of his files that you'd really like him to see. And do it in your best mobster voice."

Nodding, I press my finger to his name then put the phone to my ear. He answers after two rings and immediately starts screaming that I'm supposed to be at the office. When he finally takes a breath, I tell him what I need to, and for the first time in my life, he listens.

In the middle of the conversation, Willow gets up off the bed and heads across my room toward the door. Worry builds in my chest that she'll walk out and never come back or that she'll come back with a list. And these last five years of getting us to this point will be destroyed. When she reaches the doorway, though, she turns around and smiles.

"I'll be right back. I'm just going to go make breakfast while you finish breaking up with your father." She giggles, amused with herself.

The pressure in my chest cracks as I realize that she might be okay.

I might be okay.

We might be okay.

Chapter Twenty-Four

Willow

I'm so glad Beck decided to get out of working with his father. Sure, blackmailing him might not be the best way, but honestly, I think it's the only way other than Beck selling his house.

As Beck talks to his dad on the phone and explains to him what he found, I wander out to the kitchen to make some breakfast. I feel so well-rested I don't even know what to do with myself other than smile, smile, smile and do jazz hands apparently. Honestly, I kind of feel as happy as a cartoon character as I dance my way across the spacious kitchen.

But in the middle of my best robot move, I screech to a halt, my jaw smacking to my knees.

"What the heck is this?" I mutter, plucking up a piece of paper held to the fridge by a magnet.

Task #1: Get Willow out of that house.

Task #2: Prove to her that I'm not going to destroy her.

Task #3: Tell her I love her.

The letters are written in Beck's handwriting below the

list of rules I gave him; only, my list has been scribbled out.

Tell her I love her.

Tell her I love her?

"Beck loves me?" I whisper, nearly dropping the list.

My heart rate accelerates. My palms begin to dampen. My brain is wired, soaring a million miles a minute. I'd think I was having a panic attack, except for two things: One, those god-damn flutters go elatedly crazy. And two, I don't want to run to the front door. I want to go back to the bedroom. So, that's what I do with the list clutched in my hand.

Beck is off the phone when I walk in, looking both terrified and relieved.

"Well, the good news is that he's going to sign my house over to me," he says, tossing his phone onto the bed.

I step toward him. "And the bad news?"

He rests his elbows on his knees and massages his temples with his fingertips. "I'm probably not going to be allowed to family dinners anymore."

"Aw, Beck, I'm so sorry." Another step toward him and my fingers tighten around the list. "Are you going to be okay?"

"I'll be fine. Family dinners suck, anyway." He waves me off, but I can see a tiny bit of hurt in his eyes.

"What can I do to make you feel better?" I ask, stopping in front of him.

321

He leans back on his arms as he angles his head up. "Well, if you're offering …" His lips curve into a naughty grin.

I tap my finger against my lips. "You want me to tickle your feet again?"

He gives me a tolerant look. "That's not quite what I was thinking you could tickle. Maybe go up a little higher."

"What? To your ankle?"

Shaking his head, he snags hold of my hips, lifts me up, and drops me down on the bed.

I let out a laugh as I bounce against the bed and then squeal as he rolls on top of me and tickles my side.

"Just for that, I'm going to make you pee your pants," he teases, sketching his fingers up and down my sides.

"Please, don't!" I squeal, wrestling to get out from underneath him.

Laughing, he straddles me, snatches hold of my wrists, and pins my arms above my head. "You are so going down … Wait, what's in your hand?" His gaze shifts to me, and his Adam's apple bobs up and down as he gulps. "Where did you find that?"

"On your fridge," I whisper, struggling to get oxygen into my lungs. *Breathe. Just breathe.* "Is it true …? Task number three?"

His throat muscles move as he swallows hard. "It is, but I don't want you to panic. That's just where I am, but I won't say it aloud. I know that you're not there yet, so we can wait for now. I don't want to overwhelm you or make you feel uncomfortable while you're living with me. You've already spent way too much of your life being uncomfortable in your own house. I don't want to ever make you feel that way."

Silence ticks by, filled with our heavy breathing.

"Princess, please, say something," he pleads, still holding my wrists.

"You make me feel safe," I sputter, unsure what else to say other than the truth. "All the time. You're the only one who ever has."

"Good." He relaxes, skimming a finger along the inside of my wrist right along my thrashing pulse. "That's all I've ever wanted. To make sure you feel—are safe. Ever since the first time I had you come home with me and spend the night."

"Well, you completely and one hundred percent succeeded." I aim for a light tone yet sound uncontrollably breathless.

"Now that I got you out of that house, I did." Then he leans in to kiss me.

"Beck," I whisper right before his lips touch mine.

He pauses, his eyelids lifting open. "Yeah?"

"C-can I hear you say it?" I whisper. "I've never heard anyone say it to me without a manipulative meaning behind it."

He nods, swallowing hard. "Willow, I love you."

He says it so easily, without any effort, without wanting anything in return.

I've often wondered what it would be like to hear the word love and not cringe. When I was younger, it used to happen, but only because I was so naive. Maybe I'm being naive still, but I really don't think so. And I don't cringe. I don't run. I don't think of lists and jobs and classes. I think of Beck and everything he's done for me: when he saved me from sleeping in the car, when he comforted me during the rougher days, when he didn't judge me for the bad choices I made, when he made me laugh, even when he made me almost pee my pants.

Then I hold my breath and let every single damn syllable sink into my heart.

"I love you, too," I whisper. "I think I have for a while."

His eyes widen, but that look only lasts for a heartbeat. Then his lips are on mine. His hands soon find my body, slipping underneath my shirt. His fingers brush my nipples, and my back bows up, my knees pressing against his hips. He repeats the movement again, whispering that he can stop if I need him to. I don't want him to stop, though.

Ever.

And that's exactly what I tell him.

He peels off my shirt, and I tug down his pajama bottoms and boxers. Then he lays me back down on the bed and slips his fingers inside me as his tongue parts my lips. He feels me until I can't breathe. Kisses me until I can't think straight. Loves me until everything seems right and nothing seems wrong.

I never want him to let me go.

His thoughts seem to match mine as he only moves away to put on a condom. Then he places his body over mine, kissing me slowly, as if memorizing every single brush of our lips.

"Are you sure you want to do this?" he asks, looking into my eyes.

I nod with a hint of nerves surfacing. But I shove the feeling down and wrap my legs around his waist, really wanting to do this.

"I love you," I say.

"I love you, too," he promises.

Then he kisses me as he slips inside, and I hold on to him, never wanting to let go.

It might not be perfection, but I think it's definitely close.

Chapter Twenty-Five

Willow

The next few days move by slowly, but in the best way possible. Beck and I spend a lot of time messing around, laughing, and burning dinner because I apparently suck at cooking food that doesn't come processed and in a box. Beck finds my sucky cooking skills pretty funny, even when I set off all the smoke alarms in the house, and his laughter makes not panicking a bit easier.

To alleviate even more of my stress, I decided to accept a job at the library and a tutoring job at the college. Beck tries to talk me out of taking two, but I want to be able to afford everything on my own, even a discounted, reasonable rent price. I also decide to have Van mail me my final paycheck instead of picking it up, never wanting to go back to that place again.

Van doesn't seem very happy about me quitting, but I am. And I really start feeling like myself again: the planner, the good choice maker, the girl who loves spending time with her best friend—well, I guess my boyfriend now, which is new to me and completely unplanned. That's okay. I'm starting to realize that unplanned things sometimes turn out to be wonderful.

Everything seems to be going great until I finally have to accept that I can no longer keep washing my outfit and re-wearing it. I have to return to the apartment to get my stuff and my car. So, on a very early Friday morning, Beck and I climb into his car and drive back to a place I hope to never see again.

Just being there puts me in a foul mood, and I wonder if that's how I've been for years: a walking foul mood. I decide to ask Beck this since he seems to know me pretty well.

"You're not a walking foul mood." He rolls his eyes as he grabs the blankets off my bed and stuffs them into a box. "You're not even in a foul mood right now. You're just sad because this place reminds you of too many bad times."

"Yeah, you're probably right." I open the top dresser drawer to clean out my clothes, finding the snow globe Beck gave me. I smile as I pick it up.

"What are you looking at?" Beck asks, stepping up beside me. He has on jeans that are covered with dust from moving furniture, a long-sleeved grey shirt with the sleeves rolled up, and strands of his hair are askew. He looks so sexy. I can't figure out how the hell I managed to keep my hands off him for so long.

Talk about too much self-control.

327

"The snow globe you gave me." I hold it up and give it a little shake.

He smiles at the fake snow flurrying in the water. "You know, I was really nervous when I picked that out."

"Really?" I ask, and he nods. "Why?"

He shrugs. "I think because it was just because it was the first present I ever gave you."

My fingers fold around the snow globe. "It wasn't the first present you gave me."

His forehead creases. "Really? What else did I give you?"

"What no one else ever did." I reach out and thread my fingers through his. "Safety."

His lips tug into a small, sad smile. "That's not really a present, though, princess. Well, it shouldn't be. It should be something that just is."

"It was to me. When I was younger, I thought about it a lot actually, having someone in my life who made me feel calm instead of so scared all the time." I stare at the snow globe, tipping it back and forth. "I just never thought it would happen. Then you came along and changed every-thing. Sometimes, I wonder if maybe I made it out of this place without becoming my mom because you were always there."

He fixes his finger underneath my chin and urges me to look at him. When our eyes meet, he wets his lips. "I don't really think I can take full credit for this one. I think you made it out of this place okay because you're fucking strong."

I smile then move in to kiss him. Right as our lips connect, voices rise from inside the house.

"Where are you guys!" Wynter shouts through a giggle. "And what are you doing? Because it's really, really quiet."

I hear Luna and Grey say something, and then Ari laughs.

I shake my head, my cheeks warming. While I haven't told her Beck and I hooked up, she's voiced her suspicions over the phone. Evidently, my voice has a glow to it that it didn't have a week ago, whatever the hell that means.

"As annoying as she is, I like that she made you blush," Beck says, grinning as he lightly caresses my cheek.

I smile but then my happiness quickly falters. "Wait. What are we going to tell them?"

"About what?" he feigns dumb, his brow teasing upward.

"You know what. You and me." I put my hand on his chest to playfully shove him, but he snags my wrist and jerks me to him, our chests colliding.

He rests his hands on my waist. "I'm pretty sure they already know."

"How?"

"Because it's been four years in the making, and they've had eyes for those four years."

"Yeah, maybe ..." I rub my lips together, unsure what to do.

"Why do you seem scared that they'll find out?" he asks, trying to hide his hurt, yet his eyes give the truth away.

"I'm not really scared of them finding out," I admit. "I'm just afraid that, when they do, everything will become so real. And it'll become that much harder to lose what we have."

"I'm not going anywhere," he assures me, dropping a delicate kiss on my lips. "Stop overthinking and just accept that you and I belong together. We're real, and you're not going to lose me. You want me, and I want you."

I nod, nerves creeping up on me as Wynter strolls into my room.

She's wearing a dark purple dress, her hair is curled, her makeup flawless, and she's sporting heels.

"I thought I told you to wear something comfortable," I tell her, realizing too late that Beck's hands are still on my waist. I consider stepping back then decide to stay put and accept what I want like Beck told me.

Her eyes dart to Beck's hands, and a devious smirk spreads across her face. "I knew you sounded glowy on the phone."

"What does that mean?" Ari asks as he walks into my bedroom. Unlike Wynter, he took my advice on dress attire and is wearing an old T-shirt and holey jeans. He takes one look at Beck and me, and relief washes over his face. "Thank God. It's about fucking time."

Beck grins proudly, while I grow extremely confused.

"Wait a second," I say, stepping toward Ari. "You don't seem that surprised about this."

Ari backs up with a guilty look on his face. "Look, I know what you're getting at, and I just want to say that I thought I was making things easier."

I cross my arms. "How does telling me that Beck and Wynter like each other make things easier on me?"

"Wait, what?" Wynter whirls toward Ari. "You told her that?"

Ari shrugs. "She was always freaking out whenever Beck tried to hit on her or kiss her, so I thought I'd make it easier on her and let her think Beck liked someone else. That way, she wouldn't have to stress out every time we were all together."

"Your logic is kind of warped, but I appreciate it." To prove it, I give him a hug.

"I just want everyone to be happy," Ari says, hugging me back. "And to get along."

"You're such a sap," Wynter teases him. "But that's

331

okay. It's why we love you."

Ari rolls his eyes as we step back. "I'm the sap? You're the one always bawling during movies. And while reading books. And when you see puppies."

"Hey, puppies are really cute," Wynter argues with her hands on her hips.

They continue to argue as Luna and Grey walk into the room. Then the six of us finish packing up my stuff and load the boxes into our cars. I don't take the furniture or anything else in the house, not for my mom's benefit, but to have a fresh start.

While I may not get to do things over, I can choose to let go of the past and move forward with a new, less stressful future.

"You think you got everything?" Beck asks as I take one final walk around my room.

Wynter, Ari, Luna, and Grey have all driven off to take some of my stuff to Beck's house.

I nod, grabbing a notebook and a piece of paper. "I just need to do one more thing."

He moves up beside me as I lean over the dresser to write. "What are you doing?"

I put the tip of the pen to the piece of the paper. "Writing my mom a note to let her know where I am."

"Willow, do you think that's a good idea?" His tone carries caution. "What if she tries to track you down and get money from you or something?"

"I'm not telling her where I'll be physically," I explain. "I'm telling her where I am mentally."

"Oh." He doesn't argue anymore, just moves up behind me and massages my shoulders, giving me that comforting feeling I like so much. "Go ahead, then."

I summon a deep breath, and then I write.

> *Mom,*
>
> *I'm not sure how long it'll take you to realize I no longer live here, and I'm really sorry about that. I'm really sorry that you got to such an awful point that you don't really care if you see me anymore or not. While it really hurts that you don't care, I can no longer let that hurt control me. I've spent so many nights worrying about you, wondering where you are, if you'll come back, if you love me, and fearing all the answers. But I'm tired of wondering and waiting and hoping and fearing.*

333

I've spent so much of my life afraid of this house, your boyfriends, you, becoming like you, which I know sounds harsh and maybe it is, but I'm telling you this with the hope that maybe you'll change. Maybe you'll get the help you should've gotten a long time ago since I'm no longer going to be around to do that for you. I'm no longer going to be an enabler.

I'm going to be who I should've been all along: a teenage girl going to college who is happy sometimes, sad sometimes, lost sometimes, scared sometimes, but only because of her own life choices.

And while I'm scared to walk away, I know it's for the best. I just want you to know that, if you decide to get some help and heal yourself, you

*can always call me. I'll leave
my phone number at the bottom. Only call me if you're
my mom again and not the
woman I've been living with
for almost the last thirteen
years. I really do miss her.*

> *Love,*
> *Willow*

When I'm done, I set the pen down and leave the note on the kitchen table. Beck stays at my side the entire time, holding my hand, assuring me that I'm not in this alone.

It's a very new feeling for me, one I'll take.

As we're walking out of the house, I realize I have one final problem to take care of.

"And the Mercedes returns," I mutter with a frown as the door opens and my dad climbs out.

Beck tracks my gaze, and then his hand tightens on mine. "Let's just get in the car. You don't have to talk to him if you don't want to."

I really don't. At the same time, I know the lack of clo-sure will eat me up.

"I'm just going to tell him that I want him to leave me alone."

I start toward my dad, pulling Beck along with me, and he follows effortlessly.

"Hey," he says when I reach him. "I'm really glad I caught you. I know you want me to leave you alone, but I'd really like to talk to you."

He's wearing a dress shirt with the sleeves rolled up, slacks, and shiny as hell shoes. I wonder if he just got off work. I wonder where he works. I wonder a lot of things, not knowing anything about him other than he walked out on his family without looking back.

"I just want to tell you that I don't ever want to talk to you," I tell him, relaxing a smidgen as Beck smooths his finger along the inside of my wrist.

"Deep breaths," Beck whispers, making me aware of my panicked breathing.

I do what he says. *Air in. Air out.*

"Willow, please just give me a few minutes," my dad begs, stepping toward me.

I step back, bumping into Beck. "You don't deserve a few minutes," I tell him. "And if you wanted those few minutes, you should've gotten them thirteen years ago."

"I know that," he says, fidgeting nervously with his sleeves. "I know I messed up. I really do. But the guy I was back then ... I'm not him anymore."

"Then who are you? Because all I know is the man who left me with a horrible mother."

He rubs his hand across his forehead, seeming at a loss for words. "Up until a couple of weeks ago, I didn't realize how bad your mother has been. And up until a couple of years ago, I never thought about you or your mom, too drunk to care. Then something happened to me that was a real eye opener, so I got sober and realized ..." He blows out a shaky breath. "I realized how much I fucked up my life over the last two decades. And not just my life, but my daughter's."

"If that's true, then why did it take you two years to find me?" I snap, fighting back the tears.

"Because I wanted to get my act together." He inches toward me, stuffing his hands into his pockets. "Plus, I knew you'd be all grown up now and probably wouldn't welcome my return."

A few tears escape my eyes, but I quickly wipe them away. "Then why try at all?"

"Because I want to see you." He pulls his hand out of his pocket and tugs his fingers through his hair. "Whether that makes me selfish or not, I decided to try."

"Then why didn't you just try instead of following me around or watching the house?"

"Because I was scared," he admits. "Because I knew this is how you were going to react."

"I deserve to act this way."

"I know you do."

"Do you even feel bad for what you did?" My voice cracks.

His eyes enlarge, and he starts to reach for me, but I jerk back.

"Of course I feel bad for what I did," he whispers, on the verge of crying. "It haunts me every single hour of every single day. I wish I could take what I did back, but I can't. What I can do is ask—beg for another chance. Even if it's only a few minutes of your time. Please, Willow, just let me have that."

My legs start to tremble as anxiety pumps through my veins. I should leave, should run away from this man, but I can't get my feet to move.

Beck puts his hands on my shoulders and massages the muscles, trying to get me to calm down. "Do you want to go?" he whispers in my ear.

I nod. "I really do."

Beck removes his hands from my shoulders, takes my hand, and leads me toward the car. My dad watches in panic as I move farther away from him. I don't know if that's what gets me—the panic—or maybe deep down, I just want to talk to my dad for a few minutes. Whatever it is, I stop short of the passenger door and turn back.

"Do you have a card with your phone number on it?"

He swiftly nods then fumbles around in his pocket for his wallet. "Yes, I actually do." He takes out a card and hands it to me. "It's for my work cell, but you can call me anytime."

I wonder what he does for work… who he is now … if we could ever get over the past. I'm not so sure. If I've learned anything over the last few months, though, it's that I shouldn't run away from everything simply because I'm afraid. And while my dad hasn't really earned the chance to talk to me, I kind of have with him.

"I don't know for sure if I'll call you," I tell him, tucking the card into the pocket of my jeans. "But I'll think about it."

"That's all I'm asking," he says quickly. "Can I just ask you one question?"

I don't want to give him anything, but I nod, anyway.

"You're not living in this place anymore, right?" he asks with concern. "It looks like you're moving out … to some place better, I hope."

I can't help smiling as I glance at Beck, who is standing beside me, holding my hand. "Yeah, I really am… to somewhere much, much better."

The beginning of a new list...

Epilogue

Willow

After moving out of that apartment and ditching that awful job, my life has become a lot easier. I still spend a lot of time doing homework, working at my two jobs, and probably stressing myself out more than I need to. I'm starting to realize I might always be a worrier, but I'll be okay as long as I deal with the worry instead of bottling it up. So I do. I deal with it on my own and sometimes with the help of Wynter, Ari, Luna, and of course, Beck.

I'd like to say my mom's name was on that list, but unfortunately, I haven't heard from her for two months, not since she broke all my snow globes and took off. I did drive by the apartment once when I was passing through town. I didn't stop, though, too afraid of what I'd find or what I wouldn't. The place looked empty; the lights were off, darkness haunting every window. Honestly, it kind of always looked that way.

On a positive note, my dad didn't turn out to be as horrible as he was when I was six. A couple of weeks ago, I met up with him for an hour, and he explained to me that he struggled with alcoholism since before I was born and that he took off because he was a stupid drunk who cared more about alcohol than anything else. He also told me he never hated himself more than when he found out what I'd been through with my mom. After spending so much time hating myself, I told him I didn't want him to feel that way. He could feel bad, but not hate himself. We ended our conversation with an awkward handshake and the promise to have dinner again whenever I'm ready. While I haven't decided when that will be, I don't feel like I have to rush the decision.

One step at a time, Beck is always telling me.

I don't know what I'd do without him. And although I still fear that I might be forced to find that out one day, I try not to think about it too much, focusing on the moments I do get with him.

The wonderful, amazing, breath-free moments.

Moments I almost didn't have because I was so scared.

But I'm not scared right now.

In fact, I'm really excited.

"It's ten o'clock," I announce as I enter his bedroom with my hands tucked behind my back. "And do you know what that means?"

He's sitting in bed, staring at his laptop with his shirt off, wearing nothing but a pair of jeans. I have the strongest urge to run over and touch him. And I will. But first, I need to give him something.

He glances up from his laptop, his eyes twinkling in amusement as he scans over my plaid shorts and tank top. "I thought I declared that the next pillow fight would be a naked one."

"I know. And I plan on doing that in just a second." I walk over to the bed. "I want to give you something first."

He slides the laptop off his lap and scoots to the edge of the bed. "What is it?"

I keep my hands behind my back. "A present."

"Really? Does it have lace and bows and show off that sexy belly ring of yours?" He grazes his knuckles across my waist, grinning when I shiver.

Yep, even after three months, I'm still shivering and blushing and getting all tingly whenever he touches me. That's okay, though. The sensations are really nice when I'm not fighting him.

"Sorry, but it doesn't have any lace." I giggle as his lip juts out. "I promise it's still a good present, though. At least, I think it is."

"All right, let's see what you've got," he says, rubbing his hands together excitedly.

Grinning, I move my hand out from behind my back and hand him the piece of paper.

He instantly frowns.

"It's a good list, I promise," I try to reassure him.

345

All he does is press his lips together, refusing to take it.

Sighing, I sit down beside him and open up the piece of paper. Then I read aloud what I've wanted to tell him for years but have been too afraid to say.

"All the reasons that I love you:

1. *Because you gave me the coolest snow globe ever.*
2. *Because you didn't think I was a freak the first time you came to my house.*
3. *Because you hug me all the time.*
4. *Because you believe in me.*
5. *Because you're the nicest guy I've ever met and will ever meet.*
6. *Because you make me feel safe even during the scariest times.*
7. *Because I can talk to you about sex and not blush ... Well, sometimes, unless we're talking about something really dirty.*
8. *Because you make me*

laugh.

9. *Because you make me smile.*

10. *Because you knew to make me a list.*

11. *Because you refused to give up on me even when I fought so hard.*

12. *Because you're my best friend.*

13. *Because you made me see myself for who I really am.*

14. *Because you still cared for me even when I showed you my worst.*

15. *Because you still wanted me even when I was at my worst.*

16. *Because you're amazing, wonderful, kind, caring, sweet, funny, and a complete weirdo. But let's face it, so am I.*

17. *Because you showed me how to love not just you, but myself."*

347

My voice is shaking with nerves by the end, and I quickly clear my throat. "I just wanted you to know all of that—to know how important you are to me."

His expression is blank, and I wonder if maybe I got a little too lovey-dovey. But then he smiles, and suddenly, he's cupping the back of my neck and bringing me in for a kiss. And just like that, the brief moment of worry flies away.

"I love you, too," he whispers between kisses. "But you left off one thing."

I pull back slightly to look him in the eye. "I did?"

He nods. "You forget to say that you love me because we have awesome naked pillow fights."

I chuckle, shaking my head. But the humor vanishes as he grows serious again.

"I really do love you," he says. "More than anything."

"I know that," I tell him before sealing my lips to his.

And it's the truth. I do know he loves me. I have always known. I was just too afraid to admit it. Too afraid to accept. Too afraid of things I couldn't control.

Too afraid.

Too afraid.

Too afraid.

I almost let fear ruin my life, almost let it control me. And I almost missed out on perfect moments like this one. Because, while life is filled with imperfections, perfection does exist in rare, beautiful moments. Rare, beautiful moments make life really worth living. And I'm glad I'm not so afraid of the bad anymore that I miss out on the good. In fact, I think I'm going to make that my number two rule in life, right after loving Beck.

About the Author

Jessica Sorensen is a *New York Times* and *USA Today* bestselling author who lives in the snowy mountains of Wyoming. When she's not writing, she spends her time reading and hanging out with her family.

Other books by Jessica Sorensen:

Standalones:
Rules of a Rebel and a Shy Girl
Confessions of a Kleptomaniac
The Illusion of Annabella
The Forgotten Girl

Broken City Series:
Nameless
Forsaken
Oblivion (coming soon)

Entranced Series:
Entranced
Entangled
Enchanted (coming soon)

Sunnyvale Series:

The Year I Became Isabella Anders

The Year of Falling in Love

The Year of Second Chances

The Coincidence Series:

The Coincidence of Callie and Kayden

The Redemption of Callie and Kayden

The Destiny of Violet and Luke

The Probability of Violet and Luke

The Certainty of Violet and Luke

The Resolution of Callie and Kayden

Seth & Greyson

The Secret Series:

The Prelude of Ella and Micha

The Secret of Ella and Micha

The Forever of Ella and Micha

The Temptation of Lila and Ethan

The Ever After of Ella and Micha

Lila and Ethan: Forever and Always

Ella and Micha: Infinitely and Always

The Shattered Promises Series:

Shattered Promises

Fractured Souls

Unbroken

Broken Visions

Scattered Ashes

Breaking Nova Series:

Breaking Nova

Saving Quinton

Delilah: The Making of Red

Nova and Quinton: No Regrets

Tristan: Finding Hope

Wreck Me

Ruin Me

The Fallen Star Series:

The Fallen Star

The Underworld

The Vision

The Promise

The Fallen Souls Series (spin-off from The Fallen Star):

The Lost Soul

The Evanescence

The Darkness Falls Series:

Darkness Falls

Darkness Breaks

Darkness Fades

The Death Collectors Series (NA and YA):

Ember X and Ember

Cinder X and Cinder

Spark X and Spark

<u>Unbeautiful Series:</u>

Unbeautiful

Untamed

Made in the USA
San Bernardino, CA
01 November 2016